Trapped by Love

Linda Sealy Knowles

ISBN: ISBN: 978-1-947523-70-8

Dedication

Jack and Shirley Presnall

To a wonderful couple who has supported me in every way since I began my writing career. We were school friends and have continued our friendship through adulthood. When I think of you or see you while visiting at home, you bring a smile to my heart. I shall always treasure your support, love and friendship.

.

Chapter 1

Dearest Sarah,

I am anxiously awaiting your arrival to Fort Laramie. Your apartment is ready, and the chaplain has agreed to marry us as soon as the captain gives his permission. I pray for a quick and safe journey.

With kind regards,

Sgt. George Turnberry

Sarah Sullivan folded the short note and placed it in her Bible before tucking it into her carpetbag. She whirled to take her mama's small, aged hand in hers.

"Please, Mama. Be happy for me," Sarah whispered through the lump in her throat. "I have to go to the man I love, like you did years ago. After George and I are settled, you'll come live with us." Sarah squeezed her mama's small body close.

"I'm going to miss you so much, my child. Since your papa . . . I miss him, and now you're leaving." Tears streamed down her rosy, wrinkled cheeks. "Take this quilt, my dear. It will be cold traveling in this open-windowed coach. Winter will be here soon."

~

"Load up, folks," bellowed the burly man who had opened the door to the Wells Fargo twenty-foot stagecoach. Will Hammer was a strong, courageous man who had driven stagecoaches for many years. He boasted he had driven through hostile Indian Territory

1

and was the target for many bandits. His stagecoaches had made it through narrow and rugged trails with deep sand and endless muddy roads, but he always made it to his destination. "Give your mama one more hug and allow me to help you inside. We have a schedule to keep and I like to stay on time as much as the weather permits."

~

"Mama, I'm going to miss you." She wiped her tear-stained face with her dainty hanky. Hugging her mama, she pleaded with her to take care of herself. Sarah turned to the old Black woman who had lived with her family all of her life. "Stella, please take care of Mama. I'll write as soon as I can."

"I will, missy. Be happy, child," Stella said. She stood close to Sarah's mama, wiping her eyes.

Mr. Hammer lifted Sarah's small frame into the large interior of the coach. "Please step back, ladies. Don't want the big yellow wheels to run over any toes."

Her mama moved out of reach of her daughter's hands and blew a kiss. "Bye, my child."

~

Will Hammer climbed onto the big seat next to Jack, the shotgun guard, whose voice held grave concern. "I hope the bank manager and the marshal are the only two who know that we're carrying a large government payroll. The marshal said they were keeping it a secret this time. I nearly got killed three months ago for a whole lot less."

~

Sarah waved at her mama and Stella until they lost sight of the town of Canon City, just twenty-five miles east of Lakewood, Colorado. Sarah settled back on the seat. A young woman and a little girl perched on the opposite one. She cast them a quick smile.

"Hello." The little girl smiled, her golden curls bobbing up and down from the bumping and swaying of the carriage.

"Darling, please don't bother the lady. She's sad. Let's leave her be for now," the woman gently said. She placed the girl back onto the seat.

"But, Mama, she's crying."

Sarah glanced at the child and then at the mother, a beautiful young woman who appeared in her early twenties. The lady was dressed in the latest fashion, her blond hair pulled under a green velvet hat. A thick crocheted green shawl surrounded her shoulders.

"Your little girl isn't bothering me. She's very bright to notice I'm sad, because I am. Excited and sad. See, I'm leaving my mama to meet my fiancé. We're going to be married." Sarah adjusted the quilt across her lap and tucked the corners under herself.

"How exciting. My daughter and I are going to meet my husband. My name is Julie Connors, and this is my daughter, Penny. My husband finally got settled at Fort Laramie, Wyoming, and sent for us."

"Oh, this is exciting. I'm heading to Fort Laramie, too. My name is Sarah Sullivan. George Turnberry and I are going to be married as soon as possible after I arrive," Sarah nearly shouted.

"I'm so happy you'll be stationed at the fort along with us. John said there aren't many wives living at the fort, and there isn't a lot for a woman to do. I don't need parties and dancing. I just want to be with my husband. We haven't seen John in nearly two years. He had to leave soon after we had our sweet baby girl." Julie cuddled Penny in her arms.

"I'm going to show my papa my new doll Mama bought me for this trip." Penny held the doll up to show Sarah.

"Well, I know he'll love your baby doll as much as you do." Sarah reached out and straightened the baby blanket surrounding the dolly. "I enjoy sewing, so once we get settled, maybe I can make your baby doll a new dress."

"Can it look like mine?" Penny asked as she pulled on the hem of her new dress.

"I'll try hard to make it look like one of yours." In a few minutes Penny was fast asleep in her mama's arms.

After chatting all morning and getting better acquainted, the swaying and rocking of the stagecoach made both of the ladies relax, and soon all three were asleep.

The stagecoach pulled into its first relay stop to change horses, allow the passengers a moment of privacy, and have a bite of lunch. The relay station where the passengers would spend the night was another three-hour trip.

Both ladies enjoyed the rest and lunch. They hurried through their meal so they had time for Penny to run around the area before they had to enter the coach again.

The little girl stopped in her tracks and pointed to the corner. "Why are those men looking at us?"

"What he men, dear?" Julie shielded her eyes from the sun but saw no one.

~

Seth Jenkins stood on a big boulder peering through his telescope. First he witnessed clouds of dust and then the stagecoach traveled too fast over the rugged, narrow road. The guard riding shotgun was sprawled across the top of the stagecoach shooting at the men chasing them. The man took a hit and tumbled off the stage down the side of the ridge.

The man Seth recognized as Will Hammer gripped the leather reins and used a whip on the six horses to keep the stagecoach on the rocky trail. In a flash, the lead horse stumbled and struggled to balance on the edge of the mountain, but slipped off the trail with the other animals down the embankment. The coach tumbled slowly over and over until heavy brush and small trees helped to stop it. Will Hammer disappeared down the mountainside, but Seth had no idea where.

Seth was sure the three men chasing the stagecoach belonged to the notorious gang he'd been warned about by his Indian friends and other trappers. The wanted posters stated the three men were murderers and thieves who preyed on isolated farms and lone travelers. They'd made a name for themselves. In the past weeks, they left a trail of dead, innocent farmers and their families. They killed a young sodbuster and his younger sister, who had pleaded for death long before it came. Fortunately, they failed to find a young boy hiding in the barn loft. He identified the three men.

Seth looked to the heavens and mummed a silent prayer. The passengers were sure to be dead. There was no way he could get to the scene of this terrible crime in time to save any of them. The valley in the center of the mountains offered no way to the other side except to go around the top edge on the man-made trail. He had to guide his horse and three pack mules safely across the mountainside.

Chapter 2

"Open the door on the top and see if those women are still alive. Back at the relay station, two fine looking gals got aboard. Shoot fire, I ain't had no fun in a long time," the gang leader yelled.

"Joe, get the boot open and take the money bag. Grab the mailbag too. There might be something of value in it. Mercy, look at all these green backs. We hit the jackpot, fellows," the toothless old gang member yelled as he walked around the coach with his hands filled with money.

"We shore did, men. Those pretty women at the station are still alive. I intend to have myself some fun before we leave this here site." He lowered his tall frame down into the open window of the stage, grabbed the mother of the child, and lifted her out onto the side of the coach. The woman slapped the man across his face, stunning him for a second. He retaliated by hitting her with his fist, knocking her backwards off the coach.

She landed onto the hard ground, and her head started bleeding. He watched her lying on her back with her eyes closed. When they opened, the man jumped to the ground and thanked her for being accommodating. "Well, little lady, me and you are going to have a good time." He tossed her skirt over her head while jerking down her bloomers. Her screams were irritating as he had his way with her.

Fighting like a tigress, she clawed, kicked, and screamed, which made her more of a catch. He lowered his head to give her a kiss, but she bit him.

Angry, he grabbed his knife and sliced her throat. As he rose, her wedding ring glistened in the sunlight. He pulled on the ring, and when it wouldn't come off, he cut off her finger. "There's more than one way to skin a cat," he howled and held up the small diamond. He shook the blood off and placed it on his little finger.

~

Sarah and the little girl were lifted out of the stage by one of the bandits, who seemed to be surprised that there was a child aboard. He backed away from the woman.

Sarah stood with her back to the stage holding the little girl. The child, still half asleep, had buried her face in her shoulder. Sarah held her tight while shielding her from the savage violence taking place in front of them.

Two other men were stuffing their saddlebags with money and preparing to leave the scene of the crime. The boss man, grinning and wiping blood off his mouth, advanced toward Sarah when a blast of gunfire exploded on the mountainside.

"Damnit, it's Indians," one of the men yelled.

"You fool, Indians don't have that kind of gun."

"You idiots can fuss, but I'm getting the hell out of here."

"Let's git." One of the men jumped on his horse. The other two men followed and rode up into the mountains out of sight.

~

Seth neared the scene and saw one of the men approach the woman cuddling a child. He knew he couldn't get there in time to save her from the man, so he fired his double-barreled buffalo gun. The blast of his gun scared the men away, but he waited to make sure they were gone.

Seth jumped off his horse and tied it and the pack mules to a large tree before he approached the stagecoach. He took in the scene with one glance. The horses that were still alive were suffering. A dead woman was on the ground and another woman holding a child stood rooted near the stage.

He nodded at the young woman and walked past her to the horses. Two of the six animals were dead while the other four were bloody with broken legs. Seth closed his eyes and paused for a second before he put the animals out of their misery.

The gunfire caused the child to start crying, but the woman

didn't flinch. She stood as still as a statue. Her face was pale and her full lips were white as snow. Her eyes held a blank expression.

"Miss," Seth called, receiving no response. He looked at the whimpering child she was holding. Blood ran down the side of the woman's face, and blood was on the arm that held the child's head close to her breast. He wasn't sure if the child belonged to the woman holding her or the dead woman lying in a puddle of blood.

He knew the stagecoach was headed to Fort Laramie. The weather was getting colder every day, but it would take him weeks to carry them to their destination. He had no choice but to bury the woman. Besides, a human corpse is not something a loved one wants to receive. Seth looked to heaven and prayed, "Help me, Lord, to do the right thing."

"Miss," he called and walked closer to her. "I've got to bury your traveling companion." Again, no response. He walked into the woods and retrieved his horse and pack mules, grabbed a short shovel from one of the packs, and smoothed out a clearing. The ground was hard, solid rock and root-bound, but he continued to dig until he was waist-deep. Even with the cool air, he worked up a hard sweat that glistened off his bronze chest. The woman had slid down to the hard earth with the sleeping child in her arms. He could feel her eyes on him.

Seth untied a blanket from a bedroll and stooped down beside the dead woman who was missing a finger. Her attacker must have cut off her finger for a ring. *Sorry scum of the earth.* He sucked in a deep breath while spreading the blanket open. As he prepared to roll the body into the rough blanket, he noticed a chain under the collar of her dress. He removed it before he rolled the bloody body into the blanket.

He glanced over at the young woman and child sitting on the ground. She had begun to hum and rocked back and forth with lackluster eyes.

"Madam, Miss," Seth tried again. She stopped moving but didn't glance his way. Instead, she sucked in her breath and gripped the child tighter.

~

Sarah had heard him, but she was lost in her own place. A beautiful world with her fiancé waiting for her at the end of a shining white light. All the horrific images that had taken place before her were just a nightmare and she would wake from it soon.

~

Seth had witnessed burials without ceremonies before. The young woman was in shock, and she wouldn't take part in the burial. After smoothing the hard dirt over the mound, he leaned on the shovel and said a silent prayer for the dead woman and her family. In time the prairie grass would cover the hard-packed dirt. He needed to make some kind of marker in case someone wanted to come back to see their loved one's resting place. He gathered six large rocks and placed them in the formation of a cross.

At first, Seth had planned to go after the men once he found a place to leave his pack mules. They'd killed Will Hammer, the shotgun guard, but after discovering the woman and child, he couldn't follow the murdering men. He'd have to care for the living until he could take them to Fort Laramie.

Realizing the woman wasn't going to be any help, he searched through the trunks that had fallen off the stage. The men had searched through them and dumped most of the things onto the ground, but the clothes were still useful. He chose as many things as he could carry and placed them in an empty feed bag.

He peered in the damaged stagecoach for anything that might belong to Will and the guard, but he didn't see anything. A small carpet bag was lying unopened on the floor. It must have belonged to one of the women. He grabbed it and tied it to one of the pack mules.

Seth surveyed the beautiful mountains and dark green valley. *Such a shame to have to leave the crumbled stagecoach and six dead horses still hitched together. And a lonesome grave that may never have anyone visit it.*

Chapter 3

The man eased his way over to the young woman and child. "Miss," his words were soft but firm. "You and your little girl are going to have to come with me. I'll try to take you to Fort Laramie soon—when I can."

Sarah didn't move an eyelid, but she saw him. She also heard the bear of a man, but she didn't trust him.

"Please, let me put you on one of my mules, and I'll carry the child in front of me on my horse. She'll be safer with me."

When Sarah didn't respond, he reached for her elbow. Her body began trembling and her breathing was rapid. Even through her long sleeve dress, she felt clammy.

"I'm not going to hurt you, Miss," he tried again to get her attention. When she didn't move, he reached for the little girl and took Sarah's arm and pulled her toward the mules.

She allowed the monster to lead her without fighting. Sarah walked like a person who was being led to slaughter but didn't care. The man placed the child on the ground, but she grabbed him around the leg and held onto to him.

~

At least the child isn't scared of me.

Seth took a clean cloth from his saddlebag. He poured water over it and tried to wipe blood off her face, but she jerked away. He lifted the woman on top of a pack mule and placed her hand on the saddle horn. "Hold tight while I lead the mules. We'll be at my cabin soon." He headed to his big gray horse and placed the young

9

girl on its neck until he climbed onto the saddle. Lifting the child onto his lap, they began their short journey.

Seth kept glancing back at the young woman, who looked like she might faint and fall head-first off the mule. After two hours, they rode into a clearing and were met by his barking black and white dog.

The animal danced around the mules until Seth called to him. "Hush, Buster. You're going to scare the girls." The dog immediately stopped the loud noise and ran to post guard on the porch.

Seth threw his leg over the saddle and lifted the little girl down from the horse. He held her and approached the woman. With one hand, he lifted her to the ground. She appeared dizzy, then grabbed his arm to keep from falling. When she glanced up at him, she loosened her grip on his arm.

He told her to stand still while he looked around. He circled his cabin and saw someone through the window. A lantern cast off a dim light inside. With his fist, he pounded on the door.

It flew open and a round Indian woman was standing in the doorway. "Why did you not signal, like always?" The woman stepped onto the porch.

"I have a sick woman and child with me, and I didn't want to scare them with the gunfire. I'm happy you're here. Can you stay a spell?"

"Maybe, Red Feather comes soon."

"The lady is not well. I think she's had a spell. She hasn't spoken a word since she witnessed another passenger being murdered in front of her and the child. Their stagecoach was robbed, and it tumbled down the mountainside. Later, I'll tell you more, but I need help with her now."

"I stay." The woman walked over to the small child and picked her up. Using soothing words in her Indian language, she carried the child into the cabin.

Seth took Sarah by the elbow and led her into the dim one-room cabin. Guiding her to a rocking chair, he set her down and placed Penny in her lap. "Sit here for a minute while I bring in some fresh well water." He tossed another log onto the fire, hurried outside, and returned carrying a pail.

"I've got to pee," Penny whispered loud enough for Seth to

hear her.

Seth bent down on one knee and pointed at the Indian woman. "This is Blue Sky. She'll take you to the privy."

Blue Sky approached Sarah. When she didn't blink an eye, she took her hand and reached for Penny's, then led both of the girls to the outhouse and stayed with them.

Seth was happy Blue Sky, wife to his friend Red Feather, was at his cabin when he arrived. He was already worrying how he was going to care for the young woman and child. He'd take them to the fort, but he needed to get his furs ready to take to the trading post before it snowed. He'd worked all spring, summer and part of the fall on his hides, and these were the largest and best furs he had ever caught. His future depended on selling them.

~

When back inside, the woman named Blue Sky took Sarah and set her down on the big bed. She removed her shoes and stockings and pushed on her shoulder to lie down. Sarah obeyed immediately. The woman placed her rough palm over Sarah's eyes and chanted something she didn't understand. "Sleep," Blue Sky said.

Penny pulled on her skirt and said she was hungry just as Seth started out the front door. "Let me wash up and I'll cook us some flapjacks. How does that sound, princess?"

Blue Sky smiled at the little girl and asked in broken English. "What your name?"

"Penny. I want my mama. Where's my mama?" Tears welled up in her eyes. Blue Sky took her in her arms and rocked her.

"What is her name?" She looked to Sarah as she rocked.

"Lady," Penny replied after removing her two middle fingers from her mouth.

"You call her Lady?" Blue Sky cocked her head.

"Mama said I can't talk to strangers. Are you a stranger?" Penny cocked her head to one side.

"No, not a stranger anymore. We are . . . What you say . . . friends?"

~

Seth moved his pack mules into the barn and unloaded the furs and other supplies. He fed each mule and gave them a good rubdown. He checked his henhouse, the pigs and the new litter, the two goats and the other mules in the corral. Blue Sky and Red Feather took good care of his place whenever he left for weeks at a time.

A little while later, Seth returned to the cabin, and Blue Sky had already prepared a light meal of bacon, eggs, and flapjacks. Penny had fallen asleep on a pallet beside the bed.

"Sorry I was so long. I took care of my mules and I lost track of time. It looks like both of my house guests were exhausted."

"Papoose cried herself to sleep. She wants her mama. Mama's dead?"

"Yes, I think so, but not sure. I'm afraid I wasn't able to save one of the women. I was on top of the east mountain, and the gang ran the coach off the other side. One man killed one of the women, but I did scare them off with my buffalo gun. I'm afraid this one—" nodding to Sarah, "—witnessed everything. She hasn't spoken a word since I found her. Although she must hear because she follows instructions."

~

Sarah lay in the bed listening to their voices. She knew it was the man who had saved her and the little girl. She peeked through her eyelids, pretending to be asleep. She'd gotten a good look at the bushy-faced man who had saved their lives. He had long, dark hair tied back with a leather strip. He was a foot taller than any man she'd ever met, and his arms were muscular. She was sure he was a handsome man under all that bushy facial hair. She needed to snap out of the fog surrounding her mind, but every time she closed her eyes she saw that awful man torturing Penny's mama.

"I'm going to sleep in the barn. The bed is big enough for both of you to sleep in. You don't need to lie on the hard floor, Blue Sky," the giant whispered.

Sarah closed her eyes and tried to think about George, the man of her future. The mattress sloped down on one side and she rolled to the center. She opened her eyes and saw the big Indian woman looking at her. They stared into each other's eyes. Sarah wasn't afraid of this stranger. She smiled and drifted off to sleep.

Grinning with tobacco-stained smile and a few missing teeth, the monster sauntered toward her. His big hands were held high in the air and he smacked his lips like he was going to devour something—her.

In the wee hours of the next morning, blood-curdling screams came from Sarah's throat. Trembling and shaking, she hid under the fur rug and begged, *"Please, no. Why, oh why wasn't it me . . . instead of her?"* she continued to scream.

~

Buster was howling and pawing the front door. Seth pushed past the dog and burst through the door, carrying the lantern from the barn. He couldn't believe what was happening in his cabin. Sarah was screaming with her head under the fur cover while the child stood whimpering beside the bed in a puddle of pee. Blue Sky stood at the end of the bed with her tomahawk waving in the air.

"What the hell, Blue Sky? Put that axe down before you hurt someone. You're scaring the child."

"Mama, Mama, I want my mama," Penny screamed.

Blue Sky shook her head, lowered the tomahawk and said something in her language. She picked up Penny and carried her outside to the privy.

Seth pulled the heavy fur cover off Sarah's head. He sat down on the bed and pulled her into his big arms. Sarah fought him until he shoved her head down on his shoulder. He held her struggling body tight while soothing her with reassuring words. "You're safe now. No one will ever hurt you. I'm your protector now. The bad men are gone."

~

Sarah was awake and hoped she was safe in the big man's arms. She tightened her grip on his shirt and held on with clenched fists. Her crying turned to whimpering and hiccupping. "Are . . . you . . . sure . . . they're gone? Poor Julie. . . I should have helped her, but I was afraid they would hurt her little girl."

~

"Miss, what happened yesterday wasn't your fault. You aren't to blame." He reached for a cup of water on the table next to the bed. "Drink. Water will help you." Sarah reached for the tin cup.

Seth held Sarah in his arms and rocked while sitting on the edge of the bed. He stared down into Sarah's face—her lovely, natural complexion with pale blue veins in her eyelids. She had relaxed and fallen sound asleep in his arms. He laid her down gently.

Early the next morning, Blue Sky entered the cabin holding Penny. "Is the child alright?" Seth asked.

"She misses her mama. She's not afraid of me. I will give her a warm bath after you gather fresh eggs and bring in some fresh goat milk." Blue Sky carried Penny with her out to the well to get water.

Seth returned with a small pail of fresh goat's milk and a dozen clean, fresh eggs. "Now we'll have flapjacks in just a few minutes."

He took the pail of water and set it in the fireplace to heat it for Penny's bath.

In fifteen minutes, Blue Sky undressed the child and had her placed in the warm water. The child seemed to be enjoying herself until it was time for her to have her hair washed.

"Don't want my head wet."

Blue Sky continued to pour warm water over Penny's head while she sputtered and spat water. "If you want flapjacks, you'll settle down." The girl quieted down after that.

~

While the bacon was sizzling, Sarah lifted her head smelling the wonderful aroma of food being cooked. She looked over the room. The woman named Blue Sky dried the child off and dressed her in a fresh pair of bloomers and a dress lying in her lap. The big man was bending down over the fireplace and cooking. Her stomach growled from the wonderful smell in the room.

"Good morning, again," Seth said as Sarah attempted to sit up on the edge of the bed. She felt covered from head to toe in the long white nightgown that Blue Sky must have dressed her in while she slept.

"Mister, my mind is still foggy. I don't know who you are," Sarah said, feeling anxious and confused.

"Folks call me Seth. I'm a fur trapper during the fall and spring. Do you remember your name?"

Sarah thought for a moment and nodded. "Yes, I'm sorry to say I remember . . . everything." She watched Seth spooned up the bacon from the black skillet.

"My name is Sarah Sullivan and I was going to the fort to meet my fiancé, George Turnberry. We were to be married as soon as I arrived. Whenever his captain gave his permission, that is."

"So you aren't married? What about the little girl?" Seth asked, his brow furrowed.

"Penny isn't my child. Julie . . . the other woman traveling with me, is . . . or was her mama. They were going to the fort to meet her husband, John."

"John who? I might know this man because I know many of the soldiers. But, I don't know a soldier called George Turnberry."

"Julie's last name was Connors. John Connors was her husband." Sarah's heart ached for the young mother. Sarah gazed at the flames dancing in the fireplace. "I just met them on the stage. May I go out to the privy once more, then after I eat, lie back down? I'm exhausted."

"I'm sure you're tired. Your nightmares kept you awake last night."

~

While Sarah and the child took a morning nap, Seth went out to the barn and opened the bag of items he had picked up around the stagecoach. There were many women's items, and he was sure Sarah could use them.

Chapter 4

Will Hammer wasn't dead even though he felt like he should be. An Indian scout from Fort Laramie had come upon the scene of the accident and discovered Will lying on the side of the mountain where the stagecoach had gone over. Will had been shot and couldn't control the horses. He knew if found alive the gang of men would have killed him so he prayed and jumped. A bullet lodged in his shoulder, his leg was broken and several ribs were cracked, but he was alive.

~

The scout made Will as comfortable as he could before he went down the mountain to view the scene of the crime. He found the stagecoach empty and six dead horses. Several of them had been shot in the head. Will had said there were two women and a child aboard the stagecoach, but they were missing. Walking around, he discovered a fresh grave and ladies' items scattered all around the boot of the stage. The bank's money and mail bag were missing, too. Dried blood was on the ground near the coach, and this disturbed the man. Probably the reason for the grave, he thought.

When he returned, the Indian Scout made a travois, placed Will on it and rode into Fort Laramie with the unconscious man. He took Will to the fort hospital and went straight to the captain's office to give a report of what he had discovered.

The captain sat down at his desk and placed his face in both of his hands. "I was afraid something like this might happen. I wanted this kept a secret and have a dozen outriders guarding that payroll.

The fool. Now the men won't get their paychecks again. More men will be deserting, and I can't blame them."

"What are you going to tell Sergeants Connors and Turnberry about their women? Both are missing from the stagecoach and there's a grave. John's wife was bringing his child."

"Now that is two more fools. I warned them both about bringing their women-folk to this damn isolated place. What can I say? *Oh, by the way, your wives are dead or they have been carried off by a gang of men.* Should I give them leave to go out and find their wives? Hell, this is a mess, and it's not my fault. I'm retiring in a month, and I can't fix this problem with so little time."

The Indian scout stood as stiff as a carved wooden Indian in front of a hotel. His blood ran cold as he listened to the heartless man.

"Tell Corporal White to summon the two men to my office immediately. Let me get this over with."

~

Sergeant George Turnberry had seen Will Hammer being carried into the hospital on a stretcher. Where was the stagecoach? Just as he started to the hospital, Corporal White called to him.

"Sir, the captain has requested your immediate attention in his office."

"Do you know why the driver of the stagecoach is here without the stage? He always drives the coach from Lakewood to here."

"Sorry, Sir. I'm not at liberty to say," the corporal replied.

When George arrived at the captain's office, John was about to enter. "I hope we have good news about our wives." George patted John on the back and agreed.

"Good morning, men. I know you both were expecting the stage to arrive yesterday, as I was. I was waiting on a thirty-thousand-dollar payroll, so I could pay the men their last three months' wages. That is not to be as your wives will not be arriving today or any time soon, if at all."

John leaped forward to the captain's desk, spitting and sputtering in his face. "What are you saying or not saying? Where is the stagecoach, and more importantly, where are my wife and child?"

George froze in place. He couldn't form any words. He was expecting Sarah, the woman he had loved for years, to arrive and become his wife. "What happened?" a whisper came from his throat as he listened to John scream at the captain.

"Will Hammer, the driver of the stagecoach, told one of our Indian scouts that the stagecoach was chased by rustlers when the coach and horses went over the mountain. The scout went down the mountain and searched the stagecoach, but it was empty. Your women and the child were missing. He did say there was dried blood everywhere and a fresh grave with no name."

"I understood a dozen men were guarding the stage or I would have never allowed my wife and child to travel with the Cavalry payroll."

"I was told the same thing, you fool. Don't come in here raising your voice to me. I'll have you put under the jail." The captain pulled on his coat and smoothed his mustache. He strode to the front of his desk and looked both men in the eyes. "Now," clearing his throat before he spoke, "I know you're disappointed, so I'm going to give you both a month's leave of absence to go in search of your loved ones. That's all I can do. You are dismissed. Please get on with your business as I have a lot to do."

Both men stood looking at each other, stunned at the way the captain had told them about their wives. He didn't offer any help from the Cavalry—no scout or men to help search. Just time off for them to hunt on their own.

Thank goodness, this old man was retiring in a month. Hopefully, he'd be gone by the time they returned with their women, George thought.

~

Sergeant John Connors and Sergeant George Turnberry were issued their leave of absence from their units. They found the Indian scout who had carried in Will Hammer and bartered with him to help lead them to the site of the accident. "We're going to need a scout to stay with us until we find the men who took our wives. Can you help us?"

"I know two young hunters who can find a rabbit hole in the wilderness. They live outside fort. They will want flour, sugar, and other supplies for their family to eat. Can you provide that? Before trip?"

George and John agreed. "We'll get it this afternoon and be ready to leave at first light. Is that enough time for you?" John asked.

"Time is something we don't have a lot of," George said. "Please, we must hurry. We don't want the weather to wash away any tracks."

"Apish and Askook will be happy to lead you. You call them Coyote and Snake. They good boys and great hunters. If those men can be found, they will find them."

Early the next morning before the sun came up, the four men were on the trail to the scene of the accident in hopes of finding some clues as to which way the gang rode away.

Chapter 5

Sarah and Penny slept most of the day. Seth hoped that Sarah's sleep was from exhaustion and not a head injury caused from the accident. After a gentle knock on the door, he placed the bag of items from the stagecoach next to the door.

"Who is it?"

"I just put a bag by the door. I'll take care of the animals and bed down in the barn. You don't need to lock the front door. Buster is a good guard dog, and he'll warn me if something is in the area."

As he stepped away from the doorway, Sarah called to him, "Thanks, mister."

"Seth. My name is Seth." He grinned and closed the door.

~

Sarah investigated the feed sack and was surprised to find her new cotton gown—the one she planned to wear on her wedding night. She lowered her face into the soft fabric and cried, "Oh, George, will I ever see you again?"

Gathering her strength, she undressed and used the water in the pail to wash. She dressed in the new gown and looked at herself. This was not the wedding night she ever expected. Easing toward the bed, Sarah removed the child's shoes and placed her on the pallet beside the bed. The child turned over, pulled her dolly close and sighed.

Sarah removed the heavy fur quilt that covered the bed and slipped under the other one. The bed felt like heaven. After a few hours of restless sleep, screams tore from her throat. She was stabbing a man over and over. Blood was spewing like a fountain from his ugly body. She tossed and turned and kicked out from under the cover. Penny began to cry, and her cries became screams.

~

Buster was barking and jumping on the porch. Sarah was writhing in the bed making frightening sounds while the child stood in the middle of the floor screaming for her mama at the top of her lungs.

Seth grabbed the child and held her tight, whispering soothing words while attempting to care for Sarah. Penny hiccupped and stuck two fingers in her mouth, then lay down with her dolly.

Seth stooped down beside the bed on one knee and lifted Sarah into a sitting position. "You're safe now, Miss. The bad dream is over. Wake up." Seth looked around the room, but Blue Sky was nowhere in the cabin.

Sarah grabbed Seth around the neck and placed her tear-soaked face into his naked chest. "I'm sorry."

"It's alright. Here." Seth lifted her off the bed and placed her in the rocking chair. "I'm going to fix you some hot tea that will help you rest."

~

Sarah wiped her face with the tail of her gown and watched him crush tea leaves and pour hot water over them. He stirred the cup and held it out to her. "This is an old Indian recipe. You'll rest and feel better in the morning."

~

Blue Sky entered the back door. Peering at Sarah, she knew instantly from all the screaming the woman had had another bad dream. The little one had carried on too by the way she hiccupped. For now her eyes were closed, and she sucked on two fingers.

Sarah finished the hot liquid and walked back to the bed. She smoothed the hair away from Penny's face and patted her shoulders.

Blue Sky reached for Penny and laid her next to her in the bed. Penny's eyes opened, she sniffed and begged for her mama. Pulling her into her arms, Blue Sky placed her across her bosom and patted her until she fell asleep.

21

~

Early the next morning, Seth carried an armload of firewood and put it in a box next to the fireplace. He glanced at the bed and saw the little girl peeking out from under the covers. She smiled at him and held up her arms. "Got to pee-pee, now."

Seth reached over Sarah's sleeping body and pulled the child into his arms. He motioned for Blue Sky to be still. "I'll take her out to the privy. It turned cold last night, so stay in bed until the cabin is warmer." He helped Penny with her clothes and set her inside the outhouse.

"I finished," she called.

Seth took her inside and set her down in front of the fire. He took a soft cloth and washed her face and hands. "Are you hungry, Princess?"

"My name ain't . . . princess. Mama calls me Penny. I want my mama. Where's Mama?" Tears clouded the child's eyes.

"Are you hungry, Penny?" Seth asked again, pulling on a blond curl. He didn't want the child to start crying again. Sarah would have to tell the child about the accident soon.

Bending her head to one side, the little girl managed a small smile and demanded a biscuit.

~

Sarah had awakened and was listening to the pair discuss breakfast. She stretched under the covers. The child would have to be told about her mama soon, but how?

"Penny, Sarah's awake. I wonder if she's as hungry as a bear."

"Sarah ain't no bear, silly. You ain't no bear." she pointed to her.

"I'm going to step outside while you get dressed, Miss. I'll fix some bacon and eggs this morning and flapjacks if Penny wants them. I'm not good at baking biscuits."

Sarah watched him from the front window. After he'd walked into the barn, she hurried and removed her gown. Seeing her carpet bag in the corner thrilled her. Pulling a blue dress out of the bag of things Seth had gathered from the stagecoach, she decided it didn't matter if it was wrinkled. "Thank goodness, this was saved." Sarah reached inside and retrieved her comb and hairbrush. Taking the brush, she swiped at her long hair and tied a ribbon to hold it back out of her eyes. She slipped on her shoes and waited for Seth to come back inside so she could go to the privy. Blue Sky was still asleep, which surprised Sarah.

Seth knocked before he entered the cabin. He carried a bucket of goat's milk and a few more clean eggs.

Excusing herself, she went outside to have a few minutes of privacy. When she returned, she stood watching the big man slice a slab of bacon. Blue Sky was sitting in a rocker holding Penny and her dolly.

"Would you like for me to fry the bacon and eggs? I can cook and I need to stay busy." Sarah moved toward him and took the eggs.

"If you're up to it. I would love someone else's cooking."

Taking the large skillet down from the wall on the fireplace, Sarah wiped it and placed it over the grate in the fire. Seth had sliced a big hunk of smoke pork and placed it on a plate next to her. She lay the meat in the hot skillet and cracked a half dozen eggs, then glancing at Seth, decided she'd better cook more. The big six-foot plus, muscular man could eat a dozen scrambled eggs.

Buttering some old bread, she laid pieces into another flat-iron skillet and toasted them. She flipped the bacon and removed some of it onto a large plate. Finally, she poured the eggs into the hot grease, and the room smelled delicious.

~

Seth had made a fire outside for coffee. He carried a steaming granite pot inside and poured two cups. Then he poured about an inch of coffee in a cup and filled it to the brim with goat's milk for Penny. The warm drink would make her feel good on the inside. "This old cabin has never smelled so good," Seth declared.

"Everything is ready. Please sit down next to Penny and her dolly." Blue Sky continued to sit in the rocker but declined anything to eat.

Sarah poured a glass of water into the skillet before she sat down. Seth glanced at the skillet with a questioning look.

"Just a habit. It's easier to wash after the meal that way. Our skillet is my mama's prized piece of cooking utensils."

"Miss, do you mind if I call you Sarah? Miss Sullivan sounds so formal." Seth gave her a big grin.

"Sarah is fine. I've been calling you Seth. What's your last name?"

"Jenkins. Seth Jenkins."

"Seth Jenkins, do you have a wife and kids?"

"No, Sarah Sullivan." Seth smiled at the lovely lady. "I'm a loner up here in the mountains, but I do have a farm in south Texas my brother takes care of for me." He stared at Penny, who sat in the middle of the bed playing with her doll.

"Sarah, I know you're in a hurry to get to Fort Laramie. Since the stagecoach hasn't arrived at the fort, a search party is out looking for it. I'm going to take you and the child to Fort Laramie before it starts snowing. But first, I have to prepare my furs for sale before we leave, and I need to get someone to care for my animals while I'm gone. It will be a hard trip because we'll have to travel on horseback. I wish I could take a wagon, but the trails and roads in these mountains aren't made for wagons."

"Can I help you with anything that will help us leave sooner?"

"I hope to be ready to leave in three days. I'm sorry, but that's the best I can do. I was heading home when I saw the men and your stagecoach." He watched Sarah's expression. When she didn't reply, he continued. "If you feel like cooking, that will be a great help."

"I haven't thanked you for saving us. We're at your mercy, sir, but I feel safe here with you. I'll cook and do anything else I can before we leave."

"I have something I removed from the other woman's body. It was tucked down in her dress. I hope it will be a nice keepsake for the child or her papa. Maybe you can show it to her when you talk about her mama not coming home."

"Not coming home? I guess that would be a way to begin telling her about her mama." Sarah watched Penny play with her dolly in front of the fireplace.

Chapter 6

"Penny, why don't you and I get dressed in something warm and go outside this morning? Seth has chickens, a litter of pigs and goats. Let's go see them and get some fresh air."

"Oh boy. Can I feed the chickens?"

"May I feed the chickens, Penny?" Sarah corrected her English.

"Sure you can, if you aren't too scared of them." Penny slipped her feet into her shoes.

~

Seth laughed and went out the door pulling on his fur-lined vest. This was a good time for him to be moving back south to his farm. He didn't know if he could spend another winter all alone in this isolated cabin when the snow became too deep for trapping. He didn't realize how much he'd missed companionship with other people.

Sarah, along with Blue Sky and Penny, stepped outside into the bright sunshine when a crisp cold breeze hit them in the face. The clean air felt wonderful to Sarah. She held Penny's hand as they strolled around the small pens. Blue Sky gave Penny a handful of feed to scatter about for the dozen golden and white laying hens.

Penny called to them, "Here chick, chick, chick. Come get something to eat." Penny laughed at the big hens pecking at her white shoes.

"Come see the little piglets, little one," Blue Sky called.

Penny watched as the big mama sow laid on her side and nursed her six little babies. They rooted and pushed each other out of the way, eager to get to a teat. The mama pig raised her big head and glared at the women outside of the wooden pen. "Look at the baby goat. I want one for my very own," Penny yelled at the top of her lungs.

~

Seth cast his eyes at Sarah. He could tell she didn't know how to respond to the child. Her heavy-hearted expression said she didn't want to deny the child a new pet.

Sarah frowned at Seth, piercing him with a look that pleaded for help since the goats belonged to him.

Great, he thought. Now I'm the bad guy. "Penny, while you're here, you can help me take care of the baby goats. They'll have to stay here when we leave."

"Why?" Penny grabbed Seth's hand and pulled him toward the fenced area where the baby goats frolicked.

"When we leave here, the baby can't ride a horse and it's too far for him to walk."

"Sarah can hold it and you can hold me." Penny's held a confident determination.

With a grim expression, Seth walked into the barn, leaving Sarah to take care of the situation about the goat. "Women," he said out loud to himself. "They always have an answer for everything they want."

~

After surveying Seth's small farm area and his summer garden that had mostly turned to weeds, Sarah sat on a large tree stump in front of the cabin. She watched Penny chase the goats, and the chickens chasing her. It was wonderful to see the sparkle in the child's eyes again.

The thought of having to tell this precious child her mama wasn't ever coming home nearly broke her heart. The sooner she told her, the better it would be for her when reunited with her father at Fort Laramie.

The air was getting cooler, but it was about an hour before she had to prepare lunch and put Penny down for a nap. Sarah slid off the stump and called to the little girl, "Come with me, sweetheart, and let's take a short walk." She could feel Seth's and Blue Sky's sad eyes on their back as she and Penny strolled hand in hand down the trail away from the cabin.

A short distant from the cabin, Sarah smoothed a patch of grass for both of them to sit. "This is a lovely spot to overlook the mountainside, isn't it?" Penny nodded and smiled down at a bug crawling on the ground.

"Penny, did your mama or papa ever tell you stories about Jesus and Heaven?" Sarah asked quietly.

"Yep, I talk to Jesus at night and Mama took me to a place where we singed, and you know what?" Penny asked while looking over her shoulder.

"What?" Sarah asked concerned.

Penny wide eyes were shining bright. "A scary man screamed, 'Bad people go down there.'" She pointed to the ground. "'And fry like a chicken.' Sometimes he yelled, 'hell, hell, gonna go to hell.' He said, 'no drinking' too." Penny looked around to make sure no one was listening. "But, you know what?" She didn't wait for a reply. "Mama gave me milk and water all the time, but I didn't tell."

Sarah tried to look serious at the way she described the preacher at the church she and her mama attended. "So, did the man say anything good about a place called Heaven?" Sarah asked, hoping her mama had spoken about it.

"Don't know 'cause I put my hands over my ears like this." She demonstrated. "Mama would pull my hands down and make me sit still beside her on the hard bench until my fanny hurt."

"Sweetheart, Heaven is a wonderful place to go and live with Jesus. If a person has been sick for a long time or hurt badly in an accident, when they go to Heaven, they're made well. They aren't in pain and they are happy again. It's a lovely place with pretty flowers, lovable animals of all kind, and only nice people live there. Jesus is there with his arms open and waiting on them to come to him. He was there for your mama."

Penny held her hand over her eyes to shade them from the sun. "You mean that place up there in the clouds?"

'Well, that's what I learned when I was little like you."

"I don't wanna go there. Do I have to?" she asked, still not understanding.

"No, darling, you aren't hurt or sick, but your mama was hurt bad in the stagecoach accident. You were sleeping when the stage rolled over and down the mountain. Do you remember that happening?"

"No, but I heard mama screaming."

"Yes, she was crying because she was hurt . . . from the accident. When Seth came, he buried your mama and she went to be with Jesus in Heaven."

"I don't want her up there," Penny wailed. "I want her here with me." She cried as Sarah held her close and rocked her back and forth until there were no more tears.

"Seth is going to take us to Fort Laramie so you can be with your papa. I know you haven't seen him in a long time, but honey, he's going to be thrilled to see you."

"Are you going to stay with me?" Penny hiccupped and wiped her eyes.

"Yes, I'm going to be married and live at the fort with my new husband. I will visit with you." Sarah tried to reassure the child that she wouldn't be alone at her new home.

Chapter 7

Sarah and Penny strolled back to the open space in front of the cabin. Blue Sky was speaking in her native language to a giant of an Indian man. This man wasn't a stranger because Buster didn't run around barking at him.

Sarah stopped, pushed Penny behind her skirt, and called to Blue Sky, "Hello."

The Indian couple broke apart from where they'd been huddled.

"Come, Sarah, this is my man, Red Feather. He will not harm you. We'll be leaving for our teepee in the valley after lunch. Seth is preparing some hides and furs for us."

"Why do you have to leave? I thought you lived here with him," she said, nodding toward the barn.

"No," Red Feather spoke for the first time. "We hunt and fish together in the fall and spring, but winter is no good. Snow is too deep to move about. We go before snow falls and traps us here."

"I see." Sarah looked off into the distant. "I'll be here alone with Seth?"

"Not alone. You have girl child here." He peered down at Penny.

~

Seth had come out of the barn and listened to the conversation. He knew the concern that Sarah felt. If the soldiers found her living with him alone, her reputation would be smeared. She would be a tainted woman no other man would want to marry.

"Sarah, I see you met Red Feather. He has been my good friend for many years. He taught me everything I needed to know about trapping. We have always lived apart during the worst of the winter. This year Blue Sky and Red Feather will go back to their home and I'll travel to my home in south Texas. I have a small farm I'm planning to build into a cattle ranch. Today we'll share lunch and say good-bye. Tomorrow, we'll pack our things and head to Fort Laramie to reunite you with your fiancé and the little one's papa."

Sarah approached him. "I'll be happy to help you pack, but now I'll help Blue Sky finish lunch. I'm going to miss her."

"Yes, me too." He turned to go back into the barn. Red Feather passed her and entered the barn.

The lovely clouds had turned dark as Red Feather led his pony down the rough path with Blue Sky in the saddle. It was hard holding back tears when Sarah hugged the big Indian woman who had cared for her and Penny. She would never see this woman again. Maybe she should keep a journal like she had read sea captains did while sailing the seas.

~

Seth walked softly up beside her. "Maybe tonight, you can gather your personal things into one bag, so we can get an early start in the morning. I want to get off this mountain before dark so we can camp on level ground."

"Yes, I'll do that. I'm excited about reaching the fort. The men have probably been searching for our stagecoach. I'm surprised they haven't found us up here in the mountains."

"This is rough country, which you'll see once we start traveling. I'm sure they're probably still looking, and we might even run into them on our way."

After supper, Seth sat at the table and wrote a note to trappers that they were welcome to the cabin and anything that was left.

Seth went to the barn to prepare extra feed and plenty of water for the animals he had to leave behind. Many trappers stopped by, so he wasn't too worried about them starving. He decided to pull the goats behind the mules and leave the gate open for the sow and her piglets. The mama sow would root and forage for food until her babies were grown. Seth wished he could haul them all home, but the trails were impossible for wagons to make the trip.

The following morning, Seth and the girls had said goodbye to the cabin, and were making good time on the trail down the mountain. He placed the younger goat across the blankets on one of the mules' backs. Poor little fellow's legs had given out on him.

After several long hours, they stopped and made camp for lunch. While the girls were seeking privacy, Seth built a nice fire and made a pot of coffee to help warm everyone's insides. The air had turned chilly. After a cold lunch of ham sandwiches and hot coffee, Seth dipped some water from the stream that ran beside the mountain trail to water the animals.

Moments after he sat on a smooth boulder to rest, a blast rattled the ground, shaking him to the ground. Dynamite.

Sarah and Penny lay huddled against each other. "What was that?" Sarah's eyes were as big as saucers.

"I'm not sure, but it's not good. It's about a mile from here, in the same direction we're headed. Will you be alright while I ride ahead and find out what caused that blast?"

"Yes, please hurry before another blast takes place."

Chapter 8

Sergeant John Connors and Sergeant George Turnberry followed the young Indian guides. After several days, the guides had discovered the place where the stagecoach went over the mountain. After scouting around the stagecoach and the awful stench of the partially eaten animals, they soon found a grave. Wolves and coyotes were fighting in and around the big hole in the ground.

George Turnberry pulled out his revolver and fired several shots into the pack of wild animals, killing several while the others scattered but didn't move far away.

Sergeant Connors hurried to the hole, fell down on his knees, and looked inside. The awful smell nearly caused him to gag but he viewed several strains of blond hair tossed around in the bottom of the pit. His beautiful wife had blond hair and now she lay in a hole in the ground with wild breasts fighting for her body.

"NO!" he cried, screaming over and over. He ran at the wild critters who had only moved out of sight. "Get away, you stinking varmints." He fell to his knees again and screamed, "Julie, my beautiful Julie." Suddenly he stood, whirled, and raced to his horse like a wild man. He searched into his saddlebag until he found several sticks of dynamite.

~

George and the two young scouts watched John run around tossing everything out of his saddlebags until he found what he needed.

George rode over to John. "What are you doing?"

"I'm going to blow this place up so nothing will ever hurt my wife again." John ignited the blasting caps on the sticks of dynamite. Screaming he waved the dynamite. "If you don't want to die, you'd best get back. I can't live without my wife."

George watched as the two young guides rode their horses away from the site as fast as lightning. John ran to the gravesite with the dynamite still burning. He couldn't keep John from committing suicide, so he kicked his horse in the flanks and hurried after the scouts.

In a matter of seconds, the whole side of the mountain exploded into the air with tons of mountain rocks sliding down over the stagecoach, dead horses, gravesite and Sergeant John Connors.

A gigantic hole appeared where the mountain trail had stood. Partials of sandy dirt, wood, and hard rock filled the sky with dusty rain that floated for miles into the air. Many trees that had stood in the valley for years were blown over, blocking the side of the mountain's passageway to the valley.

George and his two guides lay on the ground covering their heads while holding their horses' reins with all the strength they had. When it was over, they stood and looked down over the covered valley. Their clothes and hats were covered with dirt.

"Thank goodness we got far enough away." Snake breathed a sigh of relief while glancing at his brother.

"Come men, we can't do anything more here. Let's get back to the fort."

The two young guides glanced at him. "Sir," Snake caught up to him. "You don't want to look for your woman and the child? I'm sure we could find them, and the money those men stole."

"I wish my fiancée had been in that grave. I'd rather know she's dead than captured by those rustlers. You know how she'll be treated." Disgust dripped from his voice.

"But sir, we might save her and the little girl."

"Don't you understand? She's already dead to me. They'll probably sell the child. Don't ever mention her name to me again. Let's go to the fort. I might get a promotion since Sergeant Connors is dead and the captain will be leaving soon."

~

The Indian scouts sat staring at the man who had searched for his woman day and night for nearly a week and now showed no remorse. "White man is like the other one—crazy, but without heart." Coyote shook his head in sadness.

Seth couldn't believe his eyes. The trail was nothing but a big hole, and the sky was raining dust and debris. Trees that had stood for years had been ripped up blocking the west trail that circled the mountain down to the valley.

He studied the area and realized his only option was to return to the cabin and remain there until some of the other trappers came along to help him dig a fresh path. Surely every man within a ten-mile radius would have heard the explosion. With winter coming and heavy snow, he wouldn't be the only trapper who had plans to go below but now was forced to stay up on the mountain until spring.

He hated to have to tell Sarah there wasn't any way down the mountain until other trappers could help clear a new trail. She'd been so excited about leaving and joining her new husband-to-be.

Seth rode into the camp area where Sarah sat with Penny's head in her lap sleeping. He looked around, satisfied his mules, dog and goats were fine. Sarah was a good helpmate and he was thankful for that. It was going to be a hard winter, and he hoped she would be able to endure the long, cold days and freezing nights.

Seth eased down onto the hard ground beside Sarah and the child. He tossed a piece of dry wood into the fire and glanced at the lovely lady with mahogany brown hair that sparkled. He had tried hard not to pay any attention to her beauty, but this was certainly going to be a long winter. Gazing into her face, he saw her frown.

"The news is not good. The road down to the valley is blocked with huge boulders, piles of sand, rock and fallen trees. We're going to have to return to the cabin and spend most of the winter there, if not all of it. I'm hoping some of the other trappers will come and help me clear a pathway so we can reach the valley come spring. I have no idea who blew up the mountain or why."

"Do you think they were panning for gold?"

"That never crossed my mind, but surely they would know how to handle dynamite," Seth commented as he stood. "I figured you'd be having a fit because I can't take you to the fort."

"I would like to scream because I'm disappointed, but it isn't your fault. I can't blame you for this delay. George most likely thinks I'm already dead."

"I'm sure some other trapper will tell the fort about this roadblock. They'll have to find another way for the stagecoach to travel back and forth between Fort Laramie, Wyoming, and Canon, Colorado."

Seth reached for Sarah's hand and helped her up from the ground with the child in her arms. "We'd better get back to my cabin before someone else homesteads it. I did leave a note giving permission to anyone who came along." He smiled and helped her onto the pack mule. "I'll carry the child."

He hurried to his horse and climbed up while holding Penny.

~

Sarah trailed behind him. *That is one strong man.* She smiled.

Chapter 9

Settling back into the mountain cabin didn't take long. Sarah unpacked her personal items and placed her bag of clothes under the bed. She unloaded the food items, skillet and coffee pot and began preparing some supper.

Seth took his mules and the goats into the barn and fed them oats and hay. They seemed content to be back in their home. The mama sow and her babies were still in the stall fast asleep. Everything seemed to be back to normal, but it was going to be a hard winter and he hoped Sarah and Penny would fare well.

The next morning, Seth dressed in warm clothes while Sarah packed him an extra-large lunch with a big canteen of fresh water. He carried an extra sharp axe and several big shovels on his pack mule. Most of the trappers would be gathered where the explosion had taken place. They would make plans to begin digging a trail down the valley.

"Sarah, it will be dark when I arrive back home. Buster will stay behind with you. He'll warn you if there's trouble around. Remember what I said about how to fire the buffalo gun. Don't get it down unless you plan to use it."

After he picked up the pack mules' reins, he called again to her, "You don't have to wait up for me. Go on to bed. I'll be spending the night in the barn after I come inside and get something to eat."

Sarah and Penny waved good-bye while holding Buster's leash. The dog strained against the rope, trying with all his might to follow his master.

~

Long after Seth was out of sight, they went inside the cabin to enjoy another cup of coffee and decide what they would cook for lunch and supper today. Cooking was the biggest chore each day because dry beans and fresh meat had to simmer for hours.

While Penny played with her dolly, Sarah counted the days on her make-shift calendar on the wall. They were going to spend Christmas up on the mountain. Thanksgiving had come and gone without any fanfare, but Christmas was going to be different.

Once the dry beans were boiling in a pot with a big piece of salt pork and another pot simmered with two squirrels Seth had caught in a snare earlier that morning, Sarah reached into her bag of clothes. She found a lovely gold and white blouse that had belonged to Julie and decided to cut it apart and make several pieces of doll clothes.

After a lunch of hot toast and ham with warm goat's milk, Sarah dressed Penny in her warm coat. They went for a short walk around the cabin and barn. Penny loved the piglets and the mama sow didn't seem to care. The goats wanted to jump around and butt Penny playfully. She ran from them in the barn and they chased after her. Sarah sat on a bale of hay and watched. Penny needed to get outside and exercise her legs, so she would rest well.

Later in the day, Sarah sat by the fire, sewing the doll clothes while Penny took a long nap. She cooked supper and they went to bed late into the night. If Seth came home, she didn't hear him.

The couple had gotten into a routine and every day, Seth did chores before he went to work to help clear the mountain trail while Sarah prepared good meals and readied the place for Christmas.

Chapter 10

Every afternoon, Sarah put the goats, laying hens, sow and her litter into the barn and locked them inside. She closed the mules up in their stalls, with extra wool blankets tossed across their backs.

"Now that the goats have wraps, are you going to make them earmuffs, too?" Seth teased while watching Sarah and Penny cuddle the solid white animals one morning.

"No, but if it starts snowing, I'll come out and place another blanket over the mules. I can't stand to know that they're cold out here."

"You are too soft-hearted. These are working animals that are used to this climate. If they belonged to some other trapper, they'd be out in the corral, not in a tight barn like mine."

"Well, they belong to you, not some other trapper."

The snow clouds appeared to be a good distance away, so Seth was headed with the other men to remove debris and big trees off the trail about two miles away. While feeding the animals, he noticed bear prints near the cabin. He decided to set a bear trap close to the door of the barn before he headed out.

Before Seth left, he called to Sarah. "Listen to me. I'll be gone all day, but if you hear an unusual noise, don't dare come outside. Understand? Don't let Penny out here alone at all."

Sarah nodded, giving him a smile. "I have made you a dozen sandwiches with the fresh bread I made yesterday to take with you.

I'm going to use the last of our fresh vegetables today and make a big pot of soup for supper." Sarah stared down at her feet. "Please be careful. I don't know what Penny and I would do without you."

"Well, just remember we aren't alone on this mountain. There are many trappers living up here, some with families, but most are alone. Many of the trappers know you're here. Red Feather will be with me today. So, if something happens to me, someone will come and get you off this mountain as soon as possible. Does that make you feel better?"

"Yes, but please be careful. We'll miss you."

He glanced back at the two of them, waving, then he rounded the curve of the wide trail.

~

"Come on Penny, let's go pick the carrots and potatoes. We need to cook a big supper for Seth because he'll be working hard today. Maybe we can make something sweet to have for dessert. Would you like to do that?"

"Yep. My mama and me made cookies. I love cookies."

She watched Penny skip around the cabin, stooping to the stringy, withered green leaves from the buried carrots. She twisted the green tops and pulled up two carrots. "Look, I have baby ones."

Sarah laughed at the pitiful carrots. "You got them just in time. Another day and they would have rotted in the ground."

After a long afternoon of cooking a big pot of squirrel stew, Sarah discovered a jar of blackberries that Seth had traded for with another trapper in the valley. After picking out the dried berries, she had enough left to make a blackberry roll. She mixed flour, salt and grease together well, then added enough cold water to make a stiff dough. The berries were left soaking in a cup of sugar water while she rolled out a thin dough. She sprinkled the berries into the dough and rolled it partially closed before adding more berries, then she placed it in a greased skillet in the fireplace to bake. If only she had real butter to mix with sugar to pour over the top, but living in the mountains wasn't like living in a small town or community. A person had to make do with what they had.

After giving Penny a good sponge bath and a clean gown, she tucked her into bed. Gardening and cooking had worn the little girl out, but she'd not mentioned her mama all day, and for that

Sarah was thankful.

The snow started falling again. She hurried and slipped on the heavy fur coat Seth had made for her, put her shoe boots down into his big black wader boots and hurried to the barn. Buster was on her heels, jumping and peeing on everything in his path. After placing another blanket on each mule and adding more hay to the hens' nests, she quickly placed each little piglet closer to their mama.

The two goats followed her all around the barn playing with Buster. She stooped and adjusted their coats she had made from extra wool blankets and hurried back outside. As she turned to make sure the barn door was closed tightly, she heard a loud snap just as quickly as she felt pain shoot through her leg. Glancing down, she'd stepped on an iron bear trap and the front of Seth's boot and her soft shoes were caught in the iron jaws.

"Oh no," she moaned. She tugged on her foot and gingerly pulled on the clamped jaws. With no luck, she lowered her body to the snow-covered ground and tried with all her strength to pull her shoe out of Seth's boot. The front part of her shoes was trapped because her big toe was burning with pain. She silently prayed the trap had not cut her toe off.

As she sat, captured by the big trap, she realized Seth must have viewed or heard a bear coming around. The bear would be after the chickens, pigs and goats. *Now I just might be his dinner.*

Buster stood at the door barking to get back inside the warm cabin. Penny had been sleeping soundly when she left the cabin to check on the animals. Sarah didn't want the dog to wake her.

"Buster," Sarah called to the little dog.

He bounded toward her. Seeing her down on his level, he began licking her face and neck. Sarah grabbed him into her arms because she was afraid he was going to bounce around and cause the other side of the trap to spring. She tucked him inside her warm coat. He was in heaven and lay quietly in her warm, soothing arms. His little furry body gave Sarah added warmth.

Cuddling Buster close in her oversized coat, she sat curled into a ball and waited as the snow peppered down harder. Several times Buster growled, which gave Sarah fright. She raised her head and peered around praying the little dog didn't smell the bear.

After several hours Buster growled and acted like he wanted to get down when she tried to contain him. Buster clawed and struggled in her arms and finally jumped loose. He raced up the snow-covered trail that led to the cabin. A horse whinnied, heavy footsteps sounded, and someone talking made its way to the barn.

"Help!" Sarah cried while Buster jumped up and down.

A gun blast close by nearly scared her to death. Sarah covered her head with her coat. Seth's voice echoed over Buster's barking. "Got him, fellow. Stand back." Another shot exploded and Sarah nearly fainted.

"Back boy, back," Seth yelled at Buster. "He won't be bothering our animals anymore."

"Help," Sarah cried again.

"Sarah, my heaven. How long have you been out here? Gosh almighty. You're caught in the bear trap."

"Thank God you've come home."

"Hold still, little one, while I unlock this trap." He tugged on the chain and released the spring, then he bent on one knee in front of her. "Are you hurting?"

With tears of relief flowing, she nodded. "Yes, my toes are in pain."

Once Seth had the trap unlocked, he pulled Sarah out of his big wader boots. Her shoe boot was smashed, and he quickly removed it but left her stocking on.

"Oh, I hurt," she moaned. "I feel like my toes are broken."

~

Seth scooped Sarah up into his arms and started toward the cabin. Her fur coat was soaked with snow, which made her heavier than she actually was. He stopped to adjust her weight and glanced down into her eyes. He had never witnessed anyone as lovely as this precious girl, and his heart leaped into his throat. *Lord help me. I've lost my heart to this little beauty.*

~

Sarah felt a change in her position while the big mountain man carried her. She looked up into his handsome face and ran her cold hand down the side of his snow-filled beard. Never had she felt such an intimate feeling for anyone. She was going to have to be careful because her heart was beginning to feel trapped with warmth, and it wasn't for the man waiting for her at Fort Laramie.

Chapter 11

Sarah sat in the rocker in front of the low-burning fire. A blast of cold wind came in with Seth with his armful of chopped wood. She noticed the bright stars over his shoulder when he stooped down to place the wood into the flickering fire.

"How long were you outside? This room is much colder than the barn. Maybe I need to go outside and get the blankets off the mules and bring them in here."

"No. I couldn't stand to know those poor animals were cold." Sarah stared into Seth's face and smiled. He enjoyed teasing her about how she took care of his animals.

~

As Seth watched Sarah hobble from the privy on her good foot, he felt like a love-starved youth. This was a woman who had already given her heart to another, but he was sure he had lost his to her. He needed to be careful around her, but he didn't give a tinker's damn about her fiancé. The man wasn't searching very hard to find his woman. If she was Seth's, nothing would keep him from finding her.

Sarah was the kind of woman any man would want for a wife. For years he felt he might die from being lonely and miserable. What frightened him the most was how much he desperately needed her. He wanted this young woman more than anything, but he had to continue to hide his feelings, for her sake.

Seth sat down in front of Sarah and removed the cold cloth that he'd placed around her foot. To hell with his emotions. He loved this woman and he was going to do everything to make her feel the same way about him.

~

"Are you alright? My foot is freezing. Are you going to wrap it in a dry rag?" Sarah could tell Seth's mind wasn't on caring for her foot.

"Of course," he mumbled. "I was making sure the swelling had gone down. Your toes aren't broken, but they'll be sore for a few days. The supper you cooked sure smells good. How about a bowl of soup?" Seth asked and lifted the lid off the big pot.

"Yes, please. I'm starving. Penny and I made you a dessert out of the last of your blackberries. I hope you don't mind, but she wanted to make cookies. The cookies might not be good using bear grease." Sarah smiled and pointed at the blackberry roll.

After ladling both of them a bowl of soup and a cup of water, Sarah continued to sit in the rocking chair while Seth positioned himself near the fire on the floor. "This is wonderful. Thank you," he said.

"Did the trappers show up to help today?"

"Yes, we had about twenty men helping, and we should have a way down into the valley in a month or so, if the snow doesn't get too deep. Most of the men are eager to get to the fort while the fur traders are there. Me too."

"A month? That means we'll still be here for Christmas."

"Yes, I'm sorry, but the men are working as hard as they can. We aren't lumberjacks and don't have the equipment to remove and drag trees away. We are working our pack mules as hard as we can."

"I understand, believe me. I know everyone wants to spend the winter in the valley."

"I'm sorry, but that's true. Do you think the child knows about Christmas and how people celebrate it?"

"She's only three, so I'm sure she won't remember or be disappointed if we don't do anything special."

"I haven't celebrated Christmas in a long time." Seth leaned back against the wall of the fireplace. "My folks always made it a special time of year for my brother and me. One Christmas, Pa built us a sled and painted it bright red. We played on the hillside, but the snow didn't stick for very long. We had a grand time." Seth sighed.

"Your pa sounds like a great man."

"He carved small animal figures and wooden play guns. We never had store-bought toys, but we didn't know the difference. Ma cooked candies, cakes and popcorn balls for us, too. She stuffed a turkey with all the trimmings and invited everyone who lived alone or couldn't afford anything special to join us. She was a caring person. You remind me of her, the way you care for the poor creatures out in my barn. Especially the way you've taken Penny under your wings in place of her mom."

"That is the nicest thing anyone has ever said about me. You are a kind man yourself." Sarah's head nodded as she ate her soup.

Seth reached for her bowl and placed it on the table. He lifted her chin and said, "It's time for bed, young lady. I hope you don't get sick from being out in the cold weather for so long." He walked around the fur-covered bed and moved Penny over to her side. Then he lifted Sarah out of the rocker and laid her down. He held the covers up so she could scoot under the blanket.

~

"Seth," Sarah whispered. "Please sleep in the cabin tonight. It's too cold to sleep outside."

"I'll see, but for now, I have a bear that I must go outside and take care of. I don't want his meat to spoil, and he has a great big fur covering his body I'll want to save. You go to sleep and don't be afraid. I am here."

After a few minutes, the door closed and the last comforting words Sarah remembered hearing as she drifted into a deep sleep were, "I am here."

Chapter 12

Seth went around the barn and found the black bear lying in a big bank of snow. He had been fortunate enough to have hit the bear in the back of his head with the first shot and then in the face when he whirled around. The rest of the bear's body was in perfect condition and would make a beautiful fur coat or a lovely warm rug.

Seth led one of the mules from the stall, tied ropes under the bear's corpse, and pulled him onto a flat table. After several hours of skinning the bear's fur hide from his body, he sawed the bear's claws off and placed them in a bucket. He'd save the claws and make a necklace for Blue Sky for Christmas. Seth had heard that Indians believed that a bear-claw necklace had special spiritual powers that gave protection and good health to the person wearing it.

After completion of skinning and gutting the beast, Seth cut chunks of the meat from the bear. He'd soak the meat overnight in saltwater and wrap the meat in soft cloth to share with the other trappers. Bear meat was tasty, cooked with dumplings, which all the men knew how to prepare.

Placing the mule back into his stall, Seth unwrapped his dirty fur coat and stretched it out over the stall's wall to dry out. He decided to take Sarah up on her offer and stay in the warm cabin tonight. He took a pail and filled it with water and carried it to the cabin with him. Easing the door open, he slid inside, quickly peering over at the bed to make sure he hadn't disturbed the two girls. Sighing with relief, he placed the pail over the fire while he stood in front of it warming his freezing body. He stooped down and added another log to the flickering fire.

Once the water was hot, Seth pulled off his furry vest and two flannel shirts and lowered the top of his red union suit down to his waist. He placed a hot cloth over his face and ran it in and around his bushy beard, removing small pieces of frozen snow tangled in it.

~

Sarah heard the door open and peeked over her fur blanket, watching Seth ease himself into the cabin, careful not to wake her. She should turn away and allow him full privacy, but she enjoyed watching him.

~

After Seth cleaned his face and beard, he took a bar of soap, placed it in the water and got it soapy. He rubbed the bar across his chest and under each armpit. He took the washcloth and rinsed himself, then reached for the warm towel and wiped his clean body. Seth reached in a bag and took out a long nightshirt, pulling it over his head. Satisfied that he hadn't disturbed the girls, he sat in the rocker and removed his boots and long stockings, then pushed his pants down and stepped out of them. He placed them in a pile beside the fire to dry. He washed his private parts and placed the dirty rag back into the warm water.

His eye caught Sarah turning over on the bed. Seth stood as still as a statue until Sarah settled down and he was sure she was asleep again. He lay another log on the fire and stretched out in front of it. He used one of his bedroll blankets as a pillow and covered himself with the other. Lying near the fire, he was asleep in a flash.

~

Once a soft snoring noise came from Seth, Sarah relaxed and smiled. Now that she knew every part of this wonderful man, she could rest.

Chapter 13

Buster's bark woke Sarah up. Penny was lying beside her awake. "Good morning, sweetheart. Did you sleep good last night? Were you warm enough?"

"Good morning," giggled Penny. "I need to go outside to pee, but it's too cold."

Sarah noticed a big blanket hanging across the corner of the room. Limping to the corner, she pulled the blanket back and saw the slop jar sitting on the floor. Seth had built them a water closet. "We don't have to go outside to the privy. Seth made us a water closet, so now we just have to go behind this big blanket. Come, let me help you over to it. Be careful and sit on the pot. There are some little rags on a table to use to wipe yourself clean."

"Now, my behind won't get frozen off." Penny laughed and climbed out of the bed.

"My goodness, child, where did you hear that?" Sarah asked smiling down at her.

"My grandma's behind got bit before."

Sarah laughed. "Do you mean she got frostbit?"

"I don't want frostbit on my hiney."

"My goodness. You've learned a lot, and you aren't very old yet."

"I know. I'm too big for my britches, but I can pull them up." Penny stood behind the curtain looking at Sarah.

"Get back under the covers while I warm some water to wash your face and hands. What would you like to eat this morning?"

"Can we eat some blackberry roll? I didn't get any last night."

Sarah smiled and said that she would warm it as she warmed the water. Opening the front door, Sarah waved at Seth. He hurried over.

"Good morning, sleepy head. You and Penny slept the morning away, but I'm glad to see you look well. How do your toes feel?"

"The toes are fine this morning. A little sore, but I'm thankful I still have them. We're both happy with our new water closet. That was so thoughtful of you. Penny won't get frostbit on her hiney now." Sarah laughed at the expression on Seth's face.

"You're welcome, I think." Smiling, he picked up the pail to get some fresh water.

"I'll start breakfast. How are the animals doing this morning? I'm happy it's stopped snowing," Sarah said in one breath.

"Breakfast will be appreciated, the animals are fine, and yes, it's good the snow stopped. I'll bring in some water." He turned her around and pushed her back inside.

~

Whistling, he strolled down to the swift branch of the stream and cracked the ice surface. He quickly filled the bucket and hurried back to the house. He knocked on the front door, then hurried back down to the branch to fill pails for the animals' water trough.

Seth gathered and washed the eggs and added more hay to their nests. If he didn't do this, Sarah would before dark. He couldn't help but smile at the way she cared for his animals. *Who had ever heard of goats wearing coats?* Red Feather would get a big laugh at that discovery.

Seth set the eggs beside the front door and started chopping a cord of wood for the barn and cabin. With the temperature dropping every night, they would use at least a cord of wood every week.

After Sarah waved at him to come in for breakfast, he placed the axe over his shoulder and entered the barn. He stood the axe on its oak handle end and made sure it was secure in the corner. A dirty axe made work difficult, so Seth kept his equipment clean and in good-working order. Seth held his hands over the fire in the barrel to warm them after removing his gloves, then reached for a clean rag and dipped it in a pail of water. He wiped his face, arms and hands, then he headed to the cabin with Buster. He could eat a buffalo.

Chapter 14

A jiggle of horse's reins could be heard coming up the trail to the cabin. Seth stood still and waited until Red Feather and Blue Sky appeared in his yard. "Hello, friend." Seth welcomed them with a wave of his hand.

"Friend," Red Feather repeated.

"You're just in time to partake of our breakfast. Sarah always cooks more than we can eat."

~

While Seth helped Blue Sky down, Red Feather led his horse, and Blue Sky's animal followed behind it. Red Feather tossed his animals a huge pile of fresh hay and let them loose to wander around in the barn.

~

Blue Sky had already disappeared into the cabin when the two men stood talking. "We agreed to take the day off and I'm happy we did. Sarah got caught in my bear trap, but she's fine. I did manage to shoot a big black bear. Wait until you see his big fur coat."

"Happy Sarah not hurt. You going to share some of that bear meat? I am sick of squirrel."

Seth nodded. "So, what brings you and Blue Sky out in the cold today?"

"Two young scouts who worked at Fort Laramie were concerned about their grandfather. They wore snowshoes and walked up the mountain to bring supplies to the old man. They said they led two men from the fort to where the stagecoach and women were attacked." Buster sniffed his moccasins. "Very sad. One man lost his mind when he discovered his wife's grave and blew up the mountain. Fool man went crazy," Red Feather said.

"What did the other man do—maybe Sarah's fiancé?"

"Scouts said they told man they could follow the rustlers and maybe find the woman and child alive. Man said his woman was dead to him."

"Are the young men still here on the mountain with their kin?"

"Yes, they stayed and helped us dig out." Red Feather headed toward the cabin.

"Red Feather," Seth called to him.

The old Indian turned.

"Don't mention anything about the two scouts and the men. Sarah doesn't need to know yet."

"My lips sealed. You'll tell her once we get off mountain and head for Fort Laramie?"

"Maybe. Her man may change his mind about wanting her back." Somehow he doubted his own statement.

Sarah's smile greeted Seth. "Isn't it wonderful we have visitors? Penny and I are thrilled to see Blue Sky again. She brought fresh butter from one of the other trapper's wives. Now I can bake cookies."

Blue Sky smiled and Penny clapped her hands, singing, "Cookies, cookies, I love cookies." Everyone smiled at the child.

"Come, men, and take a seat at the table. I have a big hot breakfast for all of us. We have flapjacks, ham, steaks, scrambled eggs and hot coffee." Sarah reached next to the fire and picked up the syrup and placed it in a small jar to pour easier.

The men devoured the food in less than ten minutes. Sarah laughed and asked if she should cook more, but the men just smiled and patted their stomachs. Red Feather burped and declared he was full.

The men rose, and Seth whispered a soft-spoken thank you, then they walked outside to the barn to view the new bear hide.

~

Blue Sky sat at the table and filled a plate with eggs and flapjacks. "Sit," she pointed to Sarah to take a place at the table next to her.

Laughing, Sarah pulled out the chair and flopped down in it. She watched Penny pretending to feed her baby doll. Sarah waited for Blue Sky to finish her breakfast before she asked about her health.

"Baby come soon," Blue Sky smiled and rubbed her big belly.

Sarah was surprised because she thought the woman too old to bear children. "How wonderful. Are you happy?"

Blue Sky grinned and nodded. "Soon. Red Feather say you help me." Blue Sky took Sarah's hand and squeezed it. Sarah felt blood drain from her face. She'd never witnessed a baby being born; in fact, she'd not heard much about the intimate facts about birthing. Her mama and Stella had always been called away to be the midwives.

Being isolated in these mountains with no other woman around, she couldn't refuse Blue Sky anything, much less not help her in her time of need. Sarah smiled at Blue Sky. "You will come her to have the baby."

Grinning, Blue Sky agreed.

Later in the day, Sarah asked Seth if he knew anything about birthing a child. He jumped up and nearly fell backwards.

"Are you with child?"

"For goodness' sake, you know I've never been married." When he didn't answer, she told him. "Blue Sky is going to have a baby."

Seth pulled the chair back to the table and sat down, breathing normally again. "I've delivered puppies, a colt, a calf, and a few kittens. A woman having a baby can't be much different."

"You're going to have to tell me a few things. She wants me to help her, and Red Feather won't allow you in the house when she goes into labor. I've never helped my mama deliver any of our friends' babies. I'm scared to death, but I'll help her."

"Is she going to have the baby soon?"

"Yes, after Christmas from the moons she counted on her fingers. Red Feather will bring her here."

"I'll help you by gathering some things I saw my mama use to help with our neighbors."

"I'll feel better knowing that you'll be near."

Chapter 15

After a few days, the snow stopped. Seth tied a rope from the front porch to the barn so they wouldn't get lost going back and forth. Sarah only went outside when she was going stir-crazy. Now was one such time. She had to have a breath of fresh air even if it froze before she traveled to the barn.

Seth placed a fire burning in a barrel to help keep the animals warm. Sarah sat on a stool and placed two blankets on the mules and cuddled the goats in her lap near the fire.

After collecting the eggs, she viewed the small doll cradle Seth had built for Penny. "She's going to be thrilled with her new doll bed. We were thinking the same way. I made a small quilt and stuffed a pillow with hay for her dolly. She adores that doll, and she'll be delighted. I also made a new sleeping gown for her and a matching one for her dolly."

"I wish we had some candy for her stocking. My mama always stuffed mine and my brothers' with candy canes, an apple and an orange." A wistful smile came over his face.

"Maybe in years to come, Penny will remember how fortunate she was to be rescued by a brave mountain man who made her Christmas special." Sarah kissed one of the goats on the head and placed it on the barn floor.

Seth helped her put her warm fur coat on. "I hope that special child is still asleep while you're out here."

"I'm sure she is. She was sound asleep before I came out." Sarah walked to the barn door and turned to look at Seth. "When will you get us a Christmas tree? Penny and I have been making a few decorations."

"I'll bring one in this afternoon. There's a couple small trees not too far from the barn. I'll cut one down but it won't be big."

"We'll love anything that will help us to celebrate Christmas. Don't stay out too long. I have a big pot of beans and cornbread pones ready."

Sarah was shedding her damp clothes when a blast of a gun went off. She raced to the frosty window. Seth held a big bird up high. Buster was nipping at the wingspread on the critter. Seth's loud voice scolded the dog, and both barged into the warm barn.

~

A little while later, Seth and Buster stormed onto the front porch. Seth stomped his big boots and slid them off, then he carried his bundle into the house. "Look what I found walking along the fence line while I was chopping down the tree." Seth unwrapped the cloth and laid a large, cleaned turkey on the kitchen table.

"My," Sarah mummed. "This is going to be a grand Christmas. A turkey with most of the trimmings."

Seth hurried back to the porch and brought in a four-foot tree with thick limbs and a large trunk. "I cut this from the top of a big tree. What do you think?"

~

"My goodness, it's the prettiest tree I've ever had." Sarah eyes filled with tears at the memory of the ugly, skinny trees her pa had always chosen.

Penny raised her head from the covers on the bed. "Is it Christmas yet?"

Sarah laughed and lifted the child from the bed and cuddled her close. "No, sweet girl, not yet. Look, Seth has brought us a turkey to cook for our Christmas dinner and a Christmas tree to decorate. After we eat, we can place our gifts under it."

"Can we tie the bows on the branches tonight?"

"Yes, Sweetheart, we can do that right after supper. Let's feed Seth for all of his hard work."

"I want some, too. Can I have jam on my corn pones?"

"I want some of that too, little girl. Will you share some jam with me?" Seth's eyes sparkled with glee.

Penny leaned over and whispered something in Sarah's ear. Sarah stood for a minute, pretending to think while the child giggled.

Shaking her head yes, Penny declared to Seth he could have some too. Sarah filled several bowls full with hot beans and spread jam on the hot bread.

~

While Sarah and Penny washed the few dishes, Seth rushed back to the barn and hammered two short boards together to make a stand for the tree. He tilted the tree and nailed the board onto the bottom of the trunk and stood it upright.

"Perfect." Sarah and Penny both clapped their hands when he brought it in.

"You girls get busy while I sit and drink a big cup of hot coffee. I enjoy watching people work." Seth tossed another log into the fire and sat at the table.

Sarah and Penny laughed while they tied bows to cover the tree. Penny screamed *surprise* as Sarah pulled out a string of red berries they had strung together to make a long garland to hang around the tree.

Seth was pleased to see the girls so happy. Sarah was a protector for Penny and made his life more comfortable while she was under his roof. Under most circumstances, he would have expected to have a screaming, demanding woman on his hands, but she was understanding and patient.

"You seem to be far away tonight. Are you feeling alright?" Sarah observed Seth while dressing Penny in her nightgown.

"I'm fine, sweet lady. I was just thinking what a strong, independent woman you are. Since you've been trapped in my cabin, I haven't heard a complaint out of you. When you couldn't get outside for days on end and had to eat wild critters of all kinds, you never fussed. Having to wear the same clothes day in and day out and having no one to talk to but Penny and me, I never heard one complaint. Most city gals would be pulling out their hair by now and making ridiculous demands on me." Seth smiled at Sarah, and her face glowed a bright pink.

"Thank you for your kind words, but you've made life here safe and easy. It isn't your fault that we haven't been able to leave. You tried to take us off the mountain. Why blame you when I know differently?" Sarah turned her attention to the girl. "Penny, do you like your first Christmas tree?"

"I love it." Penny jumped down and reached under the bed. "Look, Seth, I made you something to go under the tree."

"I can't guess what you could have made me. Are you placing it under the tree now?"

"Yep. Do you have something for me to go down here too?" Penny crawled under the tree to place his gift.

"Penny, it isn't polite to ask for something."

"What do you mean?" Penny peered at Sarah. "You give me a lot of rules."

Seth grinned at the confusion on the little girl's face. "Well, I might. Tomorrow night is Christmas Eve and I'll put my gifts under the tree then. Is that alright with you?"

"I guess." Penny looked forlorn, but Seth picked her up and began rocking her close to his chest.

~

Early the next morning, Seth hesitated for a moment before he knocked on the door. He had slept on the floor in front of the fire in the cabin, but he got up and headed to the barn when the sun came up. Stomping his feet, he worked his way back to the cabin when he saw a flash off to the side of the trail leading to the cabin. Taking his time to remove his boots, he squinted toward where he'd seen the flash. An Indian sat on a horse just out of rifle range.

The Indian wasn't wearing a heavy coat. He had to be nearly frozen. Seth couldn't imagine what the man wanted. The man disappeared, which caused Seth to feel uneasy. Suddenly, the man made an appearance again. He had placed a white rag on the tip of his rifle and waved it toward Seth.

Seth slipped his boots back on and stepped off the porch signaling the man forward. When the Indian entered the yard, Seth waved him toward the barn. The Indian jumped off his horse, hurried inside and headed to the fire in the barrel.

"Warm barn." The man surveyed his surroundings and Seth.

"What are you doing on the mountain this time of year and how do you plan to get back down to the valley?" Seth went directly to the point of the Indian's visit.

"We come up on the east side and will go back down same way. It's miles away from Fort Laramie but we're scouting for rustlers."

"Surely rustlers wouldn't be up here in all this snow."

"We search for a white woman with a girl child, too." He looked at Seth for some kind of reaction.

Seth didn't blink an eye. "Who is the woman?"

"She was in the stagecoach robbery. There's a reward for her return. Have you seen or heard anything about her up here?"

"Trappers spoke about the stagecoach accident and the rustlers, but no talk about a woman or child. Is her husband looking for her?"

"No, the new captain of Fort Laramie is paying for their return, dead or alive. If woman not here, I go. Thanks for your fire."

"Can I get you anything else to help you on your trip?"

"No, I go back to camp. We have supplies. I saw your smoke. Hope woman might be here."

Seth watched the Indian ride away on his horse, fighting the knee-deep snow. He didn't look back, so Seth hurried onto the porch and removed his boots.

~

Sarah had been watching the barn and prayed the Indian man wasn't dangerous. She was relieved when she saw the man ride away. "Who was that man? I noticed he was an Indian who wore a military coat." Sarah poured Seth a cup of hot coffee.

"He's a scout on a search party looking for a woman and child. He asked if I had seen you. I didn't give him a direct answer."

"Why didn't you tell him I was here?" Sarah's eyes widened.

~

"Do you trust me when I say I'm going to take you to Fort Laramie?" He didn't give Sarah time to answer. "The search party is sleeping out in the freezing weather. I couldn't bear to know that you and Penny were placed in a thin tent for cover." Seth watched for Sarah's reaction to his comment. "Sarah, you do believe that I'm looking out for you and Penny? I'm going to take you to the fort, but I want to do it when we can ride down on the west side of the mountain. We'll be a lot closer to the fort than traveling down the snowy, rough terrain those men are traveling."

"Of course I believe you. I was just surprised men were out in these snowstorms searching for me."

"For the next few days, please stay away from the door and the windows. I don't trust this Indian or any of the other men in the search party. There's a reward for your recovery, and men get desperate when it comes to money. They might decide that I wasn't telling the truth."

"A reward? I never imagined someone would offer money for my return. Maybe George believes I'm still alive."

"He has no reason to believe you're dead." Seth opened the door and struggled through the snow back to the barn. He needed to clear his head about Sarah. He knew he couldn't do anything about his heart.

Chapter 16

Seth stood at the window, watching the sun come up behind the mountain. What a glorious sight to witness. When he left here, he'd miss this wonderful experience. As the sun came up, he always felt God was speaking to him.

It had stopped snowing, some of the snow had already melted, and water was running beside the porch. Maybe he and the other trappers could continue to clear the pathway down to the valley. Sarah was eager to reach Fort Laramie. He saw that in her expression yesterday when she learned that there was a search party looking for her. Today was Christmas Eve, and he was determined to make it one she would never forget and then, maybe, she'd never forget him.

He glanced at the bed and watched the two girls sleeping. Penny was snuggled up against Sarah, who had her arms wrapped around the child. He implanted this scene in his mind to remember the love between these two.

Sneaking out the door, he headed to the barn. The two goats greeted him with a toss of their heads while the mules swished their long tails. Hens flew from their coops, pecking the floor in search of feed.

"Merry Christmas to all of you, too. Years ago, several of you were in a stable, welcoming our Lord Jesus into the world. What a glorious day that was for sure."

Seth wasn't a church-going man, but his mama took him to

church each Sunday and read the Bible to the family every evening before bedtime. He was a believer, and he could recall his mama's telling him and his brother, *"You boys, believe in the Lord and you'll never be alone. He'll be with you always in good and bad times. Always look to Him."*

There had been many times, especially on the mountain, when he called upon the Lord to help him, and the next day would be better. His prayer this morning was for Sarah. He wanted her to be happy.

As he fed the animals, he couldn't stop humming the hymn, "Away in the Manger." The animals snorted, and the piglets came running and surrounded his boots like frisky puppies. The sow strolled to the feed trough and began eating. The piglets were growing, and he didn't know how Penny was going to feel when she had to leave them behind. She played with them every day and had named each one.

From the woodpile, he tossed several logs into the barrel to build up the fire. Around noon today, if the sun stayed out, he would open the back of the barn and allow all the animals to go out into the corral for fresh air. Keeping the mules locked inside the barn made extra work for him, but with freezing temperatures, he couldn't allow them to freeze. Besides, he could tell they appreciated the warm barn.

As Seth and Buster had started their way back to the cabin, he stopped. Smoke was coming from the chimney, and he could smell frying bacon. Sarah was awake now and cooking breakfast. Hot coffee would be ready and waiting for him. "Sarah has surely spoiled me, Buster." The dog jumped and barked. "You like her scraps too." Seth rubbed the dog's head and both headed to the porch.

~

When Sarah heard Buster, she opened the door and gave Seth a bright smile. "Merry Christmas. Hurry inside before you freeze. I have a hot breakfast all ready."

Once the wet boots and jacket were removed, Seth and the dog hurried inside and moved to the fireplace. "This cabin smells so good. Do you have the turkey in that pot already?"

"Yes, it will take a few hours to cook so I placed it in the fireplace first thing. We're going to have a delicious Christmas dinner. I only wish Blue Sky and Red Feather could be enjoying it with us."

"Me too, but he wanted to wait until Blue Sky's time was closer before he traveled with her here."

"Come and sit down and enjoy the coffee and hot cakes. I have the syrup warmed, but Penny wants jam on hers."

"Come here, sweet pie. Give me a Merry Christmas hug this morning." Seth lifted Penny from the bed and placed her at the table. "Are you ready to open presents this afternoon?"

"My name ain't Sweet Pie. You're so funny."

"Me? Funny? Why do you say that?"

"Cause you can't remember my name. It's Penny, not Prin'ess, Sweet Pea, or Pie. Penny, Penny, Penny."

Sarah and Seth laughed at the little girl trying to correct him.

"All right, Pumpkin, I won't call you anything but Penny from now on."

Did you hear that, Sarah? Now he calling me a big orange pum'kin."

"Calm down, darling, and eat your breakfast while it's hot. Seth likes to tease you."

"Can I go to the barn and play with the goats and piglets after breakfast? The goats like to chase me and the little piglets let me hold them like babies."

"You eat a good breakfast and I'll take you out there while I muck the stalls. The sun is shining and melting some of the snow. I'm going to turn the mules out into the corral while it's daylight and not snowing,"

"While you're outside, I'll prepare the other dishes for our dinner. I am so pleased Blue Sky gave me some real butter. You don't know how much you appreciate something until you don't have it any longer."

~

Seth riveted his eyes upon Sarah. *She doesn't know the reality of her statement. When she disappears from my life, I'll be alone again. Oh, I do prefer her company.*

Seth and Penny spent a good portion of the morning outside in the warm barn. Penny tried to set each piglet in a row and teach them to lie down. "Lay down," she repeated, but one of the piglets would escape while she was attempting to get another to obey her command. Seth was surprised the little girl had so much patience with the small, untrainable animals. After the lesson was over, she marched around the barn, singing with a trail of pigs behind her.

Seth mucked each stall and placed clean hay in the deep bins for the mules and his big bay horse. He rubbed his horse down and checked for sores or other bruising, lifting its hooves to check them over. Satisfied the horse was in good condition, he led him to the open back door of the barn. The horse ran around and kicked his hind legs for good long while. Then Seth went back to the stall and placed several buckets of oats in the bin for the horse to enjoy when he brought him back in later. *A full belly will help keep the animals warmer*—he remembered the old wives' tale he'd heard from an trapper who dropped by his cabin often.

Seth watched Penny sitting on a bale of hay with one of the goats. Her head was so still Seth realized she was fast asleep.

Lifting her into his arms, she raised her head, and then immediately placed it down on his shoulder. She sighed and tried to cuddle close. Seth checked the barrel fire before he opened the barn door and carried Penny back to the warm, cozy cabin. When Seth opened the door, the aroma of food nearly caused him to go to his knees. "Man, it smells wonderful in here."

Sarah hurried to the bed and pulled down the covers so Seth could lay Penny in the bed. "She played hard this morning." Seth straightened and smiled at Sarah.

"Good." Sarah tucked the covers around the sleeping child. "She's so excited about opening her presents. When she wakes from her nap, the food should be ready for us to eat."

Seth hurried back to the porch and removed his wet, snowy boots. "Sorry I tracked up the floor." He stood in front of the fireplace in his socks, feeling like he was at home. Today, he was happier than he'd been in the two years since he'd settled on the mountain to trap and hunt. Being here with Sarah was only temporary, but he was going to enjoy himself while they were trapped together. A wonderful Christmas feast was well on its way and later, a small child would share the gift of giving. What else could a man ask for on top of a snowy mountain?

~

Later in the day, when Penny woke from her nap, she needed to use the water closet and eat. Penny adjusted her bloomers and held up her hands for Sarah to wash.

"I could eat a bear."

Sarah and Seth laughed. The child repeated everything she heard, and that statement was one Seth said most every day when he returned from working outside.

"All right, honey. The turkey is ready, along with beans, baked yams, and corn pones." Sarah helped Penny sit at the table. "Seth, will you place the turkey on this clean board and slice it? It is tender and may not slice well."

"No matter how it's served, it smells wonderful and I'm sure we'll enjoy it."

~

As the Christmas feast sat on the table in front of the man, woman and child, if a person was looking in the window, they'd think they were viewing a happy little family.

Sarah glanced around at Seth and Penny and felt her heart beating fast in her chest. How was she going to be able to walk away from this wonderful man and this lovely child when she arrived at Fort Laramie?

"Seth, would you like to ask the blessing?"

Seth looked at Sarah. He reached for Sarah's and Penny's hands and nodded.

"Close your eyes, darling, while Seth prays."

~

"Lord, thank you for this warm cabin. Thank you for the food that Sarah has cooked for us to enjoy. Thank you for all our blessings and for all the ones that will come to us." As he prepared to say amen, he peeked at Penny who held her eyes closed tightly. *"Lord, thank you for Penny. She's a good little girl. Amen"*

"I am good. Will I get to open a present tonight?"

"Yes, only after you eat a good supper." Sarah spooned some beans and turkey on her plate.

"I like this." Penny stuffed a big piece of meat in her mouth.

"Slow down, darling. Take smaller bites. Your presents aren't going away."

Seth ate a large portion of turkey and a double helping of yams. "This food is delicious. You make cooking in the fireplace look easy, and I know it isn't."

"It takes practice." She laughed and filled a small bowl of

beans and added a piece of corn pone on top. She held it out to Seth, who gladly accepted it.

After Buster was fed, and all the food was covered and put away, it was time for the presents under the tree to be exchanged and opened.

"Penny, are you ready for a present?"

"Yep." She scooted off the bed and fell on her knees to crawl under the tree.

"Wait, little bit," Seth said, as he quickly picked up Penny off the floor. "Sarah will pass out the gifts."

Sarah gave Penny a large, soft package wrapped in yellow material with a matching bow.

Penny smiled and quickly untied the bow and removed the material. She unwrapped a small pink gown for her and a small matching gown for her dolly. "Oh look. Me and Dolly will look alike."

Seth opened the door and brought in a feed-sack bag. He placed it on the floor in front of the child.

"For me?" Penny touched the bag and jerked her hand back. "Oh, it's cold."

"Well, maybe. I'd best put it back outside." Seth reached for the bag, but Penny screamed.

"It's mine. I don't care if it's cold." She opened the bag and her eyes widened. "Oh, look, Sarah. A bed for Dolly. Oh my. Dolly has been a good girl."

Sarah and Seth laughed at the serious expression on the child's face.

"Look Seth. It has a small pillow and quilt to go on the bed." Penny placed Dolly in the small cradle and covered her with the patchwork quilt.

Seth reached high on a branch on the Christmas tree, and removed a small gift wrapped in burlap material. "This one has Sarah's name on it."

"Open it, open it, Sarah." Penny excitement was contagious.

~

Sarah looked at the gift and felt a blush rush to her face. She never dreamed this man would have a Christmas gift for her.

"Do you want me to open it for you?" Penny reached for the box in Sarah's hand.

"No, darling. I can open it." Her voice was soft as she glanced at Seth. She unwrapped the small box and lifted the lid. "This is . . . lovely." Sarah stared at a small bear claw, threaded on a thin piece of soft leather.

"Indians believe a necklace like this has spiritual powers that will bring you protection and good health. I want these things for you."

"It's so smooth and shiny. How did you manage to get it this way?"

"A lot of rubbing it with a soft cloth." He smiled and said it didn't matter how much time it took. "I wanted you to have something that will help you remember your time on the mountain."

"I will always treasure it. Thank you." Sarah smiled and remembered Seth's gift from her.

Sarah reached behind the tree and pulled out her carpet bag and set it in front of him. "You want me to have a lady's carpet bag?" Seth looked confused, and Sarah laughed.

"No, silly. I didn't have anything else to put your gift in, so I just placed it in my bag so you wouldn't see it."

~

"Good. I was worried for a second." Seth reached down and opened the carpet bag. He pulled out a blue crocheted neck scarf. "This is too nice." Glancing around the room, he didn't see the shawl that Sarah was wearing when she first came to the cabin. "Sarah, where is your shawl?"

"Now don't start asking questions. Just accept this gift and enjoy wearing it in the cold weather. It will help keep you warm."

"Where did you get the yarn to make this?"

"My lips are sealed."

"I demand that you tell me how you managed to make this for me?" He wrapped the scarf around his neck and felt the softness and warmth of the scarf.

Sarah sat smiling at Seth, looking pleased with herself.

"Sarah, I love my scarf, and I will wear it with pride."

Chapter 17

The day after Christmas, the sun had disappeared, and the snow was still waist-deep in many places. Seth needed to check on the trappers who lived nearby, so he dressed warmly, wearing the new scarf around his neck. He carried a dozen cleaned squirrels, three dozen eggs, and big hunks of bear meat to the older trappers who had helped him learn to survive the last two years on this mountain. "I'll be home before dark. If I'm not, don't wait up for me. I will bunk in the barn if I am real late."

"No, please don't do that. I feel safer with you in the cabin. Besides it is too cold to sleep out in the barn."

"All right. If I am not home before dark, don't come outside to care for the animals. I'll do it when I get back." He looked at her until she gave him a nod.

~

Penny and Sarah busied themselves with cleaning the cabin, then removed the small Christmas tree. It was pretty, but with the sparse space in the cabin, it needed to be removed. Penny took the bows off and placed many of them in her hair. She laughed and played with them on the bed.

Sarah put a pan of dried beans to soak for an hour before she put them in the fire. She wanted a bath, so she went to the stream, filled several buckets of water and carried them inside—one bucket at a time on the fire. After a while, she had enough water to fill the tub.

Once Sarah's hair was squeaky clean and her body felt refreshed, she dressed in freshly laundered clothes. She bent near the fire and dried her long brown hair, then brushed it until it shone.

"Come, Penny. It's time for your bath."

"No thank you. I don't want one."

"Well, I want you to have one, so let's get you undressed."

"Please, Sarah, don't make me get cold."

"The water will not be cold, I promise you."

"Shoot." Penny gave up and allowed Sarah to bathe her.

~

After lunch, Sarah looked out the window. The wind was blowing the top layer of snow in swirls everywhere. It began to look like a blizzard outside. Sarah wished Seth would return soon, or at least stay at one of the trappers' places he was visiting.

She rushed outside to the porch, carried in a pile of smaller logs and placed them near the fireplace. Seth had a special place to store wood in the cabin, but some of the logs were too big for her to drag inside. Seth would chop those logs later, but if he didn't come tomorrow, she would attempt to chop them on the porch.

The beans were cooked so she prepared some corn pones. She placed two cleaned, cut-up squirrels in a pot with a few onions to cook slowly over the fire. Later, she had Penny rested in bed with her dolly. It wasn't long until she was sound asleep. Sarah took her carpet bag and placed it in her lap pulling out a small tin photo of her mama. "Oh, I miss you so much." Holding the picture near her heart, tears rolled down her cheeks. Her mother must be in a panic by now since she had received no word about her. Had George written her mama about the stagecoach accident? Surely he had.

Buster clawed at the door and barked several times. "Hush, boy. You're going to wake Penny." Sarah unlocked the door and peeked outside. Coming up the trail was Red Feather and Blue Sky. "What a pleasant sight." Sarah was thrilled to have their company.

Sarah wrapped her fur coat around her and went out to stand on the porch. "Hello," Sarah greeted the Indian couple and watched as Red Feather helped Blue Sky off her horse. It must be time for Blue Sky to birth her baby. "Oh Lord, please guide Seth home soon."

Blue Sky waddled inside the cabin and Sarah motioned to the rocking chair. Hurrying over to the chair, she placed it in front of the fireplace. "Sit here."

Sarah rushed to the door and looked around outside. Red Feather was entering the barn with their horses. She had hoped to see Seth riding up the trail, but it would be dark before he arrived home. He was going to visit several of the older trappers and most likely chop wood for them and carry buckets of snow into their cabin to melt for water. The old men would appreciate the meat.

Sarah could tell Blue Sky was in pain. The Indian woman never uttered a sound, but Sarah felt it was time to have her friend lie down and prepare for the arrival of her baby. She didn't know about Blue Sky, but her own insides were tied into knots. Her nerves were on edge, and she prayed she wouldn't lose her lunch. "Come, Blue Sky. You need to lie down on the bed. I have placed an old quilt over the mattress.

When an Indian woman lived alone with her man, she birthed the child, and in a few hours, was ready to go back to work. Sarah wasn't going to allow that to take place here. She led Blue Sky over to the bed and had her sit down while she undressed her. Since Blue Sky didn't have anything appropriate to wear, Sarah unfolded one of Seth's night shirts for her.

"Lie down and rest." Sarah walked to the door and looked again for Seth. Moans came from the bed. She hurried back. Blue Sky was stretched out on the bed, writhing from side to side.

Buster barked and raced down the trail. Sarah rushed to the front window and thanked God for answering her prayer. Seth was riding into the barn with the pack mule trailing behind him.

"Oh Blue Sky, Seth is home. I will feed the men some supper. Would you like a few pieces of ice chips to suck on? I can get Seth to break a few pieces of clean ice for you."

"Maybe later. I would like to sleep."

"Please rest if that will make you feel better. Penny will be awake soon. She had a long nap today."

Before the men came in from the barn, Penny awoke from her nap, and Blue Sky was fast asleep. Sarah placed two bowls of beans, the soft squirrel meat, and the corn pones on the table. Red Feather ate like a starved man. Seth asked him when he had eaten last.

"Blue Sky not feel good this morning so I ate a few berries and dried jerky. You good cook, Sarah."

"Thank you. Please, there's plenty. Have some more. After Blue Sky has her baby, I'll cook her something to eat."

The men sat and talked while Sarah washed the dishes. Penny played with her dolly and cradle.

In a little while, Blue Sky sat up in the bed. "Got to pee!" Everyone jumped. The two men raced outside to the barn while Sarah helped Blue Sky to the water closet.

"Water come. Baby come soon." Blue Sky sat down in the rocker.

"Come, Blue Sky, let me help you into bed. It won't be long and you'll be holding your papoose."

After settling Blue Sky back in bed, Sarah dressed Penny in warm clothes and carried her out to the barn to play with the animals.

Seth took Penny and asked Sarah if she needed anything to help with the birthing.

"Do you have something to wash my hands besides hard lye soap? I need something that will kill germs."

"I think I might. Go back to the cabin and I'll bring you something I use."

~

Seth looked around the barn and rushed back to the cabin carrying a brown jug of moonshine whiskey. He tapped on the door and passed the jug to Sarah. "This will kill anything."

Sarah opened the jug and took a whiff. "Gracious, what do you use this for?" She fanned the smell away from her nose.

"I've used it in place of alcohol. The Indians drink it for enjoyment and to give them courage."

"Courage?"

"Yes, before they go into battle or hunt a wild beast, they will drink their fill, and this gives them courage." Before Seth closed the door, he noticed Sarah's pale complexion.

~

Sarah listened to Blue Sky's moans and cries. She placed cool cloths on her forehead, patted her hand and said soothing words to her. When she rolled from side to side and cried, Sarah knew it wouldn't be long. She was going to have to peek under the night shirt and see how far along she'd come.

When Blue Sky screamed, Sarah poured herself a tin cup of moonshine. Swallowing a big mouthful, the fiery liquid burned everything on its way down. After coughing and gagging, Sarah tried to speak but was hoarse to the point that nothing but a squeak came out.

"Coming, the babe is coming," Blue Sky said between short breaths.

Sarah knew she must help Blue Sky, but she was scared stiff. Lifting the tail of the white night shirt, the sight was much worse than she could have imagined. The baby's head was crowning. Blue Sky screamed again.

"God, please help me . . . help her," she mumbled. "Give me courage." Remembering the jug, she grabbed it, pulled the plug and turned it up and swallowed several more mouthfuls. Her mouth was on fire, but the taste wasn't as bad as before. She was beginning to feel more courageous. Blue Sky's pleading for help snapped her back into focus and she eased the gown up once again. The baby's bloody head and shoulder were protruding from Blue Sky's body.

Sarah felt her legs go weak and everything in the room began to spin, and then total darkness came.

~

Blue Sky's cries for help brought Seth racing from the barn.

"Help, it's here!" Blue Sky screamed.

Seth rushed in the cabin and glanced around for Sarah. She lay on the floor. Blue Sky screamed again. Seth snapped his attention to her. He lifted the night shirt and immediately grabbed a soft cloth. "One more push, Blue Sky, and it will be all over." True to his words, he caught the tiny baby in his hands and laid the healthy baby boy on her belly. After he cleaned the mucus out of the tiny mouth and made sure the infant was breathing well, he cut the cord.

Once mother and child were safe, he hurried to Sarah and picked her up in his arms. "What happened to Sarah?"

"She got too much courage. No help at all."

Seth laughed and smiled down at Sarah. "Poor thing. She's such an innocent young woman." He placed her on the bed next to Blue Sky and the baby.

Blue Sky smiled and closed her eyes. Seth took over the job of taking care of the infant and its mama. With warm water from the fireplace, he washed the screaming baby and struggled to wrap a soft nappy over his bottom. After completing that chore, he wrapped the child in a soft blanket and laid him in his mama's arms. He wiped Blue Sky's face and smoothed her long black hair back out of her face.

"Now, listen to me, Blue Sky. You must stay in bed for a few days, if not longer. I know Indian women go back to work right away, but you must allow Sarah to take care of you and the babe."

Blue Sky smiled and peered at the unconscious Sarah next to her. "Later, she'll take good care of me."

"Red Feather will be a proud papa. I'll tell him to come in." Seth grinned at the sweet smile on Sarah's face. "How much moonshine did she drink? She smells like she took a bath in it."

"Many cups. She needed courage. A lot of it."

Seth went to the door and called Red Feather. The Indian brave rushed inside, carrying Penny in his arms. Seth took Penny while Red Feather glanced down on his new son. He proclaimed the infant to be fine and strong. "Look at the size of his hands and feet."

"What name will you give your son?" Blue Sky would allow her man to name their first child.

"Achak. He will have great Spirit."

Yes, he'll be wise like his father."

Red Feather gazed at his lovely wife's flushed face. "Thank you for my son."

Blue Sky closed her eyes and went to sleep with her child cradled in her arms. Penny stood at the foot of the bed craning her little neck to see the baby. Seth picked her up and allowed her to peek at the sleeping papoose.

"He's red and wrinkled," Penny said.

"Yes he is, but he had a hard time getting here. After rest, he will be soft brown and smooth."

"Why is Sarah asleep?"

Seth smiled as he looked at the beautiful girl lying in the bed. "Let's allow her to sleep for a while. She helped Blue Sky bring her baby into the world, and she's a little tired."

Chapter 18

Sarah stood in front of the fireplace preparing breakfast for Blue Sky, Red Feather, Penny and Seth. Embarrassed, she hated to face the three of them this morning. Blue Sky and the baby were still asleep. Penny was sitting on the bed playing with her dolly and watching the new child sleep in her mama's arms.

"Sarah, can I hold the baby. I want to hold him."

"Let's wait one more day before we start passing him around. He needs to stay close to his mama."

"Kay, but I won't drop him." Penny frowned but didn't plead to hold the baby again.

Buster barked and ran around on the porch, welcoming Seth and Red Feather. Both men cleaned their boots on the porch and came into the cabin. Sarah bent over the fire, turned the bacon and flipped over a couple of flapjacks.

Red Feather hurried to the bed and stooped down beside his wife. She held their baby so he could see his face. "How do you feel?" He placed his hand on her forehead.

"Good, but Sarah will not let me out of bed. She says white women stay in bed two weeks. I will die if I have to lay here that long." Blue Sky gave her husband a look that said, *help me.*

"Stay here for two more days and then we must go home. Let Sarah take care of you. I will make travois for you and boy. No horseback riding for a while. I'll take care of you."

Sarah started to tell Red Feather that Blue Sky needed to have plenty of rest, but Seth grabbed her hand and motioned with his finger over his mouth for her to keep still. She ambled closer to Seth, and he whispered. "It's their way."

A few days later, with a beautiful clear sky and plenty of sunshine, Red Feather, Blue Sky and their new baby were prepared to leave. Red Feather and Seth stood together beside the travois where Blue Sky lay cuddling her newborn. The older man stared into Seth's face. A flash of understanding and respect passed between the two. "Thank you and your woman for taking care of my family."

Sadness appeared on Seth's face. "She is not my woman." He glanced at Sarah and gave her a weak smile.

"Yes, I know what your lips say, but your heart says something different." Red Feather leaped on his horse and slowly rode out of the yard.

Sarah wiped tears from her eyes and prayed for safe travel for her new friends. She hoped she would get to see them again before Seth took her and Penny to Fort Laramie.

Seth placed his hands on her shoulders. They stood and watched their friends disappear down the narrow trail. The outside sounds around them were so quiet she could almost hear both their heartbeats.

~

Seth stood on the front porch looking at the snow clouds forming behind the ridge. If the men gathered at the last patch of fallen trees covering the trail on the mountain, they could get them removed before the storm hit.

Sarah stepped outside and looped her arm into Seth's. He closed his arm quickly, catching her hand to his side. Sarah realized what she had done and jerked her hand out of his grip.

"Sarah, the sky is clouding up for another snowstorm, but if the men come out today, we can get a lot done. I hope to get home before the bad weather hits. If I'm late, you know to stay inside after you take care of the animals this afternoon."

A dull ache covered Sarah's heart. She hated for Seth to leave them alone. "Give me a few minutes to pack you a big lunch. You can't chop wood all day without something to eat."

~

As Seth prepared to leave, he stood by the door looking at

Sarah. Seth hated to leave her for a minute, but he had no choice—the men needed him. He came out of the barn leading his horse. He'd added an extra blanket to his bedroll. Sarah hurried down the steps and offered him his lunch. "Mercy gal, did you pack all the food in the cabin?" They laughed, then he leaped onto his horse. "See you tonight, if I'm not too late."

~

Sarah and Penny waved at Seth until he was a speck in the horizon. Penny held onto Buster's leash so he wouldn't follow his master. He was a good watchdog, so Seth demanded that he stay behind and guard the girls and the cabin.

The snow started an hour after Seth left. The falling snowflakes were beautiful, but Sarah worried that the men would continue to work in the bad weather.

Penny helped roll out dumplings while Sarah cut up a hunk of bear meat. She sliced the last of the onions Seth had covered in hay in the barn. The meat and onions smelled so good. Sarah decided to cook supper early in case Seth came home early.

She poured bear grease into the cast-iron skillet, dropped cornmeal by the spoonful and cooked corn pones which were Seth's favorite. Later she would allow Penny to drop the dumplings into the meat and broth.

While the food cooked over the low fire, Sarah read to Penny from her Bible. She was so pleased she had placed the book in her carpet bag. After the long story from the book of Luke, Chapter 2, Penny's eyes closed.

As Sarah laid Penny on the bed and pulled the covers up to her chin, she murmured, "I'm happy Jesus's mama and daddy found him in the templet."

Sarah smiled, kissed Penny's forehead and replied, "They found him in the temple."

"He got to go home with them," Penny said, sighing. Sarah sat beside the child for a few minutes and patted the cover. She silently prayed George would love this little girl, too.

Sarah stirred the big pot of meat, then hurried to the window. The snow was falling a lot heavier than before. Buster whined to go outside, so Sarah eased open the door to allow him to go. In just a few minutes, he barked to get back inside. Sarah grabbed up a soft rag and wrapped him inside of it. She snuggled him and wiped the wet snow off his fur. He licked her face over and over as she rubbed him dry.

"Enough now," Sarah scolded him sweetly. She placed him down in front of the fire. Oh, how she was going to miss this smart, lovable dog.

She removed the meat from the fire and dropped the dumplings into the broth with the cut-up meat. She placed the pot back over the small fire to simmer.

She was just about to sit in the rocker, when Buster started whining and clawing at the door. "What is it? I just let you out." Sarah marched over to the window and tried to see outside. The wind was blowing hard, and she prayed Seth wouldn't try to come home in the storm. Hopefully, he would wait it out in another trapper's cabin.

Buster barked and ran around the room, moving back and forth in front of the door. He growled and sniffed the bottom of the door. Sarah glanced out the window again, but the icy window and heavy snow blurred her vision.

Something was out there, Sarah thought. She raced to the fireplace and removed Seth's buffalo gun, thankful Penny was asleep. She placed another bear rug over her for protection, moved behind the bed, and then lowered herself onto her knees, then pointed the gun straight at the door and pulled back the trigger like Seth had instructed her to do.

Without warning, the front door flew open, and a frozen giant stepped into the room with outstretched arms. Sarah pulled the trigger and a blast like she had never heard boomed in the small cabin. She flew backward into the wall, nearly knocking the breath out of her body. The burly giant gasped and staggered backwards several steps. Stunned, he stared straight ahead. Suddenly, the towering man fell face down onto the floor. One large snow-covered arm slapped the table and another slammed down onto the rocker. He looked like a huge black bear stretched over the bear rug on the cabin floor.

Sarah had shot the man. *Oh, my goodness, Lord. Please forgive me. I have killed a man.* She stood frozen behind the bed, while Penny climbed out from under the warm covers. The child didn't appear afraid, only confused.

"Look Sarah, it's snowing inside the house." Sarah glanced up at the roof and couldn't believe her eyes. She had blown a hole as big as a water bucket in the roof.

"Heavens! If I shot a hole in the roof, that means I didn't kill that man lying on our floor."

Buster was sniffing and smelling the giant spread out on the big bear rug. His black bear coat was caked with icicles and snow. His bushy black beard was matted with dirt and leaves, and his boots were wet and muddy.

"Penny, please lie back down in the bed and cover up while I check on that man. He may be hurt."

"I like the snow falling inside. It looks like Christmas." Penny snuggled down into the warm covers and watched Buster lick the man's face.

"Stop Buster, get back and let me see about this stranger." Buster continued to sniff and lick the man, so Sarah picked Buster up and placed him in the bed with Penny. "Hold him, sweetheart." Sarah shivered from the snow falling inside the cabin. She knew she was going to have to repair the hole somehow and soon.

The big man was nearly frozen to death. Sarah had to get him into some dry clothes and slowly warm his large body.

First, she attempted to wake the man, but he wasn't responding. She warmed a pail of water and placed several soft rags in it, then placed the warm rags on his face. She removed his gloves, thankful his fingers didn't show any signs of frostbite. She twisted and turned him until she removed the wet bear coat from his body and placed it near the fireplace to dry. Sitting on the floor, she unlaced his boots and pulled, using all of her strength, to remove them from the biggest, nastiest feet she had ever smelled. Gagging, she quickly opened the door to set the boots outside.

The snow had let up, but the cabin was getting colder and colder from the giant hole in the roof. She got several wool blankets and covered the man.

Surveying the roof, Sarah took the old quilt, a hammer and a few nails. She moved the table over and lined it up with the hole in the ceiling and climbed on top of it. "Perfect," she said to herself. She climbed back down, laid the quilt on the table and cut a large square. With the piece of the quilt, hammer and nails, she tacked the quilt to cover the hole. "Wonderful. Look Penny. I fixed the hole."

Chapter 19

The intruder groaned and moved around. Sarah eased down to the floor. "Mister, how do you feel? Are you warm enough?"

"Where am I?" The man mumbled. It seemed hard for him to speak.

"You're in Seth Jenkins' cabin. Do you know Seth?"

"Yep. Tell him to help me up." The burly man tried to raise his head to look around the cabin.

"He'll be back in a little while. It's almost dark, and he never leaves us alone at night."

"Listen, I ain't going to harm you. Seth might not make it home. The snow is mighty deep. I almost didn't make it here." He winced when he spoke. "I saw your smoke."

"Now that you're awake, I will make you some hot tea."

"Coffee . . . no tea." The man shook his wet hair like a dog. "If you have some."

"We do. I have food on the stove if you're hungry."

"I could eat a bear." The giant tried to sit up.

Sarah laughed as she stood. "I thought you were a bear. If you can stand, I'll give you some of Seth's things to put on. You can change behind the water-closet curtain."

"I think I can stand on my legs now. I probably wouldn't have got warm in these wet clothes. Thank you for the dry ones, ma'am."

~

As the man tried to stand, he held onto the table and looked into the eyes of the child who was peeking at him from the bed. Before he could say anything to Penny, she pulled the fur quilt up to her chin. "Are you a man or a bear?"

The man laughed out loud. "I think I'm a man."

"Yep, you look like Seth. He's big too and you look like him."

"Good, now I am going to try to walk over to that quilt that is hanging down over there." The man swayed and grabbed the table, pushed down on the foot of the bed and pulled the hanging quilt back as he stepped into the small area before closing it.

Sarah held several warm, dry towels out to the man and some clothes for him to change into. "Toss out your wet things and I will hang them by the fire to dry."

Watching and listening to the big man in the water closet, Sarah was sure the quilt that she had nailed to the ceiling was going to come tumbling down, but in a little while, he came out in Seth's clothes. They were snug on his large frame and the pant legs barely reached his calves, but at least the clothes were dry.

Sarah took the largest bowl she had and filled it with dumplings and meat. She placed two cups of hot coffee on the table for their uninvited guest.

The man looked down at the food, then up at her. "Are you not going to eat?" His eyes darted from Sarah to Penny.

"Yes, but you go on and eat. We'll wait on Seth."

~

Sarah watched as the man sat down. The giant had a few table manners. "May I ask your name?" Sarah walked over to the bed and picked up Penny before she sat in the rocker.

"I am Dutch Perry. My friends call me Dutch. I trap beavers and bears mostly. I had been following a monster of a bear, but I lost his footprints in the snowstorm. My horse broke loose from the tree branch where I had tied him, so I was on foot for a couple of miles."

"I'm glad that you found our cabin." Sarah smiled.

"Our cabin? Are you and my friend hitched?"

"No." Sarah shook her head vigorously. "Seth rescued us a few months ago. Our stagecoach was chased by rustlers who caused the stage to go over the mountain. They stole the Fort Laramie payroll and did other bad things." She motioned her head toward Penny who had little ears.

"You're the woman the search party is looking for?" Dutch had come to Seth's place with one purpose in mind. He wanted what Seth had built; the cabin, hides and furs. His woman would be an added bonus.

"With you being here in Seth's place, why didn't the search party find you?"

"Seth is going to take us to Fort Laramie. He didn't want us to go with those strange men. Please, don't tell anyone that we're here." Sarah covered her mouth with her hand.

"Never would I betray Seth." He gave her his best smile. "If he said that he will take you down to the fort, then he will, whenever the trail is cleared."

"That's where he is now. He left to go work on the road earlier, but the weather got worse after he left."

~

Buster growled, jumped off the bed and went to the door. Sarah rushed to the window and looked out. A lantern light swayed in the barn.

"Seth's home." She peered up at the mountain man and gave him a big smile. "Penny, Seth's home."

"Goodie, I love Seth." Sarah was surprised at the comment coming from the child. Penny had never said anything like that before. Her heart swelled; she had special feelings for him, too.

Dutch moved away from the table and stood at the foot of the bed. He looked nervous. She opened the door and went out on the porch, not taking time to put on her heavy coat.

~

"What are you doing, woman? Are you trying to catch your death standing outside without your coat? Get back inside this minute." Seth wasn't surprised to find Sarah waiting for him, but to stand outside in zero-below weather without a coat wasn't like her at all.

"But, Seth, we have company inside."

Seth pushed the door open and shoved her gently inside the cabin. He took off his boots, caked with snow and mud. When he entered the cabin, he couldn't believe the company that stood at the foot of his bed. Dutch Perry, a man whom Seth knew a little too well, stood peering at him from across the small room.

"Welcome home, old man," Dutch called in a loud voice.

"This is certainly a surprise. We all thought you were dead." Seth stepped closer to Sarah but didn't smile a warm greeting at their visitor.

"I was nearly dead, but some Indians discovered my body in a gully, and an old woman nursed me back to health. As I was heading down the trail, I spotted smoke. Your woman took me in. She warmed this frozen body and fed me some hot grub."

She blushed bright red. "I only gave him dry clothes and fed him some dumplings." Sarah walked over to Seth and pulled on his arm. "Come stand in front of the fire while I get you a hot drink and food. I'll eat with you." Sarah dished food, then commented to Seth, "We thought you'd stay with another trapper tonight because the storm was so bad."

"Once I started home, my horse didn't seem to have a problem plowing through the snow. It took longer to get here, but there's no other place I'd rather be." Seth reached for Sarah and pulled her close to him.

~

Sarah was surprised at Seth's show of affection toward her, but she accepted it without causing a scene. She couldn't imagine his reason for it.

~

Before Seth sat to eat, he tossed a log on the fire. "This cabin is not very warm." He felt a cold draft and wondered where it was coming from. "I'd better bring in more firewood." Seth glanced around the room and noticed the gray wool blanket tacked to the ceiling. "What in the world happened to the roof?"

Sarah gasped. "Oh, I got scared when I heard…him…at our door. It sounded like a big bear outside. Buster was barking and jumping on the door. I grabbed your gun down from the fireplace and moved behind the bed just like you told me. When he came through the door, I fired directly at him. But, as you can see, I missed and shot a hole in the roof. While Mr. Perry was unconscious on the floor, I repaired the hole as best as I could."

"I'll make a proper repair job tomorrow. Hopefully, we won't have any more snow tonight and we won't freeze to death. It seems, Dutch, you're one lucky man Sarah's a bad shot and didn't shoot you between the eyes." Seth smirked and took a sip of his hot coffee.

"I have to say you're the lucky man. You've got a nice place here—a right cozy cabin and a pretty gal."

"He has me, too." Penny peered up at the big man and bounced off the bed. "I love you, Seth."

Seth picked up the child and whispered in her ear, "I love you too, pumpkin."

"If you extend me a bed for the night, I'll be on my way at first light."

"Where is your animal? I didn't see a strange horse or mule in my barn."

"I was tracking a bear and tied my horse to a branch, but he got spooked and broke loose. "Do you think I could borrow a horse or mule from you so I can ride out of here?"

"Sure, I'll be glad to loan you one of my pack mules." Seth knew he'd never get the animal back, but he didn't care as long as it carried this man away.

Seth ate three bowls of dumplings, then washed his face and hands in a pan of warm water.

Sarah prepared Penny for bed and asked if the men would go to the barn while she got dressed for bed. After a half hour, the two men returned to the cabin.

"Sweetheart, Dutch will sleep on the floor in front of our fire. It's freezing in the barn even with the fire in the barrel." Sarah and Penny were already snuggled together and warm. Seth placed another log on the fire and tossed a few quilts and a pillow to Dutch. "Those covers may smell musky because I bought them from an old trapper when I first built this cabin."

Watching Dutch get settled on the floor, Seth walked to the side of the bed and turned down the lantern. He removed his shirt and pants. Quickly, he slipped under the bed covers with his red union suit covering his long body. He leaned over and kissed Sarah as naturally as if he did it every night.

After an hour, Dutch was snoring so loud Seth thought the roof would be lifted. Sarah was still awake. He could see her eyes blinking toward the ceiling. He leaned over Penny, who was wedged between them, and whispered. "It's important he believes you're my woman. I'll tell you more after he leaves in the morning."

~

Sarah gave him a weak smile and nodded her understanding. Seth had given her a fright when he crawled in the bed. Thankfully, Penny was already asleep and didn't have a chance to say anything about Seth being in the bed with them.

Early the next morning, Sarah peeked at the floor, but Dutch had already exited the cabin. She glanced over her shoulder and saw Seth had already gone, too. She made quick work of getting herself dressed while Penny snored away under the warm bear rugs.

Sarah opened the door and stood on the porch looking toward the barn. The sun was so bright its reflection off the snow was almost blinding. Laughter came from the barn, and then the barn door opened. Dutch rode slowly out, waved at her, and continued down the trail away from the cabin.

Seth rushed over to Sarah and softly pushed her back inside.

"Why didn't he stay for breakfast?'

"He was in a hurry to get back on the bear's track, or so he said. The truth is not in that man."

"Oh." Sarah glanced at Seth's face as she poured him a cup of hot coffee. "Do you mind telling me about that statement?"

"I had only been on this mountain a little while when I was warned about him. He will steal the eyes off a dead man."

"Mercy! That's awful. Were you afraid he might try and steal your furs and hides?"

"No, I was afraid he might try and steal you." Seth sipped a drink of his coffee.

"How could he have stolen me away from here?"

"If I hadn't returned last night, you may have found out how fast you'd be headed deeper into these mountains. There are many caves a man can get lost in if he wants."

"Is that the reason you allowed him to sleep inside and then you crawled in the bed with us?"

"It's best to keep your enemies close."

Sarah couldn't help but laugh. "I'll say he was pretty close and loud."

Seth laughed at Sarah's banter. "Stay close to the cabin for a day or two. I don't trust that he won't sneak back and try something."

"Are you trying to scare me?" Sarah placed a hand on her hip and grinned at him.

"I want you afraid—for yourself and Penny."

Chapter 20

As the winter wore on and spring set in, the trappers finally cleared a pathway down to the valley. The weeks and months had passed by rapidly since Sarah arrived at Seth's cabin. The grass was already green under some of the snow patches and golden foliage was springing up everywhere.

Sarah and Penny stood in the front yard playing with Buster and the two goats. Seth came riding up the trail with Red Feather, Blue Sky and their three-month-old infant. Sarah was thrilled to see them. She had prepared a pot of soup with a batch of corn pones earlier that morning.

"Look, Sarah, look who's coming." Penny raced around mud holes in the yard, jumping and clapping her hands.

"I see them, sweetheart. Don't get your feet muddy."

"How are my girls?" Seth leaped off his horse and grabbed up Penny. He smiled at Penny's deer skin moccasins. "Good. You haven't outgrown your moccasins yet."

"We're fine and happy to see Red Feather and Blue Sky. What are they pulling behind their horses?"

"Let us get our horses settled in the barn, and I'll tell you some good news. Do you have something for lunch? I'm starved."

"You are always hungry." Sarah laughed. "Come Penny, we've got to put lunch on the table for our guests."

Sarah was thrilled to hold Blue Sky's baby. He was a beautiful, chubby infant with coal black eyes and hair. Penny wanted to hold him, so Sarah placed her on the bed and laid the baby in the middle of it. He kicked and cooed while Penny tickled him under the chin.

"Be gentle with him," Sarah instructed.

After lunch, Seth folded his hands and asked Sarah to sit at the table with him. Blue Sky positioned herself in the rocker while Red Feather stood near the front window. Sarah was becoming anxious at the expression on Seth's face. She couldn't imagine what he had to tell her.

"I have good news." Seth half-smiled at Sarah. "The trail is opened all the way down to the valley. I can now take you and Penny to Fort Laramie."

"That's wonderful news." Sarah was almost speechless. She had mixed emotions. Leaving the mountain, this cabin, would mean leaving Seth.

"We can leave tomorrow. Red Feather and Blue Sky are going to live here in our cabin. I mean my cabin." He blushed but continued on with the plans. "After I take you to the fort, I will be traveling to my farm in Casper, Wyoming, located at the foot of the Casper Mountains.

"I guess you are ready to see your farm again . . . after being away for so long." Sarah tried to be happy for herself and Seth. She was failing. Sarah glanced over at the bed. Both of the children were fast asleep. Penny held the baby close to her tiny body. She stood and covered both of them with a light quilt.

~

"There's something else you need to know before we get to the fort." He waited until Sarah sat at the table. "Penny's papa is dead. He was with a search party and when he discovered his wife's grave, he lost all reasoning and blew up the side of the mountain."

"Was that the day we were headed down the valley and that explosion happened?" Sarah's eyebrows furrowed. "How do you know what happened that day?"

"A couple of young Indians scouts had led the search party. A few weeks later, they came up the mountain to check on their papa. They stayed on the mountain and have been helping with the clearing of the pathway."

"So, you are just now telling me this?"

"I didn't think you needed to worry about this until we were ready to leave here. Maybe I should have told you sooner, but I didn't. We're going to have to decide what to do about Penny. She's an orphan now."

"There's nothing to decide." Sarah jumped up from the table. "She's mine now. I love her. I will never give her up to strangers."

"What do you think your fiancé will say about taking on a ready-made family?"

"George is a good man. He will understand. I am not worried about Penny's future. She will be our child."

"I'm going outside to the barn and arrange my furs and hides to be placed on my mules early in the morning. You can begin gathering what few items you and Penny have. The trip will be slow going down the mountain, but once we get to the valley, we should arrive at the fort in a day."

Seth went out the door without another comment. He was hurting inside, but he had promised Sarah he would take her to Fort Laramie.

~

Blue Sky walked over to Sarah and placed her arms around her shoulders. "I take care of your little home."

Sarah gave her Indian friend a tight hug. "I know you will." Sarah couldn't stop the flow of tears that rolled down her cheeks. Why wasn't she happy soon to be united with her fiancé? Soon to be married.

Chapter 21

The news spread like fire that Seth Jenkins was riding toward the fort with a white woman and a small child. Most of the residents of the fort and the fur traders knew that Seth and many other fur trappers had been trapped on the mountain for months without a clear path down to the valley. Everyone had heard the tale about how Sergeant John Connors had gone crazy after discovering his wife's grave and blown up the mountain. The other woman and John's child had disappeared until now.

A trail of men, women and children followed behind Seth and his mule train of furs and hides. Many were hollering and asking questions, but Seth and Sarah ignored them.

~

Seth rode to the livery stable, leaped off his horse and placed Penny on the ground. "Stand right there while I help Sarah down." He lifted Sarah to the ground and asked if she was alright.

"Just a little nervous. I never thought there would be so many people to greet us."

"They're just plain nosey. Don't answer any of their questions. I'm sure your fiancé will be rushing out to meet you soon."

"Seth," Sarah touched his arm. "I'm scared. Really scared. What if he doesn't want me now? I've been missing for months."

"He'd be crazy not to still want you. I'll be near if you need any help. Remember that."

"Ma'am," a young man addressed Sarah. "Please come with

me. The captain is waiting for you in his office."

Sarah took Penny's hand. "Come, sweetheart, let's go and meet some new friends."

"Seth?" Penny looked back over her shoulder. "Come on, Seth."

Bending, Sarah whispered to the child that they would see Seth a little later, praying that would be true. She wasn't ready to depart from her savior, her friend. She arrived at the captain's office.

A young man pointed to a chair and requested she take a seat. "I will tell the captain you and a child are here."

In a few minutes, the door opened and closed. The young man told Sarah the captain wanted to see her but to leave the little girl with him.

"No, this child goes with me." She marched to the office door and opened it. Standing by the window was her love, her fiancé, the man she was going to marry.

George Turnberry slowly turned and faced her. He took a step toward her and she immediately rushed into his arms, only to be held back away from him.

"George, aren't you glad to see me?"

"Of course I am. Whose child is that hiding behind your skirt?"

"This is John Connor's little girl. I understood you knew all about the stagecoach accident and what happened to him. I have cared for her and will continue to in the future."

"I see. We'll discuss her later. How are you faring since your ordeal in the mountain with a total stranger?"

"I'm well. And blessed to have been rescued by Seth Jenkins. He took care of Penny and me without any complaint. I would have been here sooner if the mountain road hadn't been destroyed. We were on our way down the mountain when the explosion happened and blocked the trails down to the valley."

"I understand a little better now why you didn't arrive sooner. I still have a few questions that are concerning me, but I know you and this child must be tired. I'll take you over to your quarters."

George led the way to the sleeping quarters, making nasty remarks about the fort in general. One of his comments disturbed her. He said that the fort was Wyoming's little corner of Hell. No fit place for man or beast.

After seeing firsthand the living quarters, she understood what

George meant. The apartments for married couples were someone's idea of a joke. A rickety-looking, three-story building stood with a faded painted sign nailed to the front that read, "Lover's Nest" with two red hearts joined together. If he felt this way about this place and the living conditions were so bad, why had he sent for her?

After a long traumatic afternoon, Sarah joined George for dinner in the mess hall where all the married couples ate together. George finally placed a light kiss on Sarah's hand and told her one of the wives would help her settle in for the night. "We'll meet with the chaplain after he returns from a trip."

~

Sarah stood inside her small room and watched George enter his office. She walked softly over to the cot and covered Penny with a clean blanket. When she asked for another cot, she was told that there wasn't one available tonight. She could request one tomorrow from the supply sergeant.

Sarah sat at the end of her cot, read her Bible and prayed. *Lord, help me to understand George. Have I made a mistake coming here? Please help him accept John Connor's daughter as his own child after we are married. Help me to decide if marriage is the right thing for me with a man who seems so . . . what is the word, Lord? Amen.*

Chapter 22

The next morning, Sarah loitered but a moment after breakfast because she needed to see if she could find some nicer clothes for them. The clothes they had worn at the cabin had seen the end of their days, and she didn't what to shame George by wearing old, faded clothes.

Sarah longed for the trousseau her mama and Stella had sewn for her. There were yards of tatting and embroidery on the lovely white dress and underthings for a bride-to-be. She'd daydreamed many hours about her new life as a married woman as she sat and stitched seams in her new wardrobe. Now, all her lovely things were buried under piles of rock, fallen trees and dirt from the explosion. She had to be strong and not dwell on the loss of her lovely items. If George was the man she thought him to be, he would accept her no matter what she had on her back.

Upon her arrival, George had seemed distant. When she rushed to hug him, he grabbed her shoulders and held her back. He took her hand and kissed the back of it, like the men did at formal dances. She wanted to be held tight by the man she longed for, but so far he'd not shown any affection toward her.

Sarah had to decide what to do, so she took Penny's hand and hurried to the military commissary in the back of the fort.

~

Seth watched Sarah take quick steps with the child beside her. She appeared to be in a hurry, but she held Penny's hand and allowed Penny to skip along.

It didn't take him long to reach her side. "Morning, Sarah." She looked like a fresh morning breeze.

"Oh, Seth, it's so good to see you. What have you been doing since we arrived?" Sarah seemed pleased to see him. They had only been separated one day and he missed her so much.

Before Seth could answer, he felt a tug on his britches. Looking down, he saw Penny standing beside him. He bent over and picked her up. "Hello, Pumpkin. How are you doing this fine morning?"

"I've been playing with a little boy who likes to pick his nose and eat his boogers. I told him that wasn't nice, and he told me to go away."

"Goodness. You will have to show him better manners than that." Seth patted Penny's bottom and laughed. He was going to miss this child.

"May I walk with you to the store? I have to collect my money for my furs and hides." Seth peered over his shoulder at Sarah.

"I'm happy that you were able to sell them. You worked hard this past winter."

"I'm happy, too and I got a good price for the bundle. It made staying away from my farm worthwhile. The money will help me purchase more cattle and a bull."

~

Sarah was thrilled to have this short time with Seth. She enjoyed their talks and how he shared things with her. She was going to miss him.

Once they arrived at the store, Seth placed Penny on the ground and took Sarah's hand. "I want to give you some money so you and Penny will have whatever you need before you get married."

"Oh Seth, I have funds. I tucked some in the lining of my carpet bag before I left home and it's still there. I'll be fine, but thank you for the offer."

~

Several men from George's unit watched the young woman, child and bushy-faced mountain man as they stood in front of the fort's commissary. They'd heard the tale about the new captain's fiancée being rescued by a trapper who carried her off to his mountain cabin for several months. The woman didn't look afraid of the big mountain man. In fact, they looked very chummy together.

~

George Turnberry watched the mountain man and Sarah. They seemed too friendly with each other. Sarah should have been happy to get away from him after spending months in an isolated cabin together. "Too friendly if you ask me," George mumbled to himself.

"White, get in here." He was going to get rid of one mountain man today.

"Sir," the corporal responded to the captain.

"Tell the mountain man to get himself in here immediately. I have something to discuss with him."

"Yes, sir." The young man hurried and found Seth coming out of the Laramie Trading Post. He was trying to catch his breath when the mountain man passed by.

"Sir, Captain Turnberry requests your immediate attention in his office. Now, sir."

Seth raised his eyebrows and smiled at the young man. "It must be important for you to have run over here to give me his message." He smiled. "Well, lead the way."

~

Seth entered George Turnberry' s office which had little furniture inside—just an old desk and two chairs. The captain sat behind the desk, watching him. Seth glanced around, which seemed to irritate the captain.

"Why are you looking around my office? Have you misplaced something?"

"No, but the last time I was in here, there was a lot of nice furnishings. Looked like you were left with only an old desk."

"It's none of your business what I have in this office. I have called you here to tell you to pack your things and leave this fort immediately. I've watched the touching little scene between you and Sarah and so has everyone else. If you don't do as I've requested, I will have you placed in the brig."

Seth walked over to the window and glanced outside. A man could stand at this window and see all the fort's courtyard and buildings—everyone's comings and goings.

"First of all, Captain Turnberry, you have not requested that I

93

leave. I believe that you demanded that I go immediately. Fortunately for you, I 've completed my business and plan to leave today."

"Good. I want you gone as soon as possible, and I do not want you to spend another moment with my fiancée. You've been with her too much already and everyone is talking about it."

"What do you mean 'we have spent too much time together'? Are you trying to say that something improper happened between us while we were trying to survive in my cabin all winter?"

"You heard what I said. I want you gone today."

Seth stepped as close as he could to the captain's face. "Listen to me and listen well. Sarah's a lady and conducted herself like one. She told me she's known you for years, but I bet you never really knew the special lady you're planning on marrying. Sarah is the most gentle and kindest person I have ever met, and you are lucky to have her as your wife." Seth took a breath and balled his hands into fists at his side. "I am sure Sarah is as pure as the day she was born. No one, neither me nor the rustlers—and I bet my life on it—not even you, have ever compromised her in anyway." Seth stepped to the door and stopped. "Be good to her . . . or else."

The captain became braver. "Or else what, Mountain Man?"

Seth took two giant steps and stood in the captain's face again. "You don't want to know what else, sir. You have a gem in Sarah. Treat her like one."

Seth felt angrier than he had ever felt in his life. He wanted to beat this man to a pulp. Yes, he thought, George Turnberry is a little man inside who wants to be a big man outside. He acts like a tough guy, but he is as yellow as they come. His heart ached for Sarah. He prayed she would be happy, but being married to the heartless captain would only make her miserable.

Later when Seth was ready to pull out from the fort, he saw Sarah walking toward the captain's office. Seth called her name. She turned at his voice and hurried across the muddy road to join him on the boardwalk. He knew the captain's eyes were upon them, but he didn't care. He had to say good-bye. It was time to leave and head home and surrender his woman's heart into the hands of her fiancé. He wanted to grab and beg her to come with him, but he wouldn't ask her to make a choice.

As they stood close together, Sarah lifted her hand to touch his smooth, clean-shaven face. She whispered to him. "I always wondered what you would look like with your bushy beard gone." Before she could lower her hand, Seth caught it in his large, rough palm. He turned her palm up and lifted it to his mouth. He placed a soft kiss in the center and smiled into her eyes.

~

Sarah closed her hand into a small fist, sealing the kiss inside, and placed her hand over her heart. She tried to control the tears behind her eyelids, but one escaped down her cheek.

Seth used his thumb to wipe the tear away. "Don't cry, sweet girl." He immediately turned and jumped down the three steps to the ground. He turned one last time. "I'm going to my farm in Casper, Wyoming. If you need me, please write to me. I'll come."

Sarah reached out her hand toward him but dropped it down beside her. She stood and watched as Seth walked toward the livery to retrieve his horse and mules.

~

Seth's heart felt as if it was dragging on the ground. He felt empty and miserable as he entered the livery and walked to his horse. He wished he could have read the expression on her face as they said good-bye. Usually in the cabin, he could tell what she was thinking, if she was concerned about something, but today, other than the tears, he wasn't sure if she was as heartbroken as he was.

Chapter 23

Each time George tried to have a private conservation with Sarah, she had that snot-nosed young'un tucked on her hip or holding her hand. Today, he instructed Corporal White to watch the child outside his office. He told him to gather pencils and paper and play with the child while he had a long discussion with his fiancée.

~

Penny was happy playing with the corporal. so Sarah felt safe leaving her and strolled into George's office. "Good morning, George." She gave him her sweetest smile. "Has the chaplain returned from his trip?" Sarah was anxious to speak with the chaplain about her feelings for George.

George stood and glared down at Sarah. He looked from the top of her head to her worn-out shoes. He made her feel shabby.

"I'm sorry—" She pulled on her collar and smoothed her skirt. "that I don't have better clothes. All my things were left behind at the bottom of the mountain. I was able to purchase this nice dress at the commissary."

"You look fine." He motioned for her to take the chair opposite his. "I need to get a few things straight in my mind, if you don't mind discussing what happened to you while on the mountain."

"I don't mind answering any of your questions." Sarah sat and glanced around the room.

"While you were on the mountain, did you ever try to escape

from that mountain man? Did you ever attempt to get away from him?"

Sarah never dreamed in all the time she'd been at the fort that George would ask her something like that. She took a deep breath to calm her nerves and to take a moment to think about her answer. "Well, the first few days I had to adjust to my whereabouts. The first day and night I slept most of the time because I was in shock. Blue Sky, an Indian friend of Seth's, cared for me and attended to Penny, who cried all the time for her mama. I had no idea where I was. Escaping was the furthest thing from my confused mind."

His face remained expressionless.

"As far as escaping from a safe place and the man who had rescued me, I never gave that a thought. I was never a prisoner. Seth was kind to Penny and me. He was generous with his cabin and food. By that I mean he fed us, gave up his cabin and slept in the barn with his animals, and when it snowed, he made us warm fur coats and bartered warm moccasins from his Indian friends." Sarah looked into George's blank eyes. He didn't believe her.

"Why didn't you try to come to Fort Laramie?"

"Seth, Mr. Jenkins, said he would bring us to Fort Laramie as soon as he could and he kept that promise. Here we are, safe and sound."

"So, you didn't think that you needed to get away from him and try to come to me?"

Sarah was stunned. She had answered his first question as truthfully as she could. Now he was repeating the same question in a different way. "I don't understand you at all. If I had left the cabin, I wouldn't have had any idea which direction to go in the deep forest. I would certainly have been lost in a few hours. Later, the snow was so deep at times Seth could hardly get out to set his traps. Many times we were snowed in for several days during the winter." She folded her hands in a tight grip. If he asked her why she didn't escape again, she was going to scream.

"All right, I understand better now. It sounds like you had a nice *visit* with this man. Answer me this. Were you ever afraid while you were there, cooped up with a stranger in a cozy cabin?"

Before she could reply, George leaned forward, slapped his hand down on his desk, and screamed at her, making her jump. "I was disturbed every day. I wondered what could be happening to you, and all the time you were missing, you were in a nice snug cabin. I was nearly out of my mind worrying about you."

Sarah couldn't believe that her sweet, kind fiancé whom she had loved for several years was acting like a madman. "George, for goodness' sakes. I wasn't in a fancy hotel." Sarah bit her bottom lip and gave him an exasperated glance. "After I was rescued, I had no idea where I was being taken. Thank God, this stranger had a warm, yet rustic place to live. Are you angry that I wasn't having to live in a cold, dark cave or huddled under a tree left to freeze to death?"

"No, of course not.' He replied, clenching and unclenching his fists. "I just want to know if you were ever afraid of being lost on that mountain for months."

"Afraid?" She scowled. "Of course. I was terrified! Let me tell you about being afraid." Sarah leaped from her chair and circled the room. She shot him a look of disgust before she continued. "Afraid, George? When my stagecoach was being chased and shot at by bandits who didn't care if they killed anyone inside or not, we had to cover our heads and lie on top of each other on the floor." She shook her head. "We had no idea what was taking place. We prayed we wouldn't be killed by flying bullets.

"Afraid, George? When the stagecoach and six strong horses left the road and rolled over and over down the side of the mountain to land on its side. Thank God the child was asleep in her mama's arms. We didn't have time to tell if we were hurt or had any broken bones before the men were on us." She glared at him, but his face held no emotion.

"Afraid? One of the bandits pulled Julie, Penny's mama, out of the stagecoach and hit her so hard she fell nearly ten feet to the ground. While on the ground, he raped her and when she fought back, he sliced her throat." Sarah hung her head for a second. Gathering another round of wind, she tried not to shout as she went on.

"Afraid, George? I stood outside the stagecoach with a child in my arms and watched the same man, who had just killed her mama, coming for me. Thanks to the good Lord, that mountain man, whom you wanted me to be afraid of, came along and scared the men away with his buffalo gun. He fired several rounds and the robbers grabbed the money and fled." Sarah sat down in the chair, staring at her fiancé. He still didn't make a comment.

"Afraid, George? I was placed on a pack mule while the big man carried Penny in his arms. This giant of a man with a bushy beard carried us up a mountain to an isolated cabin in the wilderness." Sarah swiped a tear off her cheek. "I had no idea who this stranger was and what he was going to do to this little motherless child and me." Sarah stood in front of her fiancé.

"Afraid." She bent over and placed her palms on his desk. "When I got caught in a bear trap near the cabin, I sat outside in the snow for hours until I was rescued. I had nightmares about that bear attacking me while I was caught in his trap."

"Afraid? While Seth was gone for the day, a strange man broke into the cabin with the intention of stealing me away. Instead of shooting the intruder, I shot a hole in the top of the cabin. Seth arrived home in time to save me, again." George did raise his eyebrows with that statement.

"You ask if I was afraid? When it snowed for days on end and I had to go outside and drag in the last of the firewood, I was certain that Seth wasn't going to make it back and Penny and I would freeze to death." Sarah straightened her body and tried to stand tall and looked unafraid of the man sitting in front of her. "So, don't sit looking at me and asking if I was afraid while I wasn't here with you." Sarah stared at George, not really seeing him. Her mind was on memories of the mountain.

"I want to tell you something, George." Sarah's voice softened. "I will never forget the kindness Penny and I received from Seth and his Indians friends. How can you sit in front of me and ask if I was afraid of the man who became our guardian angel? It's unspeakable."

~

George didn't appreciate Sarah telling him what he could think and feel. He was going to be her husband, and she would do as he demanded or she would regret the day she married him. She might not have been afraid of the mountain man, but she would behave herself and obey him or she would learn about being afraid. "Well, I'm a man and I was down here in the valley hearing bits and pieces of rumors about you being on a mountain with a man. Alone, in his cabin, just the two of you. What was I to think?"

"I guess I can understand your position a little, but you have to understand mine. If we are going to be married, you have to believe me and put this behind us. You have to believe I thought of you and wanted desperately to reach the fort to be with you."

He kept his hands folded behind his back and stared out the window. "The chaplain will be here tomorrow with his wife. We'll talk with him day after tomorrow." George whirled and dismissed her as if she was one of his men.

~

Sarah left the office feeling drained. She couldn't understand the sweet man she had fallen in love with years ago. Something had happened to turn him into a cold, unfeeling man.

"Sarah, I'm hungry." Penny smiled and took her hand.

"Did you tell Corporal White thank you for helping you draw pictures?"

"Thanks, Mr. White. See you later," she said giggling.

"Later to you, Miss Penny."

Chapter 24

Early the next morning, when Sarah woke up, she didn't feel well. After dressing, she and Penny walked to the mess hall downstairs. After serving Penny a plate of flapjacks and a cup of milk, she sat down at the table with several other wives.

"Good morning, everyone." Sarah smiled at the ladies, but they only nodded at her.

Sarah removed her hanky from her sleeve and wiped her forehead. A young girl who was serving everyone coffee asked Sarah if she was feeling alright. "Your face is flushed."

"I do feel a little warm this morning, but I'm fine. Thank you for your concern." As she lifted Penny from the bench to leave the room, Sarah swayed, her legs wobbled, and she felt dizzy. She grabbed the table, hoping to steady herself but fell onto the floor unconscious.

~

"I need help here. The captain's fiancée has fainted," the young serving girl yelled.

Several of the men rushed to help Sarah. "What's happened?" Corporal White placed his coffee on the table and hurried to examine her.

"Let's carry her over to sick bay. Someone go and tell the captain." Corporal White couldn't help but notice none of the men's wives offered to help Sarah. Anger flowed through his young body. "Just wait until I tell the captain how you ladies refused to help his lovely fiancé. I'm sure he'll be happy with you all."

"Wait, Corporal." One of the ladies jumped up from the table and pleaded with him not to tell on them. "We'll go to sick bay with you and take care of her, won't we, girls?"

He glared at each of the women. "See that you do."

~

Mary Lou, one of the wives at the fort, had been taking care of Penny while Sarah was sick. Penny was a good little girl and Mary Lou enjoyed her company. She hoped she had a little girl in a few months.

Early, the next morning, Corporal White tapped on Mary Lou's door. She hoped he had come to give her a report on Sarah, but instead he requested that she dress the child and bring her and her personal belongings downstairs immediately.

"She hasn't had breakfast yet. Can't you wait until I feed her?" Why did he want the little girl downstairs so early? It was barely daylight.

"No, get her ready and hurry. She'll be leaving on the orphan wagon train in less than an hour."

"No. She's not an orphan. The captain's fiancée said they were going to raise the child. There must be a mistake."

"Do I have to dress the little girl myself?" His eyebrows formed a V. "This is not my idea. I hate it, too, but I have my orders. Please, don't make this any harder for me than it is already."

Mary Lou closed the door and dressed Penny as quickly as she could. Fighting back tears, she took her hand and led her to the porch where Corporal White was waiting.

~

He picked Penny up in his arms and reached for her brown bag of personal items.

"Are we going to eat now? I'm hungry as a bear," she said giggling.

Corporal White could not speak for the lump in his throat. He carried Penny to the livery where the wagon train waited, loaded with children and new supplies. Before he placed her in the back of a wagon, he slipped her a piece of hard candy, then turned and gave a tall, gray-haired lady Penny's things. The corporal hurried back to his barracks where he fell down on his bunk and covered his head to hide the tears that were threatening to fall. He would never understand Captain Turnberry.

~

"She'd better wake soon." Lulu stood at the foot of Sarah's sick bed. "I'm sick and tired of having to stand guard over the little princess of the fort. Just because she's the captain's fiancée, Randall made me take care of her. Do you think when they have their big wedding, a little private like my Randall will be invited to their shindig? No, although I may be asked to serve at their grand reception."

"Lulu, someone had to take care of her. I offered, but the captain refused my help. Maybe it was because I'm going to have a child."

"Well, I'm sick of caring for her. She is no better than I am. Her man wouldn't be captain if John hadn't blown himself and the mountain up."

~

Sarah couldn't believe what she had just heard about Penny's papa. She attempted to sit up. One of the ladies hurried over and asked how she felt.

"Thank you. I'm still a little dizzy but otherwise, I'm fine." Sarah swung her legs onto the floor and sat up. "What happened to me?"

"Oh honey, you had tick fever," Mary Lou Moore from Atlanta told Sarah. "The doctor found the tick after you fainted. You had a high fever. The tick was under your arm, but thankfully, he removed it. Several ladies have been taking turns caring for you. Mostly Lulu here."

"Oh, that was so nice of all of you. Thank you so much, Lulu. I know most of you live at the fort with your husbands and families. I'm sorry you were pulled away from them to care for me. I'll never be able to repay you." Sarah glanced from one woman to the next. She hated that the women had already formed an ugly opinion of her while she was sick. She was stunned to hear about Penny's papa and how he had died. Had Seth heard John Connors was the one who blew up the mountain? "How long have I been sick and who has been caring for my little girl?"

"That little girl is your child?" Lulu had a surprised expression on her face.

"No, she has been with me for months and I feel like she's mine. Sergeant John Connors and his wife, Julie, were her parents but they're both dead. Since she has no one, I intend to raise her as my own."

"How does the captain feel about raising another man's child?"

"I'm sure he'll be a good father to Penny." Sarah smiled at the jaded smirks on their faces and said she needed to go the water closet.

Sarah tottered out of the water closet, still unsteady on her feet. But her ears were working just fine. The ladies were whispering about Penny. "I'm sorry, but I couldn't help but hear you talking about Penny. Is she well?"

The ladies peered at the floor or at their hands, anywhere but at Sarah.

"Please, what's wrong?" She was ready to run out of the room and go in search of her child.

Lulu took Sarah's hands and led her back to the cot. "Please sit down. We've decided that you need to know where the little girl is . . . now."

"Please, tell me. Where is she?" Sarah pleaded.

"While you were sick, Captain Turnberry had her placed on the orphan wagon train that left two days ago." Lulu tried to break the news gently.

"No, he would never do that." Sarah screamed the words. Her eyes darted from face to face. They were telling the truth. "I must talk with George." Sarah stood and looked around the room. "Please get my dress and shoes. I've got to go and bring Penny back."

"The captain left this morning with the 'C' Patrol. He's gone into the hills to meet with some Indian tribes and have a powwow." Lulu peered around at the other women. "Well, that's what my Johnny said, anyway."

Sarah studied Lulu for a moment. "What's a powwow?"

"It's a friendly gathering of several Indian chiefs."

"When will he return?"

"Tomorrow, I believe." Lulu reached for Sarah's arm. "Please don't mention you heard this information from us." She glanced at the other women and they all looked afraid.

"I won't. George will tell me where Penny is. I won't get any of you in trouble. I can't believe he would send a small child away. She only stopped crying for her mama the last few weeks." Sarah placed her head down in her hands. "I told Seth I would raise Penny like my own child. What will he think about what I've allowed to happen to her?"

The women moved around the room, giving each other sly glances.

"Corporal White said you wanted to speak with the chaplain. He's back from his trip and he brought his wife this time. Maybe you can discuss the problem about the child with him." Mary Lou helped Sarah back to the water closet to dress.

"Yes, I'll request a meeting with him today. Thanks again for caring for me."

Chapter 25

Sarah knocked on the small church building. Corporal White had arranged for her to speak with Chaplain Sumrall. After a few minutes, the chaplain's wife opened the door and invited her inside.

"Welcome, my dear. I am Elizabeth Sumrall." Sarah took the hand of a small-framed, older woman who had sparkling blue eyes and many wrinkles on her face. She warmed Sarah with her sweet, welcoming smile. Hers was the only smile she'd received since arriving at the fort.

"My husband and I usually invite our guests into our small but cozy kitchen. Will you come with me?"

"I will be happy to join you. Is the chaplain here today?"

"Yes. He'll join us in a moment. Do you like sugar and cream in your coffee?" Before Sarah could answer, the chaplain came hurrying inside from the back of the church house.

"Hello, dear," Chaplain Sumrall spoke to his wife. "Ah, this must be the captain's fiancée everyone is talking about. It's so nice to finally meet you, my dear."

"Thank you, sir. I'm pleased to meet you both."

The chaplain motioned for Sarah and his wife to have a seat while Mrs. Sumrall placed a bowl of sugar and a small pitcher of cream in front of Sarah. "I understand from the captain's corporal you wanted to speak with me. How can I help you today?"

"I want to get my little girl off the orphan wagon train that left the fort two days ago. George, the captain, placed her on the train without speaking to me. I have been sick for the last two days. He had no right to do this. I planned to raise the child as my own and George knew this." Sarah's voice got louder.

"My goodness. Do you know where the wagon train was headed?"

"No, I have no idea, but surely someone in this fort would know." Sarah's hope of finding Penny was slowly fading.

"Miss Sullivan, Captain Turnberry told me you were traveling to the fort to marry him. He was waiting on Captain Miller to give him permission. Of course, now Captain Miller has retired, and your fiancé is the commander of the fort. He doesn't need permission. I have only been assigned to this fort for a short time, and I haven't gotten to know Captain Turnberry well."

"To be honest with you, I don't feel like I know him well either." Sarah sighed and wiped her eyes. "Since I've arrived, he acts so different toward me."

"Tell me, how has he changed?" Before Sarah could reply, Mrs. Sumrall stood and asked if she should excuse herself from their private discussion.

"Please stay." Sarah reached for Elizabeth's arm and pleaded with her. "You make me feel like I'm at home."

"Well, of course, dear. I want to help anyway I can."

"You asked how George has changed." Sarah sat for a moment and took a deep breath. "It has been over a year since he was home. He was kind and sweet to me and Mama. My mama is supposed to join us here once we are married and get settled in our home. I'm not sure now if I should send for her."

"Why do you say that?"

"Because he sent Penny away. He knew I wanted her to be our little girl. Penny was John Connors' child. His wife, Julie, was traveling with me when she was killed by those awful rustlers."

"Yes, I heard the story. You were rescued by a young mountain man and he brought you down from the mountain last week. How long were you with him?"

"I was traveling here in September and we were trapped on the mountain until last week. Seth Jenkins is the man who helped Penny and me. He's a kind man who took excellent care of us.

Seth has left the fort to go to his farm. Before he left for his home, I told him George and I would continue to care for Penny like she was ours. I spoke to George about her and he said we would talk about Penny later. He didn't agree or disagree to keep her, but I would never have given her up. I must get her back." Sarah lowered her head and cried.

"Child, if Captain Turnberry put the child on the orphan train, doesn't that tell you he doesn't want someone else's little girl to raise?" Mrs. Sumrall spoke softly.

Sarah wiped a tear. "That's what scares me. How could a man not love a precious child who has lost her parents? The George I thought I knew would be a wonderful papa."

"A good papa to his own children, not someone else's. There are people like that. There are men who father children and wish that they hadn't. I have two questions to ask you, Mrs. Sullivan. Do you love George, and do you want to marry him?" He peered over his wire-rimmed glasses and studied her face.

"I came all this way to marry George and make him a good wife. I wanted to do this with all my heart, but now, I'm not sure how I feel."

"Have your feelings changed since he gave the child away?"

"Yes. I never dreamed he would do something like that. It's a selfish side I never dreamed he had."

"I can't speak for George, but maybe he didn't know how to tell you he didn't want a ready-made family. Maybe this was his way of saving you more heartache. You need to pray about George and your feelings for him. He plans to marry you as quickly as possible. He spoke to me about performing the ceremony."

"Thank you both for listening to me. I can't let Penny stay on that wagon train. I am so disappointed in George." Sarah hugged Elizabeth Sumrall good-bye and shook the chaplain's hand.

As she walked back to her room, she never felt so heartbroken in all her life. "Please God, take care of my Penny." Sarah cried and didn't care who witnessed her sorrow.

~

After a few hours of visiting with the chaplain and his wife, she marched into the captain's office. Corporal White was filing papers when the door opened. "Good afternoon, Miss Sullivan."

"Good afternoon to you, Corporal White."

"You've heard the captain is away from the fort, haven't you?"

"Yes, but I didn't come to see him. I need your help. Can we speak privately?"

"Come, let's step inside the captain's office." He closed the door behind Sarah and got straight to the point. "How can I help you?"

"I want to go after the orphan wagon train, but I can't do this by myself. I haven't ridden a horse since I was young. It would be better if I could hire someone that you trusted to go and bring Penny back to me. If this person traveled alone, they would make better time and catch up with the train."

Corporal White hung his head. "I'm so sorry that I had to place her on that wagon train, but I had to follow orders. I did argue with the captain, but he said he would have me shot if I didn't follow his command."

"Mercy, do you think he would have done that to you?"

"Captain Turnberry is a different man since he's been promoted. I couldn't take that chance."

"I understand better now why you did it, but I need your help—not you personally, but someone." Sarah watched men and women moving around the fort from the captain's front window. George had probably stood right here, in this very spot, and watched her and Seth say good-bye.

"George had no idea how much I love that little girl or he couldn't have done this to me and her. The poor little thing is probably scared to death. She had finally stopped crying for her mama. She's grown to love and trust Seth and me. My heart is broken and I know she is sad, too."

Corporal White looked so downcast, but he really didn't have a choice—she knew this now. George had turned into an ill-tempered man who seemed to want everyone to fear him.

"Do you know someone I could hire?"

"Let me talk to a couple of men. I could get one of the Indian scouts to go in search of the train. Would you care if an Indian took on the job?"

"Heavens, no. Two of my best friends are Indians and I miss them."

The corporal smiled.

"Thank you so much. Let's keep this meeting between us.

Please let me know when you find someone to help me." Sarah left the office and went to the commissary to purchase some stationery. She needed to write her mama and let her know she was well, although it was far from the truth.

Chapter 26

Seth rode for miles until he reached the small town of
Turnersville, Wyoming. He didn't remember too much of the trip
because all he did was think about Sarah. He prayed George
Turnberry would make Sarah a good husband, but he didn't feel
good about the man. After his discussion with him, the man still
didn't believe Sarah had not been compromised by him or the
rustlers. The captain wanted to believe the worst.

After riding most of the day, his stomach was growling. He
hadn't taken time to stop and cook anything. Instead he chewed on
dried jerky. He rode to the livery at the end of the little town and
spoke to a young man who was more than willing to take his horse
and tie Buster's leash to a post. After he gave instructions to the
young man, he noticed several big wagons and a long line of small
children. They were a pretty raggedy-looking bunch. Sad, thought
Seth.

After settling his horse, he asked if there was a good place to
eat. "Yes, sir. Down the street on the left is a small café that serves
a good plate of food."

Seth tossed the boy a quarter and started walking past the
children when he saw a tall boy about ten pushing and dragging the
children into a straight line. Surprised, a little girl who resembled
Penny, fell down on her knees and began screaming for her mama.

"I want my mama. I want Sarah." The child laid down on the
dirt and screamed even louder. "I want Sarah!"

The young man who was in charge of the children hurried over to the little girl and demanded she stand and stop bawling or he'd kick her. "I'll give you something to cry about," he warned.

The child had cried out for someone named Sarah, but Seth continued on to the café. She was a loud one. He could hear her still.

"Seth, I want my Seth."

Seth stopped walking and listened to the cries of the child. Did he hear his name? He saw the boy mistreating the little girl. Seth's temper flared. He marched over to the line of children. The girl was still down on her knees looking at the ground. She lifted her head to scream again when she peered up at him.

She wiped her nose with the back of her hand and screamed, "Seth."

Seth couldn't believe his eyes. The little girl who looked just like Penny was actually Penny. Her face was streaked with dirt and her eyes filled with tears, but he would know her anywhere.

"Penny, oh my goodness. Is that really you?" The child had red eyes and a runny nose, but he knew it was his Penny. He grabbed the number pinned on her coat, tossed it to the ground, and held her in his arms as tight as he could. "Oh my child, what in the world are you doing here? Where's Sarah? Why are you here alone without Sarah?"

Before Penny could answer any of his questions, the young brute grabbed his arm. "Put that girl down, now."

Penny held her arms tight around Seth's neck and cried. "Take me home." She placed her face in his shoulder trying to hide from the mean boy.

Seth glared down at the youngster. "Son, you'd best take your hand off me. If I see or hear you mistreating another child like you did this one, I will beat the daylights out of you."

The young man stepped back away from Seth. "Why is this child on the orphan train if you care so much about her?" The boy's voice was full of anger.

"I don't know why she's here. I can't believe she's not with Sarah who's been caring for her the last few months. Who's in charge of this operation?"

"I am, mister." A tall, gray-haired woman strolled over with a notebook in her hand. "What's your problem?"

"It seems there has been a mistake. Penny is not supposed to be standing in line with a number pinned on her chest like sheep going to slaughter. Sarah Sullivan, the new captain's fiancée, has been caring for this child since her mama and papa have died. I had been helping her until we arrived at Fort Laramie last week. Sarah would never have put this child up for adoption."

"Maybe she wouldn't have, but the captain surely did. He demanded I take this child and leave before light. We pulled out from the fort after all of our supplies were loaded."

"What did Miss Sullivan have to say about this?" Seth would never believe Sarah would be willing to put Penny up for adoption and not raise her as her own. She loved the child too much.

"From what I understand, she's in sickbay back at the fort."

"Sick? My Sarah is sick?"

"Mister, I don't know anything about *your Sarah*, but the captain's fiancée has tick fever. I was told that she'd been running a high fever for two days, but she's a little better. The captain said if I didn't leave the fort this morning, he wouldn't give me the supplies I needed for the children. Excuse me, mister, but I've got to hurry and get these children unloaded." She reached for Penny, but Seth blocked her.

The older woman called to the young man. "Jeff, take the children to the public outhouses and come back here. I'll prepare lunch for them behind the livery."

"Madam, how much do you want?"

"How much do I want for what? Spit it out, Mister, because I'm in a hurry. The children are hungry."

"How much money do you want for this child? I'm taking her with me, one way or the other, but I'm willing to adopt her."

"Here now, sonny. I don't sell children."

"You said you needed supplies and you took this child because you were threatened by the captain. I have money. I can give you whatever you want and you'll not have to worry about supplies for a while."

"What else do you want?" The older woman seemed thrilled but a little dubious at the same time.

"I want you to sign a legal document giving me the right to this child." Penny had her head on Seth's shoulder with her arms tight around his neck.

"I had a home already picked out for this little girl. She was going to be a replacement child for a couple who lost their babe. They asked for a small girl with blond hair and blue eyes. They would have given me a nice donation for her."

"Don't you think that's a bit callous?" Seth couldn't believe how the children were chosen like prize cattle.

"Sir, beggars can't be choosers in this world. We came along in the nick of time to save this child from disappearing from the fort another way. The captain wanted this child gone for some reason."

"Sarah is going to be very upset to learn that Penny has left the fort." Seth still couldn't accept that Sarah had allowed this to happen to Penny.

The older woman glanced around. She motioned for him to follow her. "Walk with me to my wagon and we'll make a deal. I have a small bag of clothes that belongs to your girl."

After settling with the old woman, he carried Penny to a rooming house next door to the wonderful-smelling café. Entering he rang the bell that sat on the desk. A sweet-smiling older woman wearing a long white apron hurried down the staircase.

"Hello, young man. Who do you have with you?" The woman glanced from Seth to Penny.

"My name is Seth Jenkins, and this is my daughter. I need a room for one night and a big tub of water so I can bathe her."

"You're in luck. I happen to have one room available and I'll have my boy bring you several buckets of water. The room is two dollars and an extra half-dollar for the bath. If you roomed here for the month, the bath would be free," the owner of the rooming house said with a big toothless smile.

"Does this town have a dry goods store where I can buy my child some clothes and other things she'll need for our trip home?"

"Yep, right out the door to the right, two doors down. Mr. Roberts has a good supply of most everything."

Seth took the key and went upstairs to his room. He hugged Penny and set her down on the bed. "When the water comes up, I'm going to get some of the dirt off of you, and then we'll go get something to eat. Are you hungry?"

"Yep, I could eat a bear," she said smiling for the first time since Seth had found her. He laughed because he had heard her say that several times on the mountain.

A knock at the door, and a young boy carried in two buckets of water. "Set them over there." Seth flipped the young man a nickel.

Penny jumped off the bed and grabbed Seth around the leg as if she was never going to let him leave her.

"Let me go, pumpkin. I'm not ever going to leave you again." Seth repeated the words slowly to the child. He could only guess what she'd been through since leaving the fort with those other children.

~

Penny climbed back on the bed and watched Seth's every move. He set a bowl of water on the table next to the bed. First he wiped her face and hands. Then he moistened the cloth again and wiped her legs. Next he took a comb out of his pocket and ran it through Penny's tangled hair. After he finished, he smiled at her. "Now you look like my Penny. Let's go to the café and get something good to eat."

Chapter 27

As Sarah waited in her room, she heard loud voices and horses riding into the center of the courtyard. She raced down the stairs out onto the porch with a group of women and watched her fiancé ride directly to his office. From where she stood, she could hear his angry tone as he tossed his horse's reins to a young private. George issued orders to a few other men and stormed toward Corporal White. By his expression and the waving of George's hands, Corporal White was receiving the brunt of his anger. He stormed into his office with Corporal White following behind.

"What in the world has happened to rile up the captain?" Lulu whispered to Mary Ann who was standing next to Sarah. "I hope he doesn't make the men stand in formation for hours like he did a few weeks ago."

A loud crack of thunder interrupted Sarah's thoughts. She wanted to ask the girls a few questions about George's behavior toward the men, but lightening flashed close, so they hurried back inside.

Sheets of rain began to fall. The big windmill spun as a brisk wind blew the blades around. Several of the men were trying to shut the windmill down before the water overflowed and flooded the courtyard.

Sarah had no more than entered the front door when sheets of rain hit the side of the building. She rushed upstairs to her room and hurried to look out the front window. George was standing on the front porch over Corporal White. He clamped his hands on the front of the corporal's uniform and shook the young man like he was a rag doll. The corporal wasn't trying to get away, but George pushed the young man off the porch into the rain and pointed toward the livery. Sarah couldn't hear any of the conversation between the two men, but George was infuriated and treated the young officer disgracefully.

Corporal White saluted George and ran through the muddy courtyard. Sarah was sure the man was soaked through before he entered the livery. *What did the corporal do to provoke George's ugly behavior?*

At supper, George didn't call for her. She waited, but when he didn't arrive to walk with her to the dining hall, she went alone. A hush dropped over the room when the men and women saw Sarah standing alone at the entrance of the room.

A young man who worked in the dining hall rushed over to her and asked if he could serve her a plate of food with a fresh cup of coffee.

"Yes, please. That would be nice." He guided her to a table and held a chair out for her to sit.

Sarah sat at the end of a long table feeling alone, even though there were several couples having dinner at the same table. She overheard a word or two of their conversation as they whispered to each other. Most of their conversation was about the men's work schedule. She'd hoped to hear something about George's earlier behavior, but everyone was speaking softly, which was usual.

After supper, she smiled at everyone who looked her way and climbed the stairs to her room. Since George had not dined with her this evening, she didn't expect to see him later.

Sarah prepared for bed, then decided to write her mama a long letter. She wished she could tell her all about Penny, but not until she knew if she was going to get the child back.

~

Before daylight the next morning, Sarah heard a tapping at her door. She jumped out of bed and covered herself with her wrapper. "Who is it?"

"It's me. Corporal White. Please let me in."

Sarah inched the door open, but he pushed himself into her

room. "I'm sorry, Miss, but I only have a minute. The captain found out that you asked me to help you find the orphan train. I don't know how or why someone would tell him, but they did. I'm sorry, but I can't help you. He's sending me on a dangerous mission."

"What will you be doing?" Sarah felt so bad that this young man was being punished for something she had asked him to do.

"I'll be tracking down those rustlers who robbed the stage and killed John Connor's wife. The two Indian scouts I planned to hire to help you are going with me and a few other men. We, the scouts and I, cannot return to the fort until we have captured them. Those men have continued to rob and kill innocent people for a pence. Now they have started rustling cattle from the small ranchers in this territory."

"I am so sorry he is sending you after those men. Maybe if I spoke to George and told him I requested your help, he would reconsider sending you away."

"No. He would probably toss me in the stockade and throw away the key. Please don't let him know I came here this morning. I'm sorry, but I have to get ready to pull out. I felt you should know. You had better forget about that little girl if you're going to marry the captain."

"Thank you so much for coming to me. I'm sorry. Really I am. Please be careful. Those men are dangerous." Sarah hugged the young man. "I feel like I am losing a good friend. I'll pray for you and your men."

Corporal White swallowed with difficulty. He opened Sarah's door and peeked out in the hallway. "It's clear, so I'd better go. Bye, Miss Sullivan."

~

Sarah had not seen George since that awful morning he'd sent Corporal White away. He had not called on her for supper, nor had any of the ladies mentioned it. She was almost afraid to have to face him. A few days passed before she was summoned to George's office. In the meantime, she questioned many of the store owners about where the orphan train would be headed. No one seemed to know anything, but Sarah knew better. Rumors spread like wildfire and she knew that they didn't want to get on the captain's bad side.

Sarah dressed in her white shirtwaist and blue skirt. She shined her shoes, styled her hair in a braid and twisted it around her head like a crown. She looked in the mirror and was satisfied she looked as nice as she could with the few belongings she owned.

As she entered George's office, a tall, young man with a stiff mustache on his handsome face, jumped up from his desk chair.

"Ma'am, the captain is waiting for you. Please go right in." He hurried to the door and held it open for her.

'Good morning, Sarah dear." He appeared to choke on the word, *dear*, but she smiled.

"Good morning to you, too. I'm glad you have requested my company. I understand you've been busy, and I'm honored you made some time for me."

"Are you being sarcastic, Sarah?" He came from behind his desk and propped against it, crossing his ankles.

"Of course not. I've been concerned you would like for me to return home."

He reached into his pocket and withdrew his pocket watch and turned to glance out his window onto the courtyard. "Surely you have no reason to feel like that. I called you in this morning to discuss our marriage. The chaplain is prepared to marry us at a moment's notice."

"That's nice. But George, I am very unhappy, and I must understand your reason for placing John Conner's little girl on the orphan train. You knew I had taken care of her for months and I hoped we would raise her as our own. You knew how I felt about her."

"I wasn't prepared to speak about that this morning, but you wanted the child, not me. I wanted us to begin our marriage without someone else's child. I want my own." He stood looking down at the top of her head. "I believe you knew that I didn't want you to be burdened with a child when you'd have many responsibilities as my first lady. The child was a millstone around your neck on that mountain. Without her, you could have escaped."

"I will not speak to you again about the reasons I did not attempt to come off that mountain by myself. As far as Penny is concerned, after months of caring for her, I learned to love her. I wanted to give her a home with us. You should have talked to me about giving her away to total strangers. I insist you send some men to find her and bring her back to me."

George took Sarah's arm and held it so tight his grip bit into her skin, but she didn't flinch. "You listen to me and listen well. I give the orders here, not you. You have already stepped on my authority by asking one of my men to help you. You are the reason he was sent away on a treacherous mission. That is what he got for disobeying my orders." George whirled and walked to the window overlooking the courtyard.

With his back turned away, Sarah rubbed her arm and then quickly crossed them in front of her body.

George slowly swiveled on his heels and advanced toward Sarah. "Now, Sarah." He smiled and appeared calm. "The subject of that child is closed. Do you want to meet with the chaplain before we say our wedding vows or do you want me to choose a date and time?"

Sarah stood staring down at the floor. She wasn't sure she wanted to marry this man; a man with a cruel streak, so different from the George she came to be with.

"Sarah, dear. I have other duties this morning to attend to, so give me your answer. I hope you haven't changed your mind about marrying me. Tongues are already wagging about our relationship. People are whispering about you living with that mountain man for months. Many feel that I should not marry a tainted woman, *someone like you,* while others think I'm a loving, understanding man who has already forgiven you."

Sarah jerked her head up and faced him. "Have you, George?" She knew in her heart that this wasn't a forgiving man. She had to rethink her decision about getting married.

"Have I what, woman? I'm running out of time and patience."

"Have you forgiven me for something I had no control over?" Sarah watched the expression on his face. He merely stared at her without blinking an eye.

"I will call upon you this evening for dinner, and tomorrow afternoon we will wed. This will give me time to instruct the mess hall cooks to prepare food for the reception and invite all the men and their wives. I personally would rather not have everyone attend, but I am the captain and you will be the first lady. I have no choice but to turn our wedding into a small gala." George opened the door and patted Sarah on the shoulder. "I shall see you this evening. Be ready at six."

Sarah stood with her shoulders stiff in the doorway. "You never answered my question."

He smiled down at her, then pushed her out the door, replying, "Time will tell."

Chapter 28

Sarah stood at the window in her room and watched Lulu
and her husband holding hands and laughing as they strolled in the
courtyard. Their footsteps and voices soon faded away. The couple
looked so happy.

Sarah sat on her bed and wondered if she and George would be
a happy couple after the wedding ceremony tonight. The sun had
come out and shone down on the ugly, gray buildings in the fort.
The beauty of her wedding faded when she remembered there
wouldn't be big bouquets of lovely flowers or ferns tied with white
ribbons in the small church. She'd known when she left home to
marry George, their ceremony would be small without family or
friends. A small wedding was fine with her, but not George.

Sarah covered her face with her hands and said a silent prayer.
George insisted the whole fort be invited. Sarah knew the people in
attendance would not be there because they wanted to celebrate the
couple's happiness but because they were ordered to be there.

She sat on her bed, thinking what a sad day this was when it
should be the happiest day of her life. Oh, how she wished her
mama was here.

A light tap on the door broke her spell of daydreaming about
tonight.

Sarah moved to the door and was pleasantly surprised to see
Elizabeth, the chaplain's wife. "Come in." Sarah took the older
woman's hand and led her into her small room.

"My goodness." Elizabeth Sumrall glanced around Sarah's quarters. "I never dreamed these rooms were so cramped. Have you been comfortable here, my dear?"

"Yes. It's fine for one person." Sarah smiled for the first time all day. "It's nice of you to visit me today. You must have known I needed a friend."

"I remembered you said that your mama couldn't be here with you. I know I could never take her place, but I did want to help you with your dress and things." Elizabeth glanced around the room.

"I don't have anything special to wear. I thought to go to the dry goods store this morning and I hoped a new shipment of dresses had come in. I bought one last week, but I've already worn it. Would you like to go with me?"

~

A bustle of activity was happening in the mess hall as the ladies passed by. Employees were carrying tables and chairs outside. With a few extra touches, the reception would proceed nicely.

When they entered the dry goods store, Sarah noticed a couple of pretty nightgowns. Her soul stood still. *What would take place between myself and Seth—I mean, George? George is who I'm marrying tonight.* Sarah shook her head. Seth was gone, lost to her.

Would George carry her to his bed? Without trust, what was the possibility of sharing any joy or love? She suddenly saw a flash of how George might treat her. *He'll shun me and not share our wedding bed. He'll never spend time with me.* George practically accused her of being a fallen woman because she lived with a strange man. *Why does he even want to marry me?*

"Sarah dear, are you alright? You're as white as a sheet." Elizabeth reached out and took Sarah's shaking hand.

She smiled at the older woman. "Just bridal nerves, I guess."

"Of course, that's expected. Let's go and look at the dresses. I believe I saw a few new items."

As Sarah scanned the few dresses, it was hard to hold back tears. She remembered her mama and Stella working hours on her bridal trousseau. She was going to be the most beautiful dressed bride the fort had ever seen. "Oh well," she sighed softly. "That wasn't to be."

"Did you say something, dear?"

"No, not really. Just thinking about my mama."

It didn't take long for them to look through the dresses. Elizabeth helped her choose a soft, blue dress that had a white embroidered collar and tight-fitting cuffs with tiny, pearl buttons. The dress was a little more than she could afford, but she wanted to look like a bride. She chose a pair of white slippers.

The storekeeper asked if she wanted to charge the items on her new account the captain had opened for her. She was surprised by George's thoughtfulness, but she declined. The purchases cost her most of the money she brought from home, but she didn't want to begin her marriage being obligated to her husband.

The ladies ambled down the boardwalk with their purchases and glanced around. The courtyard was swept clean of any horse droppings, and several men sat under a shade tree practicing their musical instruments.

"Oh, Sarah, listen. It looks like we'll have a dance after the wedding. I love to dance, don't you?"

"I haven't ever danced before. I'm not sure if George knows how either."

"You'll find out tonight."

As they strolled to Sarah's quarters, Elizabeth asked her if there was something on her mind. "You've been so quiet. Do you want to talk about what's bothering you? Is it the wedding bed?"

Sarah blushed and gave her new friend a shy smile. "I'm sorry I've worried you. I do have some concerns about George." She gazed off into the distance. "He's so different from the man I remembered months ago. I've prayed and asked God for guidance."

"I knew something was wrong. Now you listen to me, child. I'm going to speak to you as if you were my own daughter." Elizabeth pulled Sarah over to sit on a bench at the edge of the courtyard. A light breeze was blowing, and the sun sat behind a few clouds.

"Sarah, if your heart in not in this wedding, please don't go through with it. Tell the captain how you really feel and go home. Marriage is a serious step in your life and a loveless marriage is like being in prison. Believe me, I know." Elizabeth reached for Sarah's hand. "I was married to a young man for several years. My pa made me marry him because he was from a wealthy family."

Elizabeth took a deep breath. "See, he was a spoiled young man who had a terrible temper. He beat me, but I could never tell my pa. I had to stay hidden for days until I recovered from the black eyes and other bruises.

"But Chaplain Sumrall isn't like that now, is he?"

"No, you misunderstand. This young man was my first husband. He liked to have a good time. He drank and played cards. One night, a rover from a cattle drive shot and killed him. They had gotten into a fight over one of the women that worked in the saloon." Elizabeth looked away and took a breath. "I was free. God forgive me, but I was happy, believe me. I remained single for years. When our town needed a preacher, Matt received the calling and it was love at first sight."

"What a beautiful, but sad story. I knew Chaplain Sumrall was a good man the first time I met him. I'm so happy you had a second chance at happiness."

"You see, my dear. I want you to be happy now. If you aren't sure about the captain, don't make the biggest mistake of your life. Please follow your heart."

"Thank you so much for listening to me and for sharing your story. I must confess to you I'm a little unsure of George. But what would he do if I decided not to marry him? He's a powerful man."

"I believe you have your answer. You should have said he's an understanding, loving man." Both of the ladies sat quiet for a few minutes. "Let's get your packages inside so you can press your dress, in case you decide to wear it this evening. Do you need any help getting ready?"

"Thank you, but no. I want to lie down for a short nap before I take a bath and get ready. I'll see you at the church. Thank you again."

Chapter 29

George walked to the front of the small church with his best man, who was his first lieutenant. He lifted his chin and glanced at his men and their families, pleased that everyone obeyed his order to be in attendance. The young man standing next to him shifted from foot to foot.

~

Elizabeth hurried down the side wall of the church and slid into the seat at the organ. She had been in the back of the church helping to calm Sarah. The young bride's nerves were shattered. Elizabeth hugged her and assured her she looked beautiful. Sarah thanked her friend and said she hoped she wouldn't lose her lunch right there in the entrance.

~

As Elizabeth played the wedding march, Sarah sneaked a peek at several of the soldiers who stood at attention and looked forward. Sarah took her first small step forward and moved slowly down the aisle. Once she reached the front of the church, George stepped toward her and eased her gently to stand in front of the chaplain. He held her elbow and pulled her close into his side. Sarah looked down at her slippers and stepped a few inches away from him. George squeezed her elbow.

~

The minister looked over his wire-rimmed glasses at the congregation and at the nice-looking couple standing in front of him. He signaled the men and women to be seated. After everyone took their seats and was still, Chaplain Sumrall said, "Let us pray." After a short blessing for the young couple, he smiled at the men and women. "The captain has requested a short ceremony so let's begin."

~

Chaplain Sumrall looked at Sarah over his glasses and asked her a question. He spoke very softly. "Will you have this man to be thy wedded husband? Will you obey him, and serve him, love, honor and keep him in sickness and in health?" The words went on and on. Could she or did she want to do all those things for this man, who felt like a stranger standing next to her?

~

When she didn't reply, George glared at her. Sarah's eyes were filled with tears. She looked sad, or possibly angry. He wasn't sure, but he squeezed her hand tighter than necessary.

~

Why had George placed her in this position? Why had he caused her so much grief by giving a child away whom she loved? Why had he wanted her to wander around in the wilderness? Why wasn't he happy she had a safe haven after the terrible accident she had endured? She was so confused.

The people in the room were so quiet one could almost hear Sarah's heartbeat. She could not confess these vows to a man who didn't love her. She could not marry this man. Sarah felt her heart surge, certain she was making the best decision for both of them. Relief flowed through her body for the first times in days.

George's firm grasp got her attention. "What is wrong with you? Let's get on with the ceremony. Answer the question now, or else." George spoke through gritted teeth, but she heard him. It appeared the chaplain did too from the look in his eyes.

Sarah could no longer speak for the lump that was in her throat. She was scared senseless, but she had to be strong and confess to God, George and the invited guests what she was thinking.

She glanced at the chaplain's wife sitting with a sweet, understanding smile on her old, wrinkled face. Her eyes were filled with tears, but they were sparkling. Sarah continued to stand silent, feeling like she was going to disgrace herself, unable to explain her reasons to George. She had to be truthful to herself and to . . .

Seth. Seth. Not George? George, the man she'd traveled miles to marry?

~

Out of patience, George grabbed her shoulders to shake some sense into her. Then he remembered what he was doing. He released the strong hold on her shoulders and smiled sweetly. "What's wrong, *dear?*"

"I'm sorry." Sarah's body was trembling. "I can't go through .. . with this farce of a marriage. You don't love me and . . . I don't feel the same about you anymore."

"Do you know what you are doing?" He hissed at her. "You're embarrassing me beyond words, and I will not forget it. You have one more chance to repeat your vows or believe me, you'll regret that you didn't."

"Do what you want with me, but I will not stand in this church before God and tell a lie."

~

Before George could say anything else, Chaplain Sumrall stepped between the couple. "Ladies and gentlemen, the captain wishes for you to file out of the church and make your way over to the mess hall to share in food and dancing. The wedding will be postponed for now, but there's no reason the good food prepared by our cooks should not be enjoyed by all. Please, quickly make your way out of the church."

The chaplain took George's right arm and reached for Sarah's, but his sweet wife had taken Sarah's hand. "Let's step into my office for a minute while everyone is leaving the church."

~

Once they entered the chaplain's office, Sarah took the closest chair. Her legs were wobbly. She wasn't sure that they would hold her up much longer.

~

George walked around the room and glanced out the window. His men were laughing as they walked toward the mess hall. He whirled around and looked at the chaplain and his wife. "I want to speak with Sarah alone. Please leave us."

~

"Not right this minute, Captain. You're in my domain now, and I will conduct this meeting." He glared at George, whom he was sure would have him transferred to another fort very soon.

"Sarah," Chaplain Sumrall addressed her, "would you like to explain to the captain why you have refused to marry him?" The chaplain was surprised with the events that had just taken place. His wife had not shared Sarah's feeling with him.

~

Elizabeth was looking at Sarah and for some reason, her presence gave Sarah courage. "No, I don't need to explain anything to him. He knows my reasons." Sarah looked directly into George's eyes. "You aren't the man I came here to marry. You aren't the man I fell in love with years ago. I plan to catch the next stage and return home."

"You'll not leave until I say you can." George's voice was harsh and demanding. He whirled around and stood straight. He stared at the chaplain. "You and I'll talk later, *mister.*" George turned and stormed out of the office, the door slamming behind him.

Sarah cried into her hands. "It seems since I arrived at this fort, all I've done is cry. I can't believe the way I spoke to him, but he's a selfish, pompous, and arrogant man—a disgrace to his uniform, too. He should be ashamed of the way he treats the men."

"You were courageous today, my dear. I'm very proud of you." Elizabeth Sumrall placed her arms around Sarah.

"I didn't feel courageous. I was so afraid. I only wish Seth was here." Sarah wiped her tears away.

"This Seth fellow," Elizabeth said, "Was he the mountain man that recused you and the little girl?"

"Yes, he made me feel safe, but I'll never see him again. I want to go home. I miss my mama."

"Well now." The chaplain cleared his throat and smiled at his sweet wife. "We'll check the stagecoach's next departure heading to Canon, Colorado. Don't fret about what the captain said about not allowing you to leave. He has no right to keep you here. I'll make sure he knows that."

Sarah knew that the chaplain was placing himself in danger to help her. "He will not be pleased with your interference."

"I know. We have already butted heads about other things that I disapproved of. He doesn't scare me."

Sarah held both of her arms tight across her body. Her insides were still trembling. She might not appear afraid of George, but looks could be deceiving. Stella, her mama's companion, would say that you have to 'bamboozle' people in thinking one way when you mean something else. *Oh, how I wish Mama and Stella were here.*

Chapter 30

Seth checked out of the rooming house and thanked the owner for her kindness. Penny was a clean, beautiful little girl. He had purchased her several outfits for the trip home. Also soft, leather shoes that came up high on the ankle with a row of brass buttons. She pranced around the lobby showing off her new duds. The store clerk asked Seth if he needed some *new duds,* too.

~

When they left the store, Seth took Penny's hand, but she pulled on it and stopped. "Are we going to go get Sarah now?" When he didn't answer her, she whined, "I want Sarah. Please?"

Seth bent on one knee and pulled Penny close. "Sarah is not going with us. We talked about this yesterday. She's staying at the fort to get married to a man she loves. She can't go with us."

"But, I want her." Pouting, she laid her head on his shoulder and began sucking on her thumb.

Seth reached for her little hand and removed her thumb. "I know. Me too." He sighed. "You, Buster and I will be happy at my farm. Let's be on our way. We've got to stop and get Buster. He'll be excited to see you."

~

When the livery owner released Buster from his leash, he jumped around and peed on everything. He leaped on Penny and licked her face over and over. She giggled and laughed.

After settling his bill with the livery owner, the threesome were on their way to Seth's farm at the foot of the Casper Mountains. Penny sat straddling the horse in front of Seth. Her little legs stuck out like wings and she gave orders to the horse, which it ignored.

Seth had sold all his mules but one, and it was loaded with their supplies. He packed a small tent, coffee pot, skillet, and food supplies to cook over an open fire. If the spring weather held, they should arrive at the farm in two days. He wanted Penny to enjoy this short adventure so she would have some happy memories.

~

The frontal attack came out of nowhere. A bullet sprayed dirt at Penny's feet while she was sitting on a log near the fire. Seth grabbed her and tossed her behind the big log. "Stay down. Cover your head."

Seth squinted over his Winchester's barrel and saw movement behind a large boulder and the flash of a rifle barrel close to a big stump. He took aim and fired. A yelp came, and he knew he'd creased one. Hopefully, this wasn't an Indian war party. A little gunshot wound wouldn't stop an Indian from continuing to attack.

As Seth kept an eye on the open landscape, he spotted the swishing of a horse's tail. He opened fire just left of the spot. The horse jerked on its reins and moved into his sight. Three horses in all.

Three horses and two men, Seth surmised. Instantly a man darted from one tree to another. Seth fired rapidly and heard another cry. He'd hit his target. At least two of them were wounded, he hoped.

Angry language came from the area, but he couldn't make out what was being said. With two of the bandits wounded and possibly a third, one of them signaled to give up the fight and leave. Without warning, the three galloped away.

Seth stood slowly to his feet. He scanned the area and prayed those men were long gone. He stood his rifle against the log and realized that his hands were shaking. With the child to think about, those men would have had to kill him before he surrendered.

Penny was rolled tightly next to the log. Her little hands covered her ears, and dirty tears streaked her pretty face.

"Come here, sweetie pie." Seth lifted her from the ground. "Did that loud noise scare you?" He rocked her back and forth.

She nodded and laid her head close to his neck.

Seth glanced at the fire he'd built earlier. It was still burning. "Are you still hungry? Do you want some flapjacks?"

"Only if it's quiet. I don't like loud noise."

Seth took his hanky and wet it with some water from the ravine. He wiped her face clean. "Let me wash your hands and wipe the dirt off your new dress."

After a pan of flapjacks, Penny was a happy, tired little girl. Seth spread out the covers inside the tent and laid her down inside. He fashioned a small pillow from some rags, but she was already fast asleep. "Bless you, my sweet girl," he said and crawled out of the tent.

Seth checked on his horse and mule. They were still where he had tied them to a short picket line between two trees. He would have normally let them graze, but he'd listened to his gut instinct this time and kept them close.

Walking around the outskirts of his camp, he found the spot where one of the men had hidden while attempting to ambush him. Blood stained the boulder and rifle cartridges were tossed on the ground. He had only heard about a few wild Indian braves robbing ranchers and farmers, but not any killings. Were the stagecoach rustlers still in the area? There were three men in on that robbery and killing, and there were three today. He was going to have to set a faster pace home. No way would he keep Penny on the trail without more protection if those men were in the territory.

The next morning, Seth woke and dressed Penny before daylight. He had not slept all night. The sleepy child rested in his arms while they rode for hours. After his arms felt numb from holding Penny, he stopped in a secluded area and made a fire. While Penny went into the bushes for privacy, he made coffee and a few flapjacks. Seth had chosen the out-of-the-way spot in case strangers drifted by on the trail. It was the custom to invite travelers to have a cup of coffee and share a meal, but Seth wasn't taking any chances with Penny along.

Seth steered his horse near a creek bed and headed to the road leading home. Just as the sun was setting, he stopped and looked down on his valley. Holding the reins in one hand, he shifted in his saddle and pointed. "Look, Penny. See that white farmhouse? That's your new home. Mine and yours. What do you think?" Buster barked at the house.

"Will Sarah be inside?"

"Oh, baby." Seth sighed and felt sadness in his heart. "Sarah will not be there." He hoped she was going to be happy married to the captain, but he was afraid for her. Sweet, kind Sarah.

Later, Seth rode his horse through the gateway of his farm. The arch connected to his fence read, "Jenkins Farm" in big bold lettering. The house was dark. The wind blew the front porch swing back and forth.

Seth stopped his horse at the front porch and leaped to the ground. He reached for Penny and placed her near him. Buster playfully leaped on her and she patted his head. "Down now," she scolded.

Seth held Penny's hand and climbed the steps to the porch and knocked. He waited but no one answered. Odd, there weren't any lamps burning on the inside. The place looked deserted. Where were Luke and Mary at this time of day? It was past suppertime.

Seth ran his hand high over the door sill and located the front door key. He opened the door and called to his brother. "Luke? Is anybody home?"

Buster began growling from the front porch. Seth turned and saw his stubby neighbor who lived on the next farm.

"Mick, old friend, it's good to see you. How did you know I was here?"

"Will and I saw you from the ridge as we were gathering a few strays. I was sure it was you."

"Do you know where Luke could be? And of course, Mary?"

"I thought he wrote to you months ago. A very sad thing's happened. Mary was sick with child. The old doc was stumped because she stayed sick. She couldn't keep anything down and slept most of the time. My Martha Ann said she and the child were just wasting away. Mary kept pleading with Luke to take her home to her mama. Poor Luke. He didn't know what to do. Finally, he took her home to Canada.

Mick stood and looked off into the distance. "Luke didn't want to leave your farm. You can look around and tell he worked hard here, but he had to make a choice. Take his wife home to her folks or stay with this place. He wanted the child Mary carried, so he didn't have a choice. He was afraid that she couldn't make the long trip, but once she knew he was taking her home, she seemed to get better. I talked it over with Martha Ann and we agreed to work both places until you returned."

"How far along was Mary with child when they left here?"

"Martha Ann can tell you more. She helped Luke care for her while he worked the farm. But she cried and cried to go home, so your brother finally decided to take her to her folks."

"I'm so sorry to hear about Mary. I was looking forward to being with them again. Luke and I worked well together, and she seemed happy." Seth sighed and looked down at Penny. "I'm kinda in a pickle for sure, now. I was hoping Mary would care for Penny while Luke and I worked away from the house."

"That's me." Penny twisted around and held out her dolly for Mick to see. "This is my baby."

"So nice to meet you, Miss Penny. Welcome to your new home."

~

Penny eased over and held onto Seth's tall leg. He reached down and picked her up.

"Who's him?" Penny asked. She giggled because the young man made a funny face at her.

"Well, Miss Penny, this is my baby boy, Will."

"Oh Pa, for goodness sakes. I'm twenty-one, not a baby anymore. Hello, Mr. Seth, good to have you home."

"Nice to see you, too. You have grown into a fine young man since I last saw you."

Will blushed but smiled at Seth's comment. "I'll put your horse and mule away, if you like."

Will walked toward the animals but Seth called to him. "I need to take a few things in the house for Penny, but the other things can be left in the barn until morning. I can't tell you both how much I appreciate all of your help with my farm. I will pay you for your help once I get settled in."

"There's no need for payment. What are neighbors for if not to step in and help each other?"

"You and your boys have done more than words could ever say thank you for. Let me do what I feel is right. Please?"

Mick peered at Seth and reached for his horse's reins while Will took hold of the mule. Seth picked Penny up in his arms, while Buster followed everyone to the barn.

Chapter 31

Early the next morning, sounds and light came from the kitchen. Seth knew he had an uninvited guest. He eased the door open and saw a woman bending over the oven's door. She was humming and turned to beat something in a big bowl.

"Good morning." Seth stepped into the kitchen. The woman jumped and whirled, holding the big yellow bowl filled with broken eggs.

"Seth, you nearly scared the life out of me."

"Martha Ann? What are you doing in my kitchen so early?" Seth walked in his bare feet to the stove to get a cup of coffee.

"You know about Mary. I came over early every morning and prepared breakfast for Luke. Mary only drank tea. There were other things I had to help her with—more personal things. I would cook breakfast here, and my boys would ride over here to eat. We had to organize our time to get everything done at both places."

"I can't believe how fortunate I am to have such great neighbors and friends. Now that I'm home, I can at least cook breakfast for Penny and me."

"Well, if you're sure. I like staying at home in the mornings, then come over later in the day to help out with your child. I'm just dying to meet her. Matt said she's a little doll. I have to admit I'm a bit curious how you came to have a little girl."

"It's a long story that I would like to tell you and Mick together later. But the sweet little thing lost both of her parents. She's adjusting as well as a little one can." Seth sipped his coffee. "Do you know of a young girl who might like to help me out a few hours a day with her?"

"None come to mind, but I'll think on it and let you know. But until then, I'll help you. I can't wait to have a grandchild."

"I appreciate your help. When I met this lovely child, I never dreamed in a hundred years that I would soon become her papa."

"I can't wait to hear that story. Oh, by the way, there's several pieces of mail for you on the mantle of the fireplace. Some of it's old." Martha Ann walked to the door and rang the bell on the front porch, signaling Mick and her boys to breakfast.

Seth headed into the parlor to get the mail. One piece was a letter dated several months ago that didn't have a return address. After tearing it open, he looked at the bottom of the page. A note from his sister-in-law, not Luke. He scanned the words quickly and had to sit down. It was like someone had hit him in the stomach. His young brother was dead. He couldn't believe it. Luke was an excellent young rider, and to fall from a horse—unbelievable. He picked up the note and reread it.

Dearest Seth,

Dearest . . . not just Seth, he thought. Odd. He read on. *I am sorry to have to inform you that Luke has passed away. Luke had a terrible accident. He fell off his horse and broke his neck. Died instantly. He left me and our son all alone and we are planning to come and live with you at the end of April. I pray you will be home by the time I arrive. If not, I will be waiting for you. My son and I need you. I am so lonely.*

Yours devoted,

Mary

Seth sighed and dropped into the rocking chair. He held the letter down by his side and closed his eyes to fight back the tears that threatened to come. His little brother was dead.

~

Martha Ann entered the parlor. Seth was holding a letter and his head bent low with his eyes closed. "Seth, what is it? Did you receive bad news?" She stood in front of him and gently took the letter from his hand. He didn't pull it away.

Martha Ann sighed after she read the first few lines. "Oh Seth, I'm so sorry. We all loved your sweet brother."

"I know. Thank you." He wiped his eyes. "May I have another cup of coffee, please?"

"Come into the kitchen. Mick will be coming in soon. He will be upset after learning this news."

~

Once the family learned about Luke's death, they sat at the breakfast table with their heads bowed. "Do you want to read the letter to us, Seth? We'd like to know what Mary's parents had to say," Mitch said, sure the letter was from Luke's in-laws.

"This short note is from Mary. She will be coming here with their new son to live—with me."

"What?" Martha Ann nearly screamed. "Why?"

"Read the letter to everyone, Mitch. I am in disbelief myself," Seth replied.

Chapter 32

Fort Laramie, WY

Elizabeth Sumrall strolled into the military outpost
and looked through the younger men's trousers. She hummed,
chose a pair and walked to the counter.

"You got the wrong size, Mrs. Sumrall. Let me get you the
right size for the chaplain. He's about the same size I am." The
manager of the store tried to take her choice and swap the pants.

"Thank you for your assistance, but these trousers are for me."
She lowered her voice. "I wear these under my skirts whenever I
go riding with Matt. I have never had one of those split skirts that
some of the city ladies wear. You see, I need a larger size." She
smiled a sheepish grin. "Old age is creeping up and so are the
unwanted pounds around the middle."

"Of course, I understand. I'm sorry. Forgive me."

Later, Elizabeth placed a plaid, flannel shirt, an old leather
belt, and a black, floppy hat in a large pillowcase marked 'laundry'
and headed to Sarah's room.

When Sarah answered Elizabeth's knock, she slid into the
room quickly. "I can't stay but a minute. I don't want anyone
putting two and two together and realize that I had something to do
with you leaving the fort. Will Hammer has agreed to help. Pack
your carpet bag. Around three in the morning, dress in these
clothes." She gave Sarah the bag. "You'll look like a young man
with your hair tucked under the hat. Leave this room and head to

the edge of the courtyard, then go to the back of the livery. The red stagecoach will be parked back there. There'll be a stepping block below the door of the stage. Climb inside and lie low on the floor. Some men will come later and hitch up the team. There will not be any other passengers. Matt and I wish you well, child. Mr. Hammer will see to your safety all the way to Canon, your hometown."

"Why is he taking this risk by helping me escape?"

"He remembers you from before. Besides, he's been on the wrong end of the captain's temper and he has no love for him."

"I pray that the chaplain won't get into trouble with George, once he discovers I'm gone," Sarah sighed. "I'm thankful the general from Washington has kept him busy the last several days."

"Yes, we are too. Oh, I almost forgot to give you this." Elizabeth reached down into her long apron pocket and pulled out a .45 colt revolver.

"Oh, my goodness. Where did that come from?"

"It's one of Matt's. He's collected guns for years. He wanted you to have it for protection. None of the guards will notice you, being dressed in men's clothes, but if one stops you, speak in a deep voice and say you're going to take a leak." Seeing Sarah's surprised look, she giggled at her comment. "That's the way men talk. Good-bye, child. Write us. If we aren't still stationed here, our mail should follow. It has in the past." She hugged Sarah. "I hope to leave here soon, too."

~

Early the next morning, Sarah dressed in the clothing Elizabeth had bought, and she looked like a slim, young man. She placed her hair in a tight bun on top of her head and covered it with the floppy hat.

A young guard was sitting in a chair tilted back on two legs, sound asleep. She crossed to the outside of the moonless courtyard and easily found the red stagecoach. She used the big block, eased into the coach and settled low on the floor. Placing her carpet bag on one side, she leaned her back against the door. A blanket and a pillow sat on the seat. She unfolded the blanket and covered herself with it.

Sarah was scared, but with God's help, along with the chaplain's and Elizabeth's aid, and Mr. Hammer's assistance, she was close to escaping George's cruel and forceful ways. Sarah prayed for a safe journey home. She couldn't wait to be held by her mama—to feel safe again.

After being rescued by Seth, she had not been as afraid as she was now. She had no idea what George would do to her if he found her cowering in the stagecoach waiting to escape from him.

Seth had comforted her from the first time he touched her. He gently placed her on a pack mule and used soothing words of assurance. She was afraid of him, but it didn't take long to know that the giant mountain man was a gentle soul and wouldn't hurt anyone.

The moment she'd arrived at the fort with Seth, she knew that George, the man she had loved, the man she had planned to marry, was not the same person she remembered. She ran to him but he didn't embrace her. He held her away with no warm greeting. That should have spoken volumes to her. George continued to treat her like a woman who had committed a crime. He acted like she had wronged him because she hadn't escaped Seth and made her way down the mountain. He didn't try to understand her relationship with Seth and Penny, that Seth was a true friend and savior.

George, her sweet loving George, was lost to her forever. Now, the man was cruel and demanded to have his way. She witnessed his highhanded orders to his young men, punishing them for the least offense. Had becoming commander of the fort changed him? Had the authority made him feel important and superior to everyone else, even her?

Suddenly a whisper came through the window of the coach's door. "Miss, are you ready to travel?"

"Yes," Sarah replied.

"The men are hitching the team and we'll be on our way. My guard, Jackson, and I will take good care of you. Just stay down until I tell you otherwise."

"Yes sir." Sarah was so relieved. She was soon on the way home. Away from George, but unfortunately, away from Seth.

Chapter 33

Casper City, WY.

Mary Jenkins stood on the boardwalk in Casper City holding her eight-month-old son who was screaming loud enough to draw a crowd. She needed a few minutes of privacy. "What are you looking at, old man? Haven't you ever seen a hungry baby?" snapped Mary at the toothless man who held his hand over one ear. The man limped away and muttered something low under his breath.

Mrs. Mattie Wallace, the dry-goods store owner's wife, placed her hand over her mouth in surprise. "Mary, Mary Jenkins? My goodness, gal, we thought we would never see the likes of you again. Come on in here and let me help with that young'un."

Mary was so relieved to see someone she knew who was willing to help her. "I've never been so happy to see anyone. Thank you. John is hungry and I need to feed him. May I sit in the back of the store for a few minutes? He's awful tired, too."

"Sure, honey. I'll have my boy bring your bags in here and put them by the door. I assume you're heading to your farm. Do you have someone picking you up?"

"Yes. He should be at the rooming house already. He was watching for the stage to arrive so he should be here soon. I really need to care for my son."

Mrs. Wallace pulled back an old green curtain and guided Mary into the storeroom. Barrels of flour, sugar, molasses, and many other boxes filled with nails and hardware were stored around the room. Mrs. Wallace dusted off a barrel and motioned for Mary to sit down on it. "Sit here on this barrel and take your time feeding that big boy. He's already falling asleep in your arms. I'll keep Mr. Wallace and Tommy up front." Mattie Wallace left her alone.

Mary unbuttoned the front of her heavy, black mourning dress which she hated having to wear. It made her look pale and sickly. Once she reached Seth's ranch, she would toss the rag in the burning barrel. She would wear the black armband only for a few more months.

~

"Willard, when Seth was in the store a few days ago, did he mention Mary, his sister-in-law, was coming for a visit?"

He rubbed his hand across his jaw, pondering his wife's question. "Can't say he said much of anything. He got his supplies like always, and oh, yes, he got a big scoop of hard candy for his girl." He smiled at his wife. "I did ask about the little girl and he said that she was making cookies with his neighbor, Martha Ann, Mick's wife."

~

A short time later, Mary returned to the front counter carrying her sleeping baby. She looked out the front window and watched her friend park his carriage out front. "Here's my ride. Thanks for your help, Mrs. Wallace." Mary lifted the tail of her long dress and scooted by the woman. She didn't want her driver to come inside the store.

~

"Tommy, carry Mrs. Jenkins' bags out to the carriage." Mrs. Wallace walked to the door and watched Mary drive away with an older, well-dressed stranger. "Willard, do you know that man who came to drive Mary out to Seth's farm?"

"Can't say I do. He has two nice horses pulling that fancy carriage."

"I'm surprised she is already with another man."

"Now, don't start that kind of talk, woman." Mr. Wallace returned to the counter after giving his wife a harsh look over his glasses. "You don't know why she has returned."

"I know," Mrs. Wallace said, biting her lip, "but remember

when she left with Luke, she was on her deathbed. She sure made a miraculous recovery."

~

Buster jumped off the front porch and barked. Martha Ann and Penny hurried outside in time to see a fancy carriage pulled by two well-bred horses arrive.

A tall, older man stepped down and took the child out of Mary's arms and offered his other hand to help her down. They placed their heads close together and appeared to be having a serious conversation. Mary patted his face and kissed the man on the cheek.

"Buster, hush and lie down this minute," Martha Ann scowled. The driver of the carriage placed the bags on the porch and returned to the carriage.

"Hello, Martha Ann. I guess you're surprised to see me." Before Martha Ann could answer, Mary turned and gave a small wave to the man who had brought her out to the farm.

Martha Ann didn't respond to Mary at first. She stared at the girl's healthy appearance. Even in that black mourning dress, Luke's wife was still very pretty and not at all sickly. "You're looking a whole lot better than the last time I saw you nearly a year ago. We were brokenhearted to learn about Luke." Martha Ann was surprised that this vain young girl would still be dressed in mourning clothes. Her mama must have insisted she dress properly.

Mary shifted the baby in her arms. "Thank you. We are all still in shock over his accident." Mary sniffed and blinked away a dry tear. "I got stronger once my mama cared for me—properly."

Martha Ann's hackles rose at that remark. She had sat by this young girl's bedside for hours pleading with her to eat and drink. She cooked three meals a day for Luke and their hired-hand. She washed clothes and cleaned their house for months until Luke finally agreed to take her away.

"I'm glad you got proper care and recovered well enough to have a healthy baby. May I see him?" Martha Ann was trying to be the Christian woman she was supposed to be. *If you can't say something nice, keep your mouth shut*, the good book said.

Mary uncovered John's face and lowered him so Martha Ann could view her son.

"He's darling and so healthy. He must be a good eater."

Mary's smile at Martha Ann didn't reach her eyes. She looked over at Penny. "Whose child is this?"

"Penny, tell Mrs. Mary who your new papa is." Martha Ann was being catty and she knew it, but Mary's remark about getting proper care grated on her.

"Seth. Seth is my papa and I love him." Penny smiled and clapped her hands. "He loves my cookies."

~

This couldn't be true. Seth couldn't have married and had a child this big. Mary was shocked to say the least. "She's too old to be his natural child. He only left here two years ago and she has to be nearly four, if not four already?"

"Seth will have to tell you all about his wonderful child. She is such a sweet and smart little girl. We all love her."

"Yes, I'm sure Seth will tell me all about her, but for now, I need to lay John down on a bed. Which room is available for me to use?"

"Seth is using the big bedroom, and Penny's room is next to his. You can use the room on this side of the house. It needs airing out and cleaning. No one has used it in a long time."

~

Mary entered the bedroom and thanked Martha Ann. "This room is fine. Not as nice as my room before, but it will do—for now." Martha Ann nodded and closed the door, leaving Mary standing in the middle of the room.

Mary laid John on the bed, unwrapping him from the big blanket. She eased down beside him and spoke softly, "Oh John, my sweet boy. One day soon, we'll be moving back into the big bedroom with your Uncle Seth." She kissed her big boy on his belly and laughed. "It won't be long before he can't resist the both of us."

Chapter 34

At suppertime, Seth, Mick and Will came into the house with clean hands and shiny wet hair, but their boots remained at the door. "Hey Papa, guess what we have in that room?" Penny pointed to the bedroom on the west side of the house.

"Well, kitten, I have no idea what you and Martha Ann have stored in there. Is it a big surprise?" He quizzed.

"You might say that, Seth." Mary had opened the door to her bedroom and stood listening to Penny as she spoke to her handsome brother-in-law. Seth slowly turned, his eyes wide at seeing her standing in the doorway with a baby in her arms.

"Mary! What a surprise for sure. It's so good to see you." Seth gave Mary a tight hug, which she tried to return. "And, who do we have here?" Seth reached for the baby and cuddled him in his arms. "My, what a handsome lad. He sure looks like Luke."

Penny raced over to Seth and pulled on his leg. "Let me see, papa. I want to play with him. Can he be my baby?"

"When did you arrive?" Seth lowered the baby down so Penny could see him. "Be careful with him," he said. Seth stood and gave Mary back the baby and led her to the dining room table. "Sit here next to me while we eat this wonderful dinner Martha Ann has prepared for us. Man, it sure smells good." Seth helped Penny into her chair on the other side of him and waited for everyone to be settled around the table.

"*Lord, thank you this day for our special blessing. Having Mary and my nephew here today is certainly wonderful. Bless this food and the hands that prepared it. Amen.*

"Mary, I'm sorry. I have hardly given you a minute to talk. Please tell us when and how you arrived in town."

"Yesterday. I rode the train down to Laramie and the stage to Casper City. It was a long hard trip, but we made it safe."

"How are your folks? Well, I hope?" Seth placed potatoes on Penny's plate. "Now take small bites and eat slowly."

"My folks are not happy with me. They didn't want me to come back here, but I had to leave. I also wanted you to get to know Luke's son."

"I would like to hear more about Luke's accident—later, when we're alone." Seth peered at Martha Ann and Mick.

"Mary, who was that nice gentlemen that brought you out to the farm? I have never seen him in town."

"Now, Martha Ann, you talk like you're in town all the time. You go twice a month, if that often." Mick smirked at his wife.

Mary couldn't hide back a yawn, so Seth suggested she should have a nice bath and go to bed.

"Everyone rises early around here," he said smiling.

~

After Martha Ann cleaned the kitchen and helped give Penny a bath, she was exhausted and ready to go home. Mary came into the kitchen and asked what time she would be over in the morning.

Martha Ann raised her eyebrows and spoke truthfully, "I will not be needed over here while you're visiting. I figured you can do the cooking and cleaning for Seth and Penny. How long do you plan on staying?"

"I am not well enough to cook three meals a day and clean this house by myself. You must continue to come and help."

Mary acted like she was supposed to be the lady of the house, not a servant. "Well, dear, I'm sorry to hear you aren't well." Martha Ann shook her head. "But Seth already told me not to keep coming over every morning. He said he could cook breakfast for himself and Penny. I'll be happy to come and get Penny for a few hours each day. She is a darling and I enjoy having her around."

"When she's not with you, who will care for her? I have my hands full just taking care of my son. He demands all my attention."

"My dear, I suggest that you speak with Seth about your

concern. It's getting late and the men have finished their conversation. Have a good night. I'll be over before lunch to get Penny."

~

Mary fed and put John down for the night. He was such a good baby and had been sleeping all night for a month. She used the bowl of water in her room to give herself a good sponge bath. Dressing in one of her nicest gowns and a robe to match, she allowed her long dark hair to fall around her shoulders. Glancing in the small mirror, Mary knew she looked pleasing to the eye. Especially to a lonely man.

Mary entered the living room where Seth was sitting in a rocker in front of the fireplace. Penny was dressed in a long white muslin gown and sat in Seth's lap, giggling at the story he was reading.

Penny saw Mary before Seth did. "Look papa, that woman is here."

Seth stopped rocking and glanced over his shoulder. "Good evening, Mary. Come and sit down in that rocker and join Penny and me in front of the fire. I always read Penny a story before she retires for the night."

"Please, continue with the story. I would love to hear you read to her."

Penny leaned forward and looked around Seth's shoulder at her with narrowed eyes.

Seth continued reading and rocking slowly. Penny's eyelids closed and a soft snore came from her. Seth closed the book, but continued to rock while snuggling the child close to his large body.

"Would you like for me to carry her to bed for you?" Mary asked, hoping to get the kid out of Seth's lap so he could concentrate on her.

"No thank you." Seth glanced down at the child. "I enjoy holding her like this at night. She misses her mama and our friend, Sarah. I like for her to feel safe and loved by me."

"Of course. I feel sad John will never know Luke," Mary said, pretending to cry as she sniffed and wiped her nose.

"Mary, do you mind telling me how Luke died? I was so surprised when you wrote he had a horse accident."

"It's not much to tell, only sad. He went off by himself to

148

round up a few strays. My pa's corral fence had a couple of broken boards and the calves had gotten out. A storm came up and there was a lot of lightning and thunder. When he didn't come home, several men rode out looking for him. They brought his body back to the ranch. His neck was broken. They found him in a gulley." Keeping her face down, Mary wiped at her eyes. "John had just been born."

"I feel better now learning how he died. A bad storm can spook an animal and make it react differently before you know it. I'm glad you were home with your folks. I know your mama was a great comfort to you."

"Well, she wasn't really," Mary snapped back at Seth a little harsher than she intended. "I was up and around in a week caring for John all by myself. Mama said John was my baby and I needed to take care of him." Mary stuck out her lip. "She's the reason I haven't gotten my strength back. I felt if I came here, you would help me get stronger."

Seth stopped rocking and placed Penny on his shoulder and stood. "Let me put her down on the pallet. Penny sleeps in my room on the floor. She won't sleep in the room next to me yet." When Seth returned, he sat back down in the rocker next to hers, which she'd moved closer to his.

"I would like to hear about Penny and her folks. I've been wondering how a single man like yourself could take on the responsibility of someone else's child." Mary pretended to be concerned about the little girl.

"It's a long story. One evening, I'll tell you along with Martha Anna and Mick the story about what happened while living on the mountain. I don't want to talk about it, but I know you're all curious." He stood and poked the fire with a long metal rod.

When she realized he wasn't going to tell her anything about Penny, she brought up another great concern. "Seth, Martha Ann said that she wouldn't be coming over to cook and clean since I was visiting with you." Glancing down at her lap, she tried to look distressed. "What will we do for food? I'm not strong enough to cook three meals a day and wash, for goodness' sake."

"To tell you the truth, I was surprised to discover you and Luke had left the farm and gone to your folks. When I decided to bring Penny home with me, I had hoped you would help me care for her.

The little one had just lost her parents. Sarah and I have been caring for her on the mountain. None of that matters anymore. If you can't care for Penny, I will find someone in town to come out a few hours each day. Martha Ann said she would care for her too while I'm working around the place. She is a good child and I will be caring for her myself a good bit."

"Who is this Sarah woman?"

"Sarah is part of the story I will tell later."

~

It was hard for Seth to even say her name aloud. His heart ached just thinking of her. How he could have allowed himself to fall in love with another man's intended, he would never know, but he had.

Mary's whining brought him out of his relapse about Sarah. He tried hard to keep her out of his thoughts.

"Will you hire someone to do the cooking and cleaning too? I'm too frail to clean this big house all by myself."

"Sorry, but I had not planned to hire a full-time housekeeper, if that's what you mean. All my extra money will be going back into this farm to turn it into a cattle ranch. I've bought a hundred head of prime beef and a large bull. They'll be arriving soon."

Seth leaned back in the rocker and watched the fire dance on the logs in the fireplace. "I have an idea. What do you think about this? I will prepare breakfast for Penny and me, and lunch, too if she's here. You can take care of yourself and John. Let's all pick up after ourselves and keep the house in order. That way I won't have to hire someone to come in. We can prepare supper together." Seth smiled at his plan, but he didn't get a response from his sister-in-law. If she wasn't happy with this idea, then she could go back to her mama. "What do you think? Are you willing to work with me?"

~

"I will try to help as much as I can." She wasn't expecting to have to work like a slave and prepare her own meals.

Seth stood and banked the fire in the fireplace. "I'd better turn in. Four o'clock comes around mighty fast and I have to get up and start the day."

"Why do you have to get up so early when you have two men working for you? Don't thcy do the morning chores?"

"Yes, they do, but this is my farm. I enjoy taking care of my stock and making repairs around the place. There's plenty to do every day to keep three men busy." Seth straightened and gave a big yawn. "Good night. See you in the morning."

"You will not see me at four in the morning." Mary shook her head and walked back to her bedroom. She could hear Seth laugh at her remark. Darn it, she thought as she checked her face in the mirror. It won't be long, and he will be treating me like a queen.

Chapter 35

Fort Laramie, WY

Early, the men stood in formation and listened to a long-winded speech from General Grant from Washington. After delivering his message and a well-deserved thank you to the men for all the good work they were doing in the territory, he left the fort with a large patrol.

George watched the men ride out the gate. He was happy to see that pompous old man leave and get out of his business. He unbuttoned the top button on his shirt, removed his dress coat and tossed it to the lieutenant. Then he walked to the dormitory where Sarah lived, marched up the staircase and knocked several times on her door with no response. He pushed the door open and entered her room. To his surprise, Sarah wasn't inside. He glanced around the neat room, his mouth agape. Sarah had moved out. He hurried down the hall and nearly collided with Lulu.

"Sorry, Captain. I didn't see you." Lulu stuttered. She stepped back against the wall to allow him to pass.

"Where's Sarah? I need to see her now," George demanded.

"I'm sorry, sir. I was just going downstairs to the mess hall. I haven't seen her."

"You're lying." The captain leaned into Lulu's pale face, sputtering and spitting. "You know everything that goes on at this fort. You are one nosey bitch and I demand you tell me now where she is, or your husband will be placed on report."

"But, sir," Tears flowed down Lulu's face as she tried to speak. "I really haven't seen Sarah at all this morning. I saw her last night but only for a minute. She was going to her room to get ready for bed. Please, I don't know."

"I'd better not find out any different, woman."

Lulu slid to the floor.

George stomped down the stairs and out into the courtyard. He looked up and down the boardwalk and flew back inside to the dining area. Many of the ladies and their children were having breakfast. The occupants practically froze in place, and mothers placed their hands over their children's mouths to keep them still and quiet.

George glared around the room, whirled and left. He entered his office and demanded that his first lieutenant search the fort. "Check the livery, horses, any form of transportation she may have used to leave the fort. Find my fiancée. Don't leave a stone unturned." George stormed to his window and watched the young man leap off the front steps and start giving orders to the men who were standing around. They scurried off in all directions.

Within thirty minutes, the lieutenant returned with information about Sarah's whereabouts. A terrified expression covered his face. "Sir, there's only one means of transportation Miss Sullivan may have taken to leave the fort."

"Well, spit it out, man. I don't have all day."

"The stagecoach left early this morning. Mr. Hammer was driving the coach with no passengers, sir."

"Was the coach stopped at the gate and searched by the guards before it was allowed to pass?"

"No, sir. They are not accustomed to doing that, sir."

"Well, Lieutenant." The captain struck his desk with his wooden baton causing the young officer to flinch. "That's exactly how she left this fort. She was on that coach." He circled the room. "Get a patrol ready and go and find that coach. Search every inch of it and bring her back. Place her in irons if needed, but bring her back. Do I make myself clear?"

"Do you want the men to bring back Mr. Hammer and the stagecoach?"

"No, that won't be necessary. No stagecoach, no more transportation." He headed to his favorite spot in the office and peered out at his courtyard and his men.

~

The patrol came galloping toward the stagecoach heading it off at the bend. Will Hammer fidgeted with the reins and told his partner to keep still and quiet. He was disappointed the patrol had caught up with him so fast, but more than that, he was fearful for his passenger.

The first lieutenant in charge of the patrol signaled for Mr. Hammer to stop and several outriders rode ahead of the stage. "Howdy, Will. It sure is a pretty day to be traveling."

"Shore is. We're making good time on the way back to Canon." Will spit a long stream of tobacco juice onto the ground. "What ya' doin' this far from the fort?"

"Oh, you know the captain. He's got us looking for a missing person."

"Really, some more of his men done abandoned the Cavalry? Can't say I blame them, none at all" Mr. Hammer gave a nervous laugh.

"I think we all feel the same way at times. I'd better get down to business. Do you have any passengers this morning?" The young man inquired with a smile.

"No sir," he yelled his reply so the others could hear him. "It's just the two of us and we're wanting to get back to Colorado before dark."

The young lieutenant got off his horse and held the reins tight. "You don't mind if I have a look inside, do you? The captain has lost his fiancée and he's mad as a hornet at her for sneaking away from the fort."

"You don't say. Well, I hope you don't find her. That's one crazy-acting man." Will spit another big chew of tobacco off to the side.

~

The officer opened the door of the coach and looked directly at Sarah. A quilt covered her body except the top of her face. Her eyes were filled with tears and fear. Poking his head inside so the other men could tell he was giving it a thorough inspection, he gave her a weak smile and winked.

He slammed the door shut and turned the handle making sure it was closed well, then leaped back on his horse. "Sorry we had to slow you down, old man, but I had to search. Ya'll be careful and we'll see you on your next trip to the fort."

The young officer raised his hand and led his patrol back toward the way they came.

~

Will breathed deeply and watched the men ride out of sight. He jumped down from the top of the coach and jerked open the door. "I had to see if you were still in here. That was a mighty close call. I'm happy that young officer searched the coach and not one of the other men. He must not have any love for the captain either."

"I was praying so hard he wouldn't open the door, and when he did, we just stared at each other. He smiled and winked. The good Lord was with us today."

"Shore was. Let's get on down the road. You hold tight and stay down." Will climbed back on top of the coach, slapped the reins, and continued their trip to Canon, Colorado.

Late into the night, Will Hammer drove the big red stagecoach into Sarah's hometown. She was home—safe. There were only a few street lanterns hanging, and all the businesses except a late night saloon were closed.

"It's mighty late to drive out to your mama's place, Miss Sullivan. Do you mind staying at Georgia's rooming house tonight? I know she'll welcome you." Will smiled. He was so pleased he'd delivered this sweet girl home.

"Yes, I'm anxious to see Mama, but it's too far to drive out there tonight. You sure Miss Georgia will open up for me? Like you said, it's awful late."

"I'll take you over and carry your bag. You traveled light for a gal." Will was hot and dusty, but this sweet lady appreciated any and all help that she received.

"I didn't have much when I was on the mountain, and I didn't purchase too many things while at the fort. Only need one carpet bag."

Will stepped up on the porch and used the door knocker. He knocked several times before Miss Georgia came to the door, covering her tall thin body with her wrap. "Will? My goodness, old man. We thought you were dead."

"Well, as you can see, I ain't. I almost died, but the doctor put me back together at Fort Laramie. Sorry it's so late, but I just drove my stagecoach into town carrying this here young lady."

"Mercy, what a surprise to see you back here, too, Sarah. Didn't you leave to get married? Is your husband with you?" She peeked around Will and Sarah.

"No, Miss Georgia, I didn't marry. I'm so sorry to disturb you tonight, but it's too late to drive out to my home. May I have a room here tonight?"

"Of course, child. Your mama is going to be so surprised to see you. How about you, Will? Do you want a bath and room?" Georgia frowned at his appearance.

"Not now, maybe early in the morning. I got a lot to do and I'll just get nasty all over again. Goodnight, Miss Sullivan." Will tipped his hat and turned to walk down the steps.

"Mr. Hammer." Sarah took him by his arm to stop him from leaving. "Thank you so much for bringing me home. I'll never forget you." She stood on her tiptoes to kiss his dusty cheek.

"It was a pure pleasure, Miss. I was happy you chose not to marry that captain. I'll be here after breakfast to take you home."

Sarah turned to Miss Georgia. "May I go straight up to bed? It's been a long trip."

Chapter 36

The sun hid behind a cloud as Sarah stood looking over Main Street, waiting to go downstairs for breakfast. Her slim, delicate hand dropped the clean white curtain at Miss Georgia's soft knock on her door. She couldn't stop the sigh that blew from her, so relieved to be home. She opened the door.

"Good morning. Are you ready for a cup of tea or coffee? Please come downstairs and we'll have breakfast."

"Thanks, I would enjoy a nice strong cup of coffee." Sarah plodded down the stairs. With an infinitely bleak future, her mama would be there to help her get back to a normal life. She wished her mama had met Seth. Such a wonderful man with a keen sense of humor. Never cruel and thoughtless like the captain. *Oh well, I'll have to tell Mama about the big mountain man who saved my life.*

Mr. Hammer arrived in front of the boardinghouse to take Sarah out to her mama's place. He'd borrowed a smaller wagon to drive the eight miles out of town. When he returned to Fort Laramie, he'd report back to Chaplain Sumrall he'd delivered Sarah to her mama's front door—safe and sound.

Sarah leaped down from the wagon seat and rushed through the small, white picket fence to the front door. She opened the door and turned the knob. It was locked, so she knocked and called, "Mama. It's me."

Stella opened the door, staggered backward and wailed. "Miss Sarah, oh my Lord, Miss Sarah!"

"Stella, what's wrong? You act like I'm a ghost." Sarah grabbed Mama's old companion and held her tight.

Stella had to hold onto Sarah while she sat down on a chair in the front room. Her old legs felt like they might give away any minute. "We...we were told . . . you are supposed to be dead, but you ain't."

Sarah looked across the room and saw her sweet mama holding onto the parlor door frame. "Mama, I'm home." Sarah rushed into her mama's outstretched arms.

"My baby, my baby. I can't believe it." Her mama went limp.

Sarah tried to hold her but she was falling.

~

Mr. Hammer heard all the screaming and rushed into the house just in time. He caught Sarah's mama as she wilted to the floor.

"Oh, Stella, Mama, I know I haven't written to you in months, but why did you think I was dead?"

Stella wiped her eyes and shook her head "George, that man you left here to marry— he sent a letter—he didn't say much except that you were dead."

Sarah rushed to the kitchen and got a glass of water. "Drink this, Mama."

After taking a swallow of water, she reached for her daughter's face. "Oh, my baby. I'm so happy you're home and well. God is good."

"Yes, Mama, God is good. He helped me to get here—home, along with my new friend, Mr. Hammer."

Mr. Hammer carried Sarah's mother into the small parlor and laid her down on the sofa. "You need to rest for a while, Mrs. Sullivan. You've had a fright for sure."

Mrs. Sullivan reached out and took Mr. Hammer's hand and squeezed it. "Thank you for bringing my baby home."

~

After awakening the next morning, Sarah lay in her bed almost forgetting where she was. So much had happened since she left home nearly a year ago. She studied the ceiling. Closing her eyes, she admonished herself to be sensible. Life goes on and she must get up and begin a new life. She had to put George and Seth in the past. It would be hard because for two years, she had planned and dreamed of marrying George, her wonderful knight in shining

158

armor. When that didn't happen, she dreamed of a gentle, handsome mountain man. A life with him was not to be either. She'd first felt like giving up on life, but God would be displeased with her if she did that.

~

The beginning of each day had nothing to inspire her to get out of bed. She did enjoy gardening, so she made herself rise before the sun was too hot so she could weed the flower and vegetable gardens near the house. Flowers were abundant this time of the year and she enjoyed arranging a vase of daffodils and putting it in the vestibule of the church on Sundays. She loved watching the honeybees spread their wings and carry pollen from one bush to another. Like seemed so simple, but oh, so lonely.

Mr. Rogers, an old gentleman who taught school, had stopped by the house and asked if she would help him. He needed someone to assist him with the younger children while he tutored the older boys in mathematics. The school board had agreed to pay someone a few dollars a week.

This would be something I might be good at since I love children.

Placing the hoe up against the house and removing her gloves and hat, she entered the backdoor. Stella was baking biscuits and frying ham steaks which made the kitchen smell delicious. "Stella, I'm going to get fat if I'm not careful. Your cooking makes me hungry even when I'm not." Sarah laughed and poured herself a cup of coffee. "How's Mama this morning?"

"Why don't you ask me yourself?" Mama smiled, walked into the room and sat down at the table. "To answer your question, I am wonderful. My soul warms every time I see my little Sarah in my garden. Since you have been home, you have revived all my plants. I almost killed everything, and you came home and saved them." She held up a cup for some hot coffee.

"Mama, you do look better today." Sarah gave her a big smile. "I've made a decision." Sarah looked at Stella, who had stopped cooking the ham, while Mama put her coffee down and listened.

"Mr. Rogers needs my help at the school several days a week, and I've decided to take the job. What do you both think?"

"About time you got something to do. Mr. Rogers couldn't get a better helper, as far as I'm concerned." Stella wiped her hands on her apron and gave Sarah a big hug. Mama smiled and nodded her agreement.

"All right, I will ride into town tomorrow and talk to him about my position and responsibilities. We'll all go. Let's have lunch at the new café." Sarah sat down and allowed Stella to serve her a big plate of steak and ham.

Chapter 37

Casper City Mountains

After a long time away from Fort Laramie, Corporal White, two Indian scouts and a few men had begun a journey into miles of unknown territory. At any place on the trail, there was opportunity for ambushes and attacks from the crazy men that they were after. They searched the countryside for hours each day, trying to find any sign of the three men who had attacked Will Hammer's stagecoach and killed John Conner's wife. They stopped at farmhouses and questioned the farmers about the outlaws, but so far the rustlers had not hit their places. He warned the families to stay on guard at all times.

One afternoon, Corporal White's men found a man who appeared to be dead, sprawled on the side of the trail. A slight movement caused the horses to move a step or two backward. The man was wearing canvas trousers and a checked shirt that opened at the neck, revealed his dirty white union suit. He covered his face from the scorching sun with a dirty, floppy hat.

He must have heard horses coming his way because he tried to stir and sit up. "Help," the old man called.

Corporal White and his men remained in their saddles about thirty feet away from the injured man. "Are you the only person around here?" The corporal called to the man. He didn't want his men to be attacked while caring for the stranger.

"Yep, I'm sure . . . they took everything . . . I was left for dead. My horse . . . was spooked when I fell off and he ran away. The sorry bastards."

Corporal White signaled for a soldier to check the man over. "Do you know who robbed you and left you for dead?" The old man's story had a ring of truth to it. The men they were after stole everything and killed people.

"Not by name, but I'm shore I heard of them skunks before. I thought they were long gone from this part of the territory."

The young soldier pulled the old man's vest back and opened his shirt. A hole oozed blood from the old man's shoulder.

"Is it bad? You don't have to lie to me."

The young soldier stood. "You'll live."

The old man smiled and said he would hold him to that.

The two Indian scouts jumped off their horses and searched the ground for signs.

"Was it Indians that did this to you?" There had been rumors several tribes of young Indian braves were on the warpath.

"Man, I wouldn't be lying here talking to you with all my hair if it was Indians. It was those three men . . . they been stealing everything that ain't tied down and killing anybody that tries to stop them. The yellow bellies jumped out of the rocks in front of me. One of them fellows grabbed the reins and held my wagon in place. If I had been on my horse, I would've given them a merry chase. My wagon was loaded with furs and hides, and two barrels of moonshine."

"Where did the moonshine come from?" Corporal White grinned at the old fellow.

"Can I have some more of that water, sonny?"

One of the other soldiers carried a canteen of water and opened the lid for him. "Don't drink too much at one time."

"Thanks, sonny," the old man said. He turned up the canteen and drank too much too fast. The old man coughed and spit water everywhere.

"The three men came from the rocks and stole your wagon filled with supplies and shot you. Did you get a good look at all three of them?"

"Shore. That's why they shot me. They don't want witnesses. I heard tell that's the reason they kill those poor farmers, wives and children. But, I seen 'em and I'll tell the marshall in Casper if you can help me get there."

"Let our medical man take a look at your wounds and patch you up so you can ride. We're a hunting party on the trail of those men. Ain't returning to Fort Laramie without them, dead or alive."

"Maybe those fools will open one of my barrels and start celebrating early. That's some mighty powerful stuff. They'll be dead drunk soon with a terrible hangover if they drink a lot of my brew."

Corporal White laughed and said he hoped the men started drinking soon. "What's your name, old man?"

"Folks call me Billy Jack." He glanced around and asked, "You ain't got anything stronger to drink than that thar water? When that young man starts digging around in my bullet wound, it's gonna hurt like the dickens."

Corporal White signaled with his hand for one of the men to get the flask of whiskey out of his saddlebags.

The men spent an uncomfortable night in the rain, but by morning the sun was out with a clear sky. After breakfast, Corporal White kept the men and horses at a slow trot. If they were attacked, he didn't want the horses too tired to run. The two young Indian scouts rode ahead and under a blistering sun led the patrol into Casper City.

The patrol rode to the edge of town and stopped in front of the town's livery. "Howdy, fellows." A big barrel of a man walked out of the shaded area of the barn and gestured to the men to get down. "How can I help you, General?"

"Only a corporal, young man." Corporal White grinned at the big guy whom he knew was teasing him. "First, we need to know if this town has a doc. I got a hurt man who needs attention right away."

"Go one block that way, turn left and pass two doors and head up a flight of stairs. The doc should be there, since he just brought his horse and carriage here. He'd been out all night. He boards his rig here."

"Shorty," Corporal White called to one of his men. "You and Jeff take the old man to the doctor's office. If he doesn't have any means to pay for treatment, I'll take care of it before we leave town." Corporal White walked over to the livery owner. "Sir, do you have space to board and feed our animals for the night?"

"Sure do. Just ride them into the barn and have your men unsaddle them. Toss the saddles over the stands I built. The stands come in right handy for taking good care of saddles and other equipment."

The two young Indians scouts walked out of the barn and spoke to Corporal White, "Do you remember Seth Jenkins, the mountain man? The man the captain demanded to leave the fort because he was too friendly with Miss Sullivan, his intended?"

"Of course, I remember. What about him?"

"He told me he has a farm somewhere near Casper City. I bet the livery owner knows where he lives. Mr. Jenkins might know something about the men we're after."

The livery owner interrupted the three men talking about Seth Jenkins. "I know Seth well. Nice fellow. He just arrived home awhile back and had the cutest little girl with him. He said she was his adopted daughter. If you want to go to his place, it's easy to find." When the men didn't ask him for the directions, he gave them to them anyway. "Go east out of town for about two miles, and his farm is the first one you'll come upon."

Corporal White walked away from the men. He couldn't believe Seth Jenkins, the man who'd rescued Miss Sullivan, lived close by. How did the mountain man find the little girl whom he had placed on the orphan train? He had to find out some answers for his own curiosity. Attempting to help Miss Sullivan was the reason the captain punished him by sending him off on this manhunt.

The next morning, Maria's Café had fresh hot-brewed coffee and bacon simmering, which made Corporal White's stomach growl. A young girl who wore a dirty apron around her swinging hips seated him and his men.

"Morning, fellows. Where are you soldier boys from and how long are you staying around?"

"Miss, please bring us coffee and a platter of bacon and eggs with some of those delicious-looking biscuits I smelled when we entered this establishment." Corporal White ignored the young lady's flirtatious ways, and his men followed suit.

"Jeff, how was the old man doing last night before you retired?" Corporal White hoped the old man wasn't going to die from his bullet wound.

"He'll live, I hope. Doc says the wound is inflamed. Infection is trying to set in but he's doing everything he can to save the old man. He was already complaining about being hungry and wanting a drink. The doc said that it would be a day or so before he could have solid food." Jeff smirked. "What the man really wanted was some hard liquor like his own moonshine."

Corporal White laughed and shook his head. "Men, I want us to get off the trail a few miles and ride out to the Jenkins farm which is only a couple miles from here. He may have seen or heard something about the men we're looking for."

As the old grandfather clock struck eight o'clock, the men rose and exited the restaurant. The waitress called to them to hurry back.

Chapter 38

Seth Jenkins' ranch

The terrain between Casper City and Seth Jenkins' farm was rough. Big boulders lined the road and tall Ponderosa pines formed a thick canopy over parts of the trail. The patrol had no problem locating the farm.

~

As the men rode under the big flat-iron arch, Seth stepped from the barn. He recognized the two Indian scouts immediately. "What a surprise, Snake and Coyote. I never thought I'd see the likes of you two again."

"Hello, Mr. Seth. It's good to see you too," replied Snake, the older of the two brothers.

"Mr. Seth, this is Corporal White from Fort Laramie. We're looking for those three men who killed Sergeant Conner's wife and robbed the stagecoach."

"Get down and water your horses. I'll have some fresh coffee prepared. Ride them into the shade of the barn. It's already a hot morning." Seth pointed to the area where he wanted the men to settle their animals while they were here. Martha Ann had come outside onto the porch. She had to be wondering why a Calvary patrol would be coming out this way.

"Martha Ann, please make some coffee for these men. They'll sit out here on the porch while we discuss business."

~

166

Martha Ann hurried back into the house and made a big pot of fresh coffee for the men. She sliced a fresh loaf of hot bread and spread soft, creamy butter over the slices. The men were most grateful. Afterward, she went back inside and allowed the men to conduct their business.

~

Corporal White quizzed Seth about whether he had seen the three men or heard about them harming anyone close by.

"When Penny and I were heading home, we spent the night on the trail. While I was preparing breakfast, three men starting shooting at us. I grabbed Penny and tossed her behind a log and began firing back at them. After many exchanges of gunfire, I'm sure I wounded two of them. They gave up and rode away."

"Where were you?" Corporal White pulled out a small notebook and wrote down the area that Seth described.

"Since I've been home, I haven't seen or heard anything, but now I'm sure it was the same three men who robbed the stagecoach, I won't be leaving my womenfolk alone. My neighbor and I help each other, but sometimes I leave my farm unguarded. I'm going to hire two men to come and work for me as soon as I can get to town."

"Mr. Seth, your little girl—is that Mr. Conner's child?"

"Well, she was his, but I adopted her from the owner of the orphan train. I have a paper that says she's mine." Seth gave the men a hard look. Nobody was going to take Penny away from him.

When no one said anything, he continued. "The captain placed Penny on the orphan train while Sarah, Miss Sullivan I mean, was ill. She and I both loved the little girl and Miss Sullivan assured me she and the captain would raise her as their own once they married."

"Mr. Jenkins, I have to confess that I was ordered to place the child on the orphan train. I felt sick to my stomach, but the captain probably would have had me shot if I didn't obey him." He took the last sip of his coffee and sat back in the straight-back cane chair. "I agreed to help Miss Sullivan get the child back, but someone told the captain of my plan. I got put in this position of leading the patrol."

"I understand, Corporal. You were only following orders. Believe me, I know all about the captain. Miss Sullivan told me he had changed, but I don't think she really knew how much, since she had planned to marry him."

"But, Mr. Seth, they didn't get married," Snake spoke up, his eyes wide.

"How do you know that?" Corporal White asked Snake before Seth could make a reply. Seth didn't think he could speak anyway. His mind was whirling. Sarah wasn't married. She was still a free woman.

"While on the trail, after we made camp one evening, I saw several Indian braves camping over the next rise. I talked to them. Several of the younger boys had watched the wedding from the loft of the church. The braves joked about it because they were happy the woman backed out of marrying the sleazy-eyed man. One boy said he saw the angry captain storm out the back door of the church, but the woman wasn't with him. I'm sorry I forgot to mention it."

Seth was finally able to pull himself together. "Do you know if Miss Sullivan is still at Fort Laramie?"

"No, I don't know that. But the boys said they still served all that good wedding food the cooks had prepared and had a big celebration."

"Snake, you didn't hear one of them mention anything about Miss Sullivan? Think. Try to remember." Seth was happy beyond words the wedding didn't take place, but he was worried about Sarah's whereabouts.

"I'm sorry. That's all I know." Snake held his head down while peeking at his brother who only shook his head.

The corporal placed his hands on his hips. "I have to admit I'm pleased Miss Sullivan didn't tie herself to the captain for life. She was so hurt when she got well and found the little girl gone from the fort. She pleaded with me to help her." He sighed. "I don't know what's going to happen in the future at the fort under that captain's leadership."

Seth stood and walked with the corporal to the barn.

"Mr. Seth," Snake and Coyote were standing in the doorway. Snake held his hat in his hands. "You said you wanted to hire two men to work on your farm. My brother and I are good with horses and cattle. We know how to plant fields and harvest crops. We ain't lazy and will work hard for you."

Seth raised his eyebrows and smiled. "This comes as a surprise. You men are scouts and good ones at that. Are you sure you want to settle down on a small cattle farm?"

"With our help, the farm won't stay small. We've worked on big cattle ranches and learned to brand and worked roundups, too."

"How are you both with a hammer? If I hire you, I'll need help building a bunkhouse." Seth looked at Corporal White to see how he felt about him hiring his two scouts.

"We're good. We've helped build several houses." Snake stood next to his brother and placed his arm around his shoulder. Seth saw the affection between the two young men.

"Well now, Snake, my neighbor has been keeping this place going while I was gone, especially after my brother left. He has a grown boy who is a good worker. They help me when I need assistance and I go to their place and help them. Would you be willing to do that?"

"Mr. Seth, you'll be our boss man and we'll do whatever you tell us to do. No questions asked."

Seth smiled and gave a little laugh. "Well, men, welcome to my family. I'll be happy to have you live here with Penny and me. I feel good already knowing you two guys will be here."

Coyote turned to Corporal White. "Sorry sir, but I'm sick and tired of being bullied around by that man at the fort. I can't hold my tongue much longer and he will have me beaten like he's done to several other braves."

Snake glanced at his brother. "I'd killed him if he ever hurt you." He stepped closer to the corporal. "Sir, I hope you understand why we don't want to return with you. You've been good to me and my brother."

"You have made a wise choice. If only I could get away, I would, too. But if I don't return, I'll be classified as a deserter and when caught, I'd be shot." Corporal White's face reddened. "I'd give anything to request another position somewhere else." The man looked over his shoulder at his other men. "We'd better get back on the trail. Hopefully, we'll find those men soon. I wish they headed to Canada. If they cross the border, we could return to the fort."

~

Seth and the two scouts stood in the front yard, watching the

169

men ride away. "Men," Seth said, "you don't know how happy I am to have you here. I want you to know you have brought me wonderful news. I'm going on a trip in the morning, and I'm going to need your help."

"Where are you going, Mr. Seth?" Snake asked.

"I tell you what. After lunch today, I want one of you to ride over to Mick's place. I'll give you a note to deliver to him. I have a story to tell and I only want to tell it one time. Since you two are going to be a valuable part of my family, you should know the reason I'll be leaving for a while."

Seth went into the house and fed Penny a bowl of soup and crackers. He took her hand and led her into his room. "Now, Sweetheart, I want you to take a nap, and this afternoon, I'll take you outside to see my new piglets."

Later when Martha Ann, Mick, Mary and the scouts were seated around the dining room table, Seth told them the story about what took place while he was on the mountain. He began with how he'd witnessed the stagecoach robbery and scared the men away from the scene. "It killed me that I couldn't get to the women sooner. I saw the results of the brutal attack that Mrs. Connors endured." He took a moment to compose himself. "I buried Penny's mama as best I could. Sarah was in a bad state. She rocked the child but was in a trance." He sighed and took a drink of coffee. No one said a word while waiting for him to continue.

"I placed Sarah on the pack mule and held Penny. We went to my cabin. Was I ever happy to find Blue Sky at my place. She took care of Sarah who was in a bad way for two days. She slept but had nightmares. When she recovered, we were on our way down the mountain to Fort Laramie when someone blew up the other side of the mountain, blocking the path. Later, I discovered it was Mr. Connors, Penny's papa. Once he found his wife's grave, the men said he went crazy."

"He did," Coyote asserted. "We were with Corporal Turnberry when he lit the dynamite and blew up the mountainside."

"Quiet, brother. Let Mr. Seth talk." Snake kicked his brother's ankle.

Seth continued. "I returned to the cabin and Sarah, Penny and I remained there for five months. Sarah was always a lady and a wonderful replacement mama to Penny. I worked with the other trappers removing trees and other debris to clear the trail down the mountainside. I'd promised Sarah I would take her to Fort Laramie to her fiancé, who was waiting to marry her."

Seth glance at Martha Ann, who used the tail of her dress to wipe away tears. "That poor baby," she said.

"After arriving at the fort, I sold my furs and hides and left Sarah in the hands of her man, George Turnberry. He'd been promoted to the captain of Fort Laramie. Sarah assured me that she and her fiancé would raise Penny as their own child. Believe me, leaving her and Penny was the hardest thing I ever did."

"Why did you find it hard? You should have been happy," Mick remarked.

"Unfortunately for me, I had fallen in love with those two." He surveyed their faces. Mary scowled.

"On my way home, I stopped in Turnersville, a small town about fifteen miles away from the fort. As I was going to get something to eat, I saw the orphan train. Standing in line with other children was Penny. My heart stopped when I saw the little girl. I grabbed her up in my arms and gave the woman in charge money to draw up adoption papers. Penny is my legal daughter now."

"Why was she on the orphan train when you left her with the lady?" Martha Ann asked.

"It seems that Sarah had taken ill and while she was at the sick bay, her fiancé made the old woman take Penny with her. If she refused, he threatened to hold back the supplies she needed for the other children."

"Maybe she didn't really want the child. She wasn't her little girl." Mary sat back in her chair.

Mick ignored Mary's comment. "Does this Sarah know that you have Penny now?" Mick asked.

"Not sure what she knows. I thought all this time she'd married Captain Turnberry. But the men said she didn't get married." He smiled for the first time since he started the story. "This is the reason I called this meeting with you. I'm going to the fort to search for Sarah and if I have to, I will travel to her hometown in Canon, Colorado."

"I hope you can find her. I bet she was upset after finding Penny gone. I would have been." Martha Ann stood and walked to Seth. "When are you leaving?"

"First light, if you will care for Penny for me," Seth said. "Will you take her to your place? It will be easier."

"Of course, we'll love having her." Martha Ann smiled.

"Mary, you'll not be alone. The boys will be here, and they will cook for themselves out in the bunkhouse. If you need anything, just ask one of them."

"I never liked being in this big house by myself. Do you really have to go on a wild goose chase after some woman?" Mary sniffed.

"Sarah Sullivan is not just some woman. I thought you understood. I love her and I'm going to marry her before we return, if she'll agree to have me."

Chapter 39

Seth stood behind the thirty-six-inch white picket fence that surrounded Sarah's little farmhouse, then reached for the latch. A brown, floppy-eared puppy dug out from the front porch. He sat back on his haunches, bared his baby teeth, and growled. Seth smiled down at the small protector and tried to flip up the latch. Frustrated, he stepped over the gate and stared down at the pup who had attacked his shiny new western boot.

~

Sarah stepped outside, holding the door with one hand, and with the other shading the morning sun from her eyes. She stomped her foot and called to the puppy. "Penny, come." The copper-haired puppy bounced to her feet and stopped barking.

"You have her trained well," the man standing in the blinding sunlight said.

Slowly Sarah walked down one step, allowing the door to slam. She lowered her hand and heard the voice clearly. Sarah's eyebrow's rose. Silent, she didn't dare move.

Seth's gaze was penetrating, and his mouth hid a smile. For a moment she prayed this man was Seth. How she longed to hug him tight and place her head on his chest.

"Seth, is it really you?"

~

Walking slowly, not wanting to alarm the puppy, he moved closer to Sarah, the woman he was dying to hold in his arms.

"Yes, it's me." His comment was spoken so soft he wasn't sure she heard. Before Seth knew what happened, his love flew into his arms with tears flowing down her cheeks, dampening his neck and shirt collar.

Seth wrapped his arms around Sarah's tiny waist, lifted her, and whirled her around. He eased her to the ground giving her a chance to look at him.

~

She had not seen Seth in nearly a year, but he had not changed one bit. His hair was longer than the last time she'd seen him, and it was dark and curly. The bushy beard was still gone, and this pleased her.

~

Seth leaned in for a kiss and felt as if he was drowning. He felt his body trembling at her touch. Whispering into her soft hair, he said, "I never thought I'd see you again. I can't believe you didn't marry your beloved George, but oh, my love, I'm so happy you didn't."

"Am I your love?" Sarah touched his chin and made him look directly into her eyes.

"When it comes to loving you, I never joke. I have the most honorable intentions in the world and when we find the preacher, I'll prove it to you."

~

Sarah could feel her body radiating through the layers of her clothes. She pushed back away from the intimacy of their embrace.

"I beg your pardon, Sweetheart. I forgot myself for a moment." A crooked smile appeared on his face. "I want to kiss you and never turn you lose, but this isn't the time or place. Your mama may come out here with the shotgun she's pointing at me from the doorway."

"Oh, Seth, mama will be thrilled to meet the man who saved her baby, as she calls me. Come, let's go inside so you can meet her and Stella."

"Before we go in, I want you to know something that will make you very happy."

"I don't believe I could be any happier than I am now. Just having you standing in front of me—" Seth placed his fingers over her lips.

Sarah's eyes widened, and when he removed his fingers, she

smiled and stayed still.

"I have Penny." Seth waited for her to understand his statement. When she made no response, he repeated himself. "I found Penny on the orphan train. She's at my farm."

"Oh, my goodness. I can't believe it." Tears filled her lovely eyes and she practically leaped back in his arms. "Oh my love, you have my Penny."

"Our Penny, our little girl." Seth corrected her.

"How did you find her?"

"After I left the fort, I stopped in the town of Turnersville. Once I placed my horse and Buster at the livery, I saw the orphan train. Children were standing in line, and there was a child screaming and crying. She called your name and then she called mine. I gave the orphan-train leader money and adopted Penny. She's our little girl now."

"Why didn't you bring her?" Sarah asked.

"If she'd known I was coming to find you, she would have been screaming to come. She's cried for you many days and nights. I didn't bring her because I wasn't sure I could find you."

"Mama and Stella are on the porch. We'd better go ease their minds."

~

The sky had darkened, and stars had come out when he rode away from the little farmhouse. He glanced back over his shoulder and saw the glow of the lantern in the window. He never wanted to leave Sarah again, but it wouldn't be proper for him to stay at their place.

Sarah's house was warm and homey just as she'd made his small cabin on the mountain. He smiled and urged his horse into a fast trot. The sooner he got back to the rooming house in Canon, the quicker the morning would come, and he could arrange to marry Sarah and take her to his home as his wife.

He had a lot to do the next morning. Sarah wanted her mama to go with them and he knew Sarah's mama wouldn't want to leave Stella behind. He was going to have to buy a covered wagon for the women to travel in. They'd want to carry some of their smaller pieces of furniture and their personal belongings.

~

The next morning, Sarah glanced around her home. She'd left

it before to marry George, but for some reason, the little haven now felt different. She was comfortable and safe here, but she had no doubt that she'd be happy as long as she was with Seth.

After dressing, she prepared to ride into school and teach one last day. She hated to have to give her notice to Mr. Rogers. He'd been so good to her and she appreciated her small paycheck every week. As she made her way toward her classroom, the children gathered around her near the steps of the building. A twelve-year-old boy spoke first.

"Is it true, Miss Sullivan? Are you leaving town to get married?"

"Mercy, news travels fast. I was just asked yesterday afternoon. How did you children hear so quickly?"

"Mrs. Georgia told my mama, who works for her in the kitchen, that a man from the Casper Mountains had come for you."

"I'd hoped to speak with Mr. Rogers. I am happy to marry a very special man, but I'm sad to be leaving all of you." Sarah glanced around at the smaller children who looked down-hearted. "Come, let's go in and make my last day special."

The children raced inside the building as she took the older boy by the arm. "I'm sure Mr. Rogers will find someone else to help him with the children while he teaches the older students."

"I hope so, Miss Sullivan. We've all learned so much since he's had the time to work with us." The boy turned and walked up the stairs into the classroom.

The day seemed to last forever. Sarah spoke with Mr. Rogers and he was understanding. Sarah mind was racing with all the plans she needed to accomplish before leaving town again.

As the children were reciting their numbers, their little faces were looking at the doorway. Sarah tapped on her book to force their focus back to her, but that didn't help. She turned to look at what held their attention. Her handsome Seth stood with his hat in one hand and a handful of wildflowers in the other. The children giggled as he walked into the room and didn't stop until he stood in front of their teacher. He offered the flowers to Sarah, knelt down on one knee and reached for her hand. He then turned to smile at the children.

The little girls giggled, and the boys hid their eyes.

"Sarah Sullivan, I love you. Will you make me the happiest

man alive and marry me?"

"Oh, Seth, how sweet. Of course I will marry you." He slid a pretty emerald ring on her finger.

"I realized on the way home last night that we talked about getting married, but I hadn't asked you properly," he said, loud enough for the students to hear.

Seth motioned for one of the older girls to come to the front of the room. He held out a large bag of penny candy. "Please pass out this candy until it's all gone." He glanced at an older boy and signaled with his head for the boy to help him. The young boy held out his hand, while Seth poured twenty-five silver nickels into his hand. "Give each child one, please."

The boy mouthed, "Wow."

"Children, I am sorry that I'm taking Miss Sullivan away from your school, but I need her. As you all witnessed, she's agreed to become my wife. I hope you will take the candy and money as a peace offering."

"Are you an Indian?" A little boy asked Seth. "Indians have pow wows and give each other peace. Ain't that right, Miss Sullivan?"

"Isn't that right, Billy?" Sarah smiled at Seth and then back at the small child. "By the gifts and candy Mr. Jenkins is giving you, he wants you to be happy for us."

The children stood and circled the couple. "We are not happy, but we understand," the oldest student spoke for the children.

Seth whispered to Sarah he would be waiting outside for her when class was over. They'd go meet with the preacher about getting married—the next day.

Chapter 40

"What?" Seth nearly yelled at the old woman who stood on the front porch of the little white church. "When will the preacher return?" Seth could not believe the preacher had been called out of town.

"He don't tell me his business. I just clean the church, but he left this morning. A man came and got him." The old woman turned and went back inside the church.

"Sarah, do you know another small town nearby that might have a preacher or judge that could marry us?"

"Ours is a traveling preacher. He's not here but one week a month, so he may go on to another town before coming back here."

"I was in hopes we could travel back home to my farm as man and wife."

~

Coming over the rise on the mountain, Seth stopped the covered wagon. "Sarah, there's Fort Laramie. Are you sure you want to go inside and purchase our supplies while I have the horses checked at the livery? We are about two days from my farm."

"Do you think we could ask Chaplain Sumrall to marry us in private? I would love for Elizabeth to stand next to me. She's a special lady and friend."

"Why don't I drop you girls at their home, and you can visit with Mrs. Sumrall while I take care of the animals?" Seth glanced around at the women.

"Sarah, dear, why don't you give me your list and Sella and I will go into the store and purchased our supplies while you take care of the wedding plans. Once we've finished, we can join you at their house. Just point us to the right one."

"Sounds like we have everything taken care of in a small amount of time. I want to get in and out as fast as we can. I hope George is on a patrol." Sarah sighed and looked at Seth. "I don't want to see him."

Seth waved at several of the soldiers who recognized him and called out to him. He stopped in front of the small church building and helped Sarah down. "Maybe, if things go well, you'll be Mrs. Seth Jenkins before we leave here today." He wanted to kiss her, but he touched the tip of her nose instead.

Sarah watched him drive the wagon to the commissary. She knocked on the front door. "Please be home." Looking over her shoulder, she only saw a few soldiers milling around in the courtyard.

The door opened and Elizabeth nearly screamed with joy. "Oh, Sarah, what a wonderful surprise. I prayed I would hear from you soon." Elizabeth scanned the area before she closed the door. "How did you get here from Canon?"

"Seth, my mountain man, came to Canon after he found out I didn't marry George. He asked me to marry him. I have to confess that I had feelings for him before I was to marry George. I was never unfaithful to George, but he had changed so much, and Seth had been so kind and generous to Penny and me." Sarah hung her head and wiped away a few tears. "Seth found Penny on the orphan train and paid money to the woman in charge to adopt her. She is at his farm in the care of his neighbor. I can hardly wait to see the child."

"This is wonderful news. I know how heartbroken you were when George placed her on the train with the other children."

"Is the chaplain home? Seth and I want him to marry us today and I want you to stand with me."

"Oh Sarah, he's not here. Some of the soldiers were on a patrol and some bad men raided their camp and several were killed. He rode out to the campgrounds to help with the burial and to pray over the young men."

"Do you think he will be back soon?"

"No, he only left about an hour ago, and the raid happened

179

miles from here. Some of the injured rode in and went directly to the doctor's."

A loud knock scared the two ladies. Both jumped and laughed. "Let me see who is trying to knock down my door," Elizabeth said.

"It's probably my mama and Stella."

Standing at the door was George. He appeared thinner and had grown a mustache which made him look like a villain from one of Sarah's book. Elizabeth stepped away from the door as George stormed into the room. "Leave us, woman."

"I will not, sir. This is my home." Elizabeth stood firm and blocked Sarah.

Sarah touched her friend's arm. "Please, Elizabeth. Leave us for a few minutes. I'm sure George doesn't have a lot to say to me."

George waited until Elizabeth left, then said, "So, you finally came to your senses and came back where you belong. As soon as the chaplain returns from the burial detail, he can marry us."

Sarah looked at George like he was a madman. "Do you really think that I have returned to marry you?"

He stood glaring at her but didn't make a response.

"Why would you want to marry a woman you don't trust? Why do you think I left and didn't say my marriage vows to you?"

"Listen to me and listen well. You embarrassed me beyond words. Now, your return will help me recover from the worst day in my life. Everyone will believe that you begged me to take you back, and you will beg and plead with me now."

He reached for Sarah before she could move away from him. He grabbed her arm and twisted it behind her back." She screamed but he only twisted it higher.

~

Elizabeth ran out the back door. She had to find the mountain man.

~

"Beg me, you slut!" George screamed.

"Never! I came here to make plans with the chaplain to marry Seth Jenkins. He will be here in a few minutes," she said, wincing from his hard grip.

"No, you'll never marry that man. You'll marry me, or so help me, I will have that man shot before the sun goes down today." He turned Sarah loose and shoved her to the floor beside a rocking chair.

~

Seth heard voices when he came in the front door with Elizabeth fast on his heels. When he spotted Sarah on the floor, he tightened his hands into fists and stormed toward George.

Elizabeth hurried to Sarah and tried to pick her up, but she gasped and whispered, "I think my arm is broken."

"So, big man, you want to take on someone more your own size? You want to tangle with me? Oh, I hope you do because I'm going to try my best to break your neck."

Before George could make a reply, Seth placed his hands under George's armpits and carried him dangling in the air to the front door that stood open.

"Put me down, you fool. My men will arrest you as soon as I give the order."

Stepping onto the porch, Seth plunked George down on his feet and hit him in his stomach. The man folded over. Seth hit him directly in the face and heard the crack of his jawbone. Blood spewed everywhere.

From his spot on the ground, the captain yelled toward the group of soldiers watching the fight. "Arrest that man." George pointed at Seth who stood on the small stoop with his hands balled into fists and his long legs spread apart.

The three men stood rooted in their place.

"Did you hear me? This man will be shot before the sun goes down." He rolled his lean body off the ground and stood on wobbly legs.

Sarah had walked onto the porch with Elizabeth and stood next to Seth.

"Men," Elizabeth called to the soldiers. "Sarah needs the doctor. Your captain may have broken her arm."

Seth turned toward his love. "Are you in a lot of pain?"

Sarah nodded, but gave him a reassuring smile.

Two of the soldiers hurried away while the other one remained. He took his rifle and pointed it directly at his captain.

"Sir, you are under arrest. Please come with me peacefully or I will have to shoot you."

"Have you lost your mind? You'll be shot right alongside of

the mountain man if you don't point that gun in his direction immediately." Every vein in George's neck protruded as he wiped his bloody mouth.

"Beg your pardon, Sir, but where I come from, a real man would never hurt a lady. Miss Sullivan is one of the nicest ladies I have ever met. You have injured her. I don't know why, but I don't care. Men ain't supposed to hurt their womenfolk."

A large crowd had gathered in the courtyard and witnessed the young southern soldier holding a gun on their fearless captain. Some of the men sniggered and made sly remarks about how happy that were that someone had beat the hell out of the captain.

Corporal Jefferson arrived on the scene and asked what was going on. Seth stepped off the porch and explained the situation to the officer.

"Jimmy," Corporal Jefferson spoke gently but firmly. "I am the office in charge now and I will handle this problem. Give your rifle to Private Freeman and he will take the captain to his office, for now. Captain, you are to remain under guard in your office until I can get to the bottom of this trouble."

"Every one of you men will be put on report and I will deal with all of you very soon." George stormed away without giving Sarah a second glance.

"Miss Sullivan, please return inside the house until the doctor comes. Mr. Jenkins, are you prepared to be on your way soon— in about an hour's time?"

"Yes, sir. As soon as Sarah sees the doctor and gets her arm checked, we will be leaving for my farm at the bottom of the Casper Mountains." Seth stepped closer to the officer. "Corporal, Miss Sullivan is my intended. We stopped here to get a few supplies and to ask Chaplain Sumrall to marry us. About a year ago, Sarah planned to marry the captain but she changed her mind."

"Yes, I heard the story right after I arrived here. The captain is not well and as soon as I can, I'm going to write to Washington and report his actions. The men here are all afraid of him and many of their wives have gone back to their families because of the way he makes their husbands work long hours. They never get to have any family time." The officer looked around at the men who had gathered to watch the fight.

"Mr. Jenkins, I need a favor of you. Will you take young Jimmy with you away from this fort? He will be in grave danger if he remains here. The captain will punish him something fierce, and I won't be able to stop him. I'll inform Jimmy that his service time has been completed and he has done an excellent job while in the Cavalry. I would like for him to go home to his family."

In less than an hour, the doctor had examined Sarah's arm and said it would hurt for a few days but wasn't broken. He tied a sling around her neck and placed her arm in it. "Wear this for about a week and you should be alright."

Sarah thanked the man but stopped him from leaving. "Doctor, please check over Mr. Jenkins' hands."

"My hand is fine, dear. I will need to soak it in warm saltwater a few times and it'll be fine. I won't be able to handle an axe for a few days, but—"

"Sit down here, son, Let me check your hands so your woman will stop worrying about you." The doctor examined Seth's hands and fingers and declared them alright. "Like he said, they'll be sore for a few days. Are you the one that busted the captain's nose?"

"Yes. He's lucky I didn't do more than that."

The doctor laughed, closed his black bag and wished them safe travel home.

With a big hug from Elizabeth Sumrall, the three women sat in back of the covered wagon while Seth sat next to Jimmy who would be driving the horses. Back on the trail, they headed home.

Chapter 41

After two long, slow days on the road to Seth's ranch, it was a joyful afternoon when they arrived. Sarah looked at the large white ranch house. She was surprised to see how big it was. Lovely plants surrounded the porch and many were still in bloom. "What a wonderful place," Sarah said aloud.

A large red barn sat beside the house with a spacious corral filled with horses and calves. As Seth began to help her down from the covered wagon, she saw the two Indian men, Snake and Coyote. She remembered seeing them at the fort before they were forced to leave with Corporal White.

"Hello. What a pleasant surprise. It's so good to see you again."

"We're happy you are here and will be Seth's woman." Snake smiled and Sarah giggled at his comment.

"Hello. Mr. Seth. So happy you home." Coyote reached for the reins of the lead horse.

"Thanks, men. Please help my ladies down from this old wagon. They're very tired. Have you seen Penny since I've been away?"

"Yes, sir. I rode her around the ranch on my horse. She loves riding. Do you want me to go tell Mrs. Martha Ann to bring her home?"

"That would be great. Sarah can't wait to see the child, and I know Penny is going to be thrilled to have Sarah home."

Sarah and the others heard the door slam. They turned to see a lovely woman standing on the porch. The young woman hurried over to Seth.

"Welcome home, love," Mary said as she threw her arms around his neck and hugged him tight. "I missed you so much."

Seth removed her arms from around his neck. He blushed fiery red from the show of Mary's unexpected affection. He cleared his throat and peered at the women.

"Sarah, this is Mary Jenkins. She's my sister-in-law and will be living with us. She was married to my brother, Luke."

"Mary, I want you to meet someone very special to me. This is my fiancée, Sarah Sullivan." Seth reached for Sarah and placed her between him and Mary.

"Fiancée? Well . . . it's nice to meet you," Mary commented, looking at Sarah's mama and Stella.

"Yes, it's nice to meet you too, Mary. Seth never mentioned we would have a houseguest for a while, but I'm happy you're here. I hope we can all be friends." Sarah stepped back and introduced her mama and Stella. "This is my mama, and our dearest friend, Stella. Mama and I couldn't do without her."

~

Mary looked Stella up and down like she was judging her ability to work. "Thank goodness, you had enough sense to bring your servant. I am sick and tired of cooking and cleaning." Mary whirled and went back into the house to check on her son who was now trying to walk.

~

Seth was the first to apologize to Stella. "Please accept my apology. You will not be a servant here, but we will all pull our weight and help around the place. I don't have any servants in my home."

"It's all right, Mr. Seth. I know my place, and she was just reminding me where I belong." Stella took Mama's arm and helped her walk into the house.

~

Mama walked into the lovely parlor. John was playing on the floor. "Is this you're your son?" Mama asked Mary.

"You don't see any other mother here, do you? Of course, this is my son," she snapped and picked her son up. "He takes many hours of care every day, and I don't have time to do anything else."

Mama ignored Mary's outburst and continued to look around the room. "Oh Seth, your home is so nice. I can't believe how roomy it is."

"Our house, your new home." Seth pulled Sarah into his arms. "I want you to make any changes you want to make. It's yours." He looked at Stella and Mrs. Sullivan. "There are enough bedrooms for each of you to have your own room. This is your home now and I want all of us to be happy together. I am overflowing with joy just having you all here."

~

A half-hour later, Sarah heard a horse ride into the front yard. She raced to the door and flew outside onto the front porch. "Penny, Penny, my baby, my baby!" She hurried to Snake and took Penny out of his arms.

~

Seth stood at the door of the barn and watched the reunion of Sarah and Penny. Both of them were crying from joy. Seth's eyes misted and he hurried out to meet Penny, too. For the first time in months, the three were back together like they'd been on the mountain.

~

Early the next morning, Seth asked Sarah if she would go on a carriage ride with him. He wanted to show her his ranch and all his land.

"Of course. I would love to go, and I would like to bring Penny along."

Seth took them around the edge of his fenced property. "After I arrived home, I went to Billings and ordered three hundred head of the finest cattle I could find. That big black monster out in the corner of the field is my pride and joy. I hope he will sire many new calves this winter."

"Oh my. You'd said you were trapping furs and hides to make money to help support your ranch. It looks like you were very successful." Sarah gazed up at him.

Seth flicked the reins and the horse walked on down the trail.

"Why didn't you mention your brother's wife, Mary, before we arrived yesterday? I was surprised to learn she will be living with us with her darling son."

Seth looked sheepishly across the pastureland. "To tell you the truth, I was hoping she'd be gone by the time we returned. She knew about you because I told her I was leaving to find the woman I wanted to marry." He patted her leg, giving her a reassuring smile.

"That was nice, but she must not have understood you. The greeting she gave you was a warning to me."

"What are you talking about? A warning for what?"

"Men really don't understand women," Sarah said to the wind. "Listen, sweetheart. Your sister-in-law had her claws out yesterday when she hugged you and called you *her love*. I could tell you were surprised by her greeting."

"Yes, that was downright embarrassing. She's never acted that way before."

"She was telling me in so many words and actions that she wanted you, and I'd better be warned."

When Seth didn't reply, Sarah asked him to tell her about her husband, Luke. "Did they have a good marriage? Were they happy?"

"I guess they were until she got with child. She stayed in bed most days. Luke asked Martha Ann to come over and care for her while he worked beside me on the ranch. This place was a two-man farm at that time. We wanted to buy a cattle ranch so we worked the fields and cared for our animals every day until dark. Money wasn't coming in like we needed it to for us to expand. That's when I heard about trapping. I talked to an old trapper and he told me what to do and where to find the most critters, like bears, beavers, deer and other small animals. After many discussions with Mick and Luke, I decided to leave the farm into their capable hands and headed to the mountains." He grinned at Sarah. "I'm glad I did."

Sarah smiled and looked at Penny who was playing with her dolly on the backseat.

Seth continued. "I never received a letter from Luke, so I had no idea Mary's condition was grave. She wanted to go home to her mother, so Luke packed their things and drove her to Canada to be with her family. Later, he was thrown from a horse and broke his neck."

As Seth turned a bumpy corner in the trail, Penny's doll fell off the seat. "Get back on this seat. I am going to beat your butt!"

"Penny." Sarah twisted in the front seat and glared at Seth.

"Don't look at me. She didn't hear that from me. And besides, I've never laid a hand on that child."

"Penny, has anyone ever spoken mean to you and said they were going to spank you?" Sarah asked.

Penny didn't answer right away.

"Please, sweetheart, tell me. Have your ever been punished by someone beating your butt?"

"Mary screams at me. She ain't hit me, but she says she's gonna do it. She does hit John on his bottom because he screams and won't stop."

"Listen to me, Sweetheart. Dolly is like a baby, and you are to love her. You should never hit her or even say you're going to do that. If she does something bad, lay her down in her cradle. Do you understand me?"

"You mean like when I'm cranky and Mrs. Martha Ann makes me go to bed until I ain't tired anymore."

"Yes, just like that."

"Okay, I'll do that."

Seth pulled the carriage to the front of the barn. Coyote rushed out and took the horse's rein. Seth lifted Sarah and Penny to the ground.

Sarah smoothed her dress. "Oh, I had a grand time. Let's do this again soon. I love this spacious ranch and I am so happy all your hard work on that mountain paid off for you. You've fulfilled your dream."

"Not yet. When you become my wife, then it will be fulfilled. I love you. Please don't fret about Mary. She is my brother's widow and the mother of my nephew. She means nothing more to me."

Chapter 42

After a few days of getting into a routine, Sarah and her mama loved the ranch and were happy. Snake and Coyote had helped mama plant a new summer garden close to the house. She was eager to go to town and pick out different seeds to put in the ground.

Stella said she liked the ranch but was uncomfortable in Mary's presence. But she loved Mr. Seth's big kitchen. He had almost all the modern equipment that helped to make baking and cooking easier. The inside sink pump was the grandest of all. She took over most of the cooking, but since Sarah enjoyed working in the kitchen, it was fun having someone helping her.

Mrs. Sullivan didn't mind washing on a washboard. She washed the ladies' light items and hung them outside to dry. She pressed the linens and folded them. Penny enjoyed playing in the dishwater every night. Seth had built her a stool to stand on to wash her hands. She was going to be a good homemaker one day. Everyone had something to do they enjoyed and selected chores to do outside.

Everyone except Mary. She felt that since she had Baby John to take care of, that was her only responsibility. Not everyone agreed with her, but to keep peace, no one said anything about her laziness.

~

Mary was sick and tired of all these people living in the house with her and Seth. She wanted her man to herself, and there was no privacy in this house with people everywhere. Time was running out. As soon as the traveling preacher returned to town, Seth and Sarah would be married. Mary had to do something to cause Sarah to leave and leave soon. Then Seth would marry her.

~

One day everyone decided to go with Seth into town. Penny needed new dress materials and shoes. She was growing like a weed and her shoes were too tight. Mrs. Sullivan and Stella had giggled that they had things to make, too. After everyone was dressed and ready to leave, Mary announced she wanted to go with them. "Stella, you stay home and take care of John. He's too heavy for me to carry and shop."

Stella raised her eyebrows and glanced at the others in the room. "Sorry, Missy. I'm not your babysitter and I have a list of things I need to shop for. You never let me take care of John before when I asked, so I'm sure you can manage today." Stella and the ladies went outside.

"Well, is she coming or not?" Snake asked. He had hitched up the two horses, and the animals were eager to go.

"Seth, dear," Sarah said, sweetly. "You'd better check on Mary. We're ready to leave. She requested to go, but she's not here. Please look in on her."

~

"Mary," Seth called as he walked into the house. He looked everywhere, then he knocked on her bedroom door. "Mary, are you in there?" With no answer, he eased the door open. She sat on the bed crying.

"Why are you crying? The girls are waiting for you to go into town."

"They hate me. They won't help me with John, and I can't have one minute of peace from him. I want to go shopping but Stella won't keep him. Doesn't she know she's only a servant and must do what we need her to do?"

Seth entered the room and placed his hands on his hips. He shook his head. "Mary, none of what you have said is true. You never allowed the ladies to help with the baby. I've seen that with my own eyes. As for Stella, she's not a servant. We have no servants. She helps take care of Mrs. Sullivan, but she is not her servant or anyone else's. Now are you going to town or not? The ladies are waiting for you."

"No, I am not going with those selfish, mean women. Tell them to go without me." She stood and pushed Seth out the bedroom door and slammed it.

Seth came outside and told Snake to load up and take the girls to town. "Mary won't be going this time." He walked over to the wagon and smiled at the three women. "I would like to ask you all to try harder to be nice to Mary. She is living with us, and we all need to get along. Will you do that for me?"

When they didn't give him an answer, he said, "All right." He slammed his palm against the wagon and said, "I'll see you later."

As they traveled to town, Stella spoke, "It was my fault she got upset. She has it in her mind I'm a servant and I should work for her. Maybe I need to wear a maid's apron and a little hat. I should bow to her and only attend to her and that precious baby."

"Over my dead body," Sarah spoke firmly. "In all my years that I've known you—and you've lived with me and Mama all my young life—you haven't been treated like a servant and you won't as long as I have breath in my body. It is not your fault that she's a spoiled, lazy, young lady. She is going to have to grow up and take care of herself like you taught me. No one is going to cater to her. Understand?"

Stella used her hanky and wiped away a tear. "Mary's going to cause a lot of heartache in this family. Mark my words."

After a long day of shopping, the women returned home to find Mary had prepared a big pot of beef stew and cornbread for supper.

"What a nice surprise, Mary." Sarah gave her a sweet smile. "Thank you so much for cooking supper for the family. We had planned to have a cold supper of sandwiches, but this is so nice."

"Well, I wanted to do something since I acted so ugly this morning. I hope you will all forgive me."

"Of course, we do. You sit in the rocker and hold John while Stella and I set the table and dip up the stew for everyone. The men will surely enjoy this hot meal after working all day outside."

Stella, Mrs. Sullivan and Sarah jumped in to prepare the table and serve everyone. No one complained that the stew tasted of salt and the cornbread could have put a hole in the wall. The boys took seconds of everything. Two pitchers of tea and all the fresh milk sat empty, so Sarah made an extra-large pot of coffee to help wash the salty food down. Mary had made a delicious-looking cake, but everyone declared they were too full for dessert.

"I want some cake, Mama . . . . Sarah, please," Penny asked sweetly. Penny was going back and forth between the two names. She was still confused, so Sarah wisely let her decide on her own.

Sarah sliced the child a small piece and cut Seth an extra big one and set them down in front of them. All eyes at the dinner table were on Seth.

"I'm not too sure I can eat all this. The stew was so filling," he said between narrowed lips to Sarah.

"Oh, sure you can. Mary worked hard all day on this food." Sarah held back her laughter but offered her sweetest smile. Seth looked so pitiful, but he dug into the cake and swallowed it down quickly. "Coffee, please." He held his cup to Stella.

After the dishes were washed and put away, Sarah showed Mary the material she had chosen for Penny's new dresses.

"This material is so lovely. I can't wait to have some new dresses made for myself so I can get out of this drab black," Mary said.

Sarah smiled and watched the others make their way to their rooms. Mary should have been in mourning but wore only a black arm band. Sarah had never seen her in a black dress or heard her mention her late husband, Luke.

Chapter 43

"Sarah, may I speak with you before you turn in? Penny is fast asleep already and I tucked her in. Let's sit on the porch swing and have a little chat," Seth said.

After wishing everyone a good night, Sarah joined Seth on the porch.

"You know, I would like to wring your pretty little neck for putting that awful cake in front of me. If you think the stew was salty, you should have tasted the baking powder in the cake. I nearly gagged, but Penny didn't seem to notice."

Sarah smiled and tried her best not to laugh out loud. "Penny only ate the sweet icing."

"How do you know the icing was sweet? You didn't eat any of the cake because I watched.

"I licked my fingers while cleaning the cake knife."

"Why do you think she decided to do something today? She's been here for weeks and hasn't raised a finger." Seth leaned back and pushed the swing with his boot.

"Mary doesn't want to be on your bad side. She knew she was really ugly today, so she had to do something." Sarah sighed and smiled at Seth. "I think she meant well. She just can't cook."

~

Everyone got into a routine while waiting for the traveling preacher to return to Casper. Stella cooked, Mrs. Sullivan worked the garden and washed, and Sarah sewed and did all the other duties a rancher's wife took care of. Mary cared for her son and complained about being bored.

Martha Ann and Mick came over for Saturday supper while their son, Will rode into town with Snake and Coyote. "When are you two planning on getting hitched?" Mick asked, getting directly to the point.

"As soon as the traveling preacher returns this way. He'd just been here when I arrived home with Sarah. We just missed him," Seth said looking at Sarah.

~

Mary ambled around in her room. She was bored out of her mind having to play the sweet sister-in-law when she really wanted to be the lady of the house. Seth may have gone to Canon and brought Sarah to his farm, but they weren't married –yet. She had come here from Canada with the hopes of marrying Seth. They could work his ranch, travel the world, and have a grand time. She was tired of sitting around and watching that woman flirt with the man she wanted. Seth belonged to her by rights. Sarah may have spent months with him on the mountain, but Seth would never touch a woman pledged to another. It was time. Tonight was the night she'd force Sarah to leave and take everyone with her. Seth would soon be hers.

Mary waited until everyone was settled down for the night. Stella seemed to stay up half the night, cleaning and caring for the old white woman who acted like she was helpless. Penny was asleep on her pallet near the fire in Seth's room and her son was sound asleep in the middle of her bed with pillows surrounding him for safety.

"How in the world could anyone have any privacy in this house?" Mary murmured as she tiptoed across the house to Seth's room.

The oil lamp was turned down low. The light cast shadows on the wall as she inched toward Seth's bed. Seth turned toward the wall, throwing the heavy quilt off his hard, firm body. Mary slipped off her house slippers and eased toward the bed. She stepped on Seth's white undershirt. Penny flopped around on her pallet and sat up, but just as quickly, she lay back down and after a minute began to snore. Mary's heart nearly stopped, then she smiled. Good. The child was sleeping soundly.

Mary gazed down on Seth's body that was turned away from

her. She removed her robe and laid it down on the chair next to the bed. The shadows of the outside tree limbs danced on the softly lit wall. She eased herself onto the bed, slid under the sheet and sighed. Seth flipped over and threw his arm across her waist. She snuggled as close to him as she could.

"Oh, you smell so good," he said as he tightened his hold on her and lifted his leg over hers, pinning her into his arms. He began nibbling on her neck. She moved her hand down his body near the waistband of his underpants.

"Oh Sarah, I have dreamed of this many, many—"

~

Penny woke up and had to pee. When she stood at the foot of her papa's bed, she saw that woman lying next to him. She raced to wake up Sarah.

"I got to go," Penny said softly, shaking her.

After the trip to the water closet, Sarah tiptoed Penny back to her pallet. "Let's be quiet, Sweetheart, so as not to wake up your papa." Sarah whispered.

"He's awake," she said softly. "I heard him talking to that woman."

"What woman? No one is in here," Sarah said.

"Is too. Look there." Sarah stared at Seth's bed through the dim light.

~

Mary had heard Penny and Sarah come back into the bedroom. She smiled. *Good, let them find me in Seth's arms. This should make Sarah leave for good.*

~

Seth was moving around under the covers and murmuring sweet words.

Sarah hurried over to the table and turned the lamp up. The light cast light over the small room.

Seth sat up, blinking from the bright light. "What's going on?" He glanced down at Mary and leaped out of the bed. Grabbing the sheet, he covered his manhood and naked, hairy chest.

"What the hell! Why are you in my bed?" He glanced from Mary to Sarah and back to Mary. He waited for a second and then stormed over to the peg on the wall, grabbed his trousers and went into another room to dress.

Mary sat up in the bed, pulling the sheet up over her naked shoulders. "Now Sarah, you see how it is. Seth is not going to marry you when he has me. You'd better go and pack up your mama, that old Black woman, and oh yes, take that brat with you, too." She pointed at Penny who stood with her face pressed between Sarah's front legs. It took Sarah a moment to understand what she had just discovered. Seth and Mary.

"Come with me, Sweetheart." Sarah picked Penny up in her arms and carried her to her mama's room. "You can get in the bed with my mama. Is that alright?"

Penny nodded. "I don't like Mary. I don't want her for a mama." Penny placed her two fingers in her mouth and snuggled next to Mama.

"You go back to sleep," Sarah whispered. "Let the grown people take care of everything." She reached for Penny's fingers and removed them from her mouth.

Shocked, Sarah was so angry her insides shook. She had to do something about Mary. Stella stood in the doorway.

"Child, do you love that big strapping man?" Before Sarah could answer, Stella continued. "You get in there and drag that piece of mourning trash out of your man's bed. That man is yours and you need to protect what's yours. You gave that man your heart. Show him how much you love him. Toss her out of this house." Stella marched back to her room.

In all the years she had known this old woman, she'd never seen her ruffled like tonight. Stella was right, but was it Sarah's place to make Mary leave? She took a deep breath. Stella's words gave her the courage to do what needed to be done. Sarah lifted her chin, used the back of her hand to wipe away the tears, straightened her muslin gown, and marched into Seth's bedroom. Mary was sitting on the side of the bed.

"Oh, I thought you were Seth coming back. Have you started packing yet?" Mary sat back on the bed, lifted one knee and gave her a smug smile.

"No, I am not packing, but you will be soon. I don't know where you'll go, but I don't care. We had planned for you to stay here and raise your son, but you've made that impossible. You must leave."

~

196

Mary yawned and turned to put on her slippers. "Listen to me, sister. I'm not going anywhere. This was my home with Luke first, and now Seth will be mine." Before Mary knew what was happening, her hair was jerked back by the roots. She hit the floor with a thump, and then her robe slapped her in the face.

"Get up and get out of my man's room. Seth is the man I'm marrying. If you think I'm going to let you move into his bed and take him away from me, you got another thing coming. Do you understand? Seth is mine and mine alone. As far as that little girl, she's mine, too. Seth may have adopted her, but she was mine first. Seth and I will make plans for you to return to your family or anywhere else you want to go, but you aren't living under this roof."

~

Sarah stormed from the bedroom into the parlor leaving Mary sprawled on the floor. She had never been so angry in all her life. Her body shook as she neared the fireplace in the dark parlor. She had never in her life lifted her hand to another person. Sadness and weariness overwhelmed her. A woman had to be desperate to stoop so low as to climb in bed with another woman's man.

"Sarah," a voice called from the across the parlor. "Am I your man? Yours and yours only?"

Sarah dashed across the room into Seth's arms. She simply had to tell him her true feelings. "Oh, I wanted to die when I saw you two in bed together, but I trust you with my life. I knew you would never betray our love."

Out of the corner of her eye, Sarah saw Mary sneaking across the dark parlor back into her own bedroom.

Seth whispered in her ear, "I promise to send her away. She'll never hurt you again."

Her heart clamored in her throat. The anger melted away with the warmth of his strong arms. She bravely raised her eyes as far as his chin. He'd shaved before going to bed and he smelled of soap. She wanted him to carry her to his bed, but she came to her senses. Quickly she turned from him. "We'd better behave ourselves before we wake the rest of the house."

"I have a feeling they're awake already." Seth smiled in the dark and kissed her forehead.

Chapter 44

Early the next morning, Seth placed Mary and baby John in the wagon. "I'm sorry, Mary. Please take care of my nephew. When he's older, I would enjoy having him come and spend the summers with me. In the future, please remember my offer. Snake is going to drive you into town. Here's some traveling money for you and the boy." Seth handed Mary an envelope, but she refused to take it.

"I don't need your money. I have a man waiting in town for me. He's older, wealthy and loves me. He knew I wanted to be with you, but he said he would wait."

Snake jumped on the wagon and Seth signaled for him to pull away. As they drove out of the yard, Sarah, her mama, and Stella stood on the porch with Penny. No one waved but watched until the wagon was out of sight.

Seth strode to the porch and stared at the ladies. Stella and Mrs. Sullivan turned and went back inside, leaving Seth and Sarah alone. "Hopefully, Mary will be happy." Seth peered at the ground but glanced up when Sarah spoke softly.

"Yes, I want her to be happy, too." She stepped down off the porch and kissed Seth on the cheek.

Later that afternoon when Snake returned from town, Seth asked about the man Mary was going to meet. "Was the man pleased to see Mary?"

"Oh, he looked nice enough. He took John from her and then helped her down from the wagon before I could jump down. I heard him say that after she freshened up, they would walk to the church and get married. The preacher man is in town for a week, but they should get married before they left town tomorrow."

"Really? The preacher is in town. That's great news." Seth was overwhelmed with excitement. "Sarah and I can be married this week. Listen, I'm going to ride into town in the morning and make arrangements for a small wedding. While there, I'll purchase some supplies. You and Coyote make a list of what is needed in the barn, and I'll tell Stella and Mrs. Sullivan about my plans. Sarah's going to be surprised."

"You don't think you need to tell Miss Sarah first?"

"You're right. Sarah first."

Snake rolled his eyes.

Early the next morning, Seth told everyone he had some important business in town, and he would be home before lunch. He gave the two men instructions about what needed to be done on the ranch, but he didn't say anything to Sarah. He wanted to have everything planned before he announced to her when they could become husband and wife.

~

Stella and Penny each grabbed a berry-picking basket and headed out into the open field where Stella had discovered a large patch of blackberry bushes. "Jams and blackberry pies shore would be enjoyed by everyone come this winter," Stella told Penny as she skipped by her side.

Before Stella knew what happened, a hand had circled her neck and foul-smelling breath whisked against her skin. A knife tip touched her cheek when she elbowed the stinking person in the ribs. She twisted around and screamed at Penny. "Run, baby, run!"

Penny dropped her basket and ran to find Seth.

~

Once the man caught his breath, he raised his fist and hit Stella in the face, knocking her to the ground. He quickly jerked her to her feet. "You're coming with me, old gal. You try anything else and I'll gut you like a pig. You'll make the others do just what I want. They ain't wanting to see your brains blown all over the front yard."

~

After Stella was steady on her feet, she slid her free hand inside her apron pocket and pulled out a small derringer. She twisted around and faced the nasty creature, pointing her gun directly at his chest.

Once he realized what she held in her hand, he roared with laughter. "What you gonna' do with that little pea shooter, gal?"

"You touch me again, ole man, and you'll soon find out." Stella didn't flinch or stutter.

Suddenly, his hand reached out and he grabbed for the gun. She side-stepped his body and shot him directly in the heart. Blood splattered his front shirt and onto her neck and blouse. He looked wide-eyed before he fell forward facedown. Dead.

Catching her breath, she calmed herself and prayed, "Forgive me, Jesus, but I had no choice." Making the sign of the cross over her chest, she wiped blood and tears from her face. Racing as fast as her old legs would carry her, she searched all around for Penny. "Please Jesus, protect the little one."

~

Stella eased herself closer to the ranch house. A gun blasted followed by a scream. She couldn't tell whose voice she heard. "Oh Lord, help us please," she prayed.

When she peeked around a large tree close to the house, two strange men with guns hid near the front of the house. Snake was firing his rifle at the men while Coyote crawled back inside the barn.

The front door burst open and a man came out dragging Sarah and her mama at gun point. Mrs. Sullivan was crying while Sarah held her close.

~

Stella rushed into the back of the ranch house. She could hear the men yelling at Snake and Coyote as she grabbed Mr. Seth's buffalo gun that he kept over the fireplace. She'd watched when Seth taught Mick how the big gun worked. Seth had told Mick that he kept the gun loaded at all times, just in case. Now was the time…just in case . . .

Easing over to the front window, she saw the two bandits standing in the front yard, demanding that the boys come out of the barn or they would shoot Mrs. Sullivan first. One of them pointed his pistol into the back of her head as she cried and struggled.

Coyote, holding his wounded side, eased from the barn first.

His rifle dangled at his side. Sarah struggled with the man holding her and both of the men laughed.

~

Snake glanced at the front porch and couldn't believe what he was seeing. Stella, the old black woman, held Seth's buffalo gun braced on her shoulder.

One of the men turned and noticed Stella and laughed out loud. "Now look what we got here." Waving his pistol toward Stella, he yelled to her, "Old woman, you'd better be careful with that big gun before you hurt yourself."

~

As the two men's attention was on Stella, Sarah eased her mama and herself away from the men. If Stella pulled the trigger, she didn't want to be hit by a stray bullet. Suddenly and unexpectedly, Snake raced from the barn firing his gun in the air and shouting an Indian chant. The distraction caused the men to train their guns on him.

~

Stella braced herself with her legs and pulled the trigger. The kick and blast of the big gun sent her backward through the open doorway onto the hard floor. The two men were hit and blown a foot in the air from the close range of gunpowder. Loud screams came from Sarah and her mama as blood spattered both of them.

~

Sarah pulled her mother and rushed to Snake and Coyote, not sure if anyone was hit by the wild bullets. After Sarah realized she wasn't shot, she reminded Snake that there were three bad men, but only two were dead. "He could be around somewhere. We've got to be careful, but we must find Penny."

~

Coyote limped inside the house to help Stella on her unsteady legs, with the others following close behind. Once they were in the house with the door locked, Stella told them the other man was dead in the blackberry patch. "I told the child to run. She's hiding somewhere."

"How do you know the other man is dead? Snake helped Coyote take Stella to the nearest seat.

"He came upon me and Penny. He grabbed me and wanted to use me as a hostage to make ya'll come out of the house. I shot him. He's dead."

Everyone stared at Stella. Coyote said, "You mean you shot the men in the front yard and now you tell us you killed the other man in the blackberry patch?" His mouth hung open.

"So, all three bad men are dead? Praise Jesus." Snake couldn't stop smiling. "I'm still trying to understand how you were able to shoot those two men outside when I know you wouldn't ever hurt a fly."

"Hush up, boy. I'll tell you later, but for now we've got to find Penny." Stella lowered herself into the rocker on the porch while everyone hurried in all directions calling the child's name.

~

Seth came riding up the lane to the ranch house and stopped in front of the open gate. His horse snorted and tried to back away. The front yard looked like a battlefield. Two men lay in a bloody bath—dead. His heart beat fast. He held a crying Penny in his arms.

Sarah rushed from the back of the house toward him with tears streaming down her cheeks. Seth jumped down from his horse with Penny glued to his chest.

"Oh, Seth, those men who killed . . . those are the same men." Seth tried to put Penny on the ground, but her little arms had a death grip around his neck. Sarah's wailing was scaring her. He wrapped one long arm around Sarah and held Penny tightly in the other.

Snake raced over to him and took Penny out of his arms. "Come with me, baby girl." Penny whimpered but allowed him to take her.

Seth held Sarah until she stopped crying and kissed her hair and face, whispering she was safe now. "I'm here and those men don't look like they could hurt a flea now."

"Where . . . where did you find Penny?" Sarah asked in between hiccups, her eyes on Snake carrying the child into the house. "We've been so worried about her."

"I forgot my money so I turned around. Couldn't believe my eyes when I saw Penny running down the middle of the road. I jumped off my horse and she ran to me screaming that Stella said to run. A bad man was in the blackberry patch. She begged me to come home and make him go away."

"I am so thankful you forgot your money. After Stella killed those men, we split up to search for her. Thank the Lord you turned around and found her."

"Stella shot those men? Is everyone alright?"

"Coyote is hurt, but not too bad. You aren't going to believe what took place after you rode away from here." Sarah smiled for the first time since Seth had arrived home.

"Mr. Seth," Snake called to him. "If you bandage Coyote, I'll ride for the sheriff. He's going to be very happy he don't have to worry about them three men again."

Seth glanced around. "I only saw two—"

"That's part of the story you won't believe." Sarah led him into the kitchen. Seth eyes narrowed when his saw his buffalo gun lying on the floor. "Who used the buffalo gun?" He looked at Sarah. "You aren't going to tell me that Stella did—?"

~

"My Lord, let me hold you." His voice was strained. Even distressed, Sarah could feel how gentle he was with her. After she told him about what had happened and how Stella had shot the men, Seth just shook his head. "You had to be so afraid of those men."

"We were terrified. I was afraid Mama might die on the spot. Her frail body was shaking so hard."

When the sheriff arrived, the men relived the whole story to him and his deputy. Both men were in disbelief. The men loaded the three dead bodies onto a wagon and carried them away. Before the sheriff climbed onto his horse to depart, he announced to Seth, Stella, Snake, and Coyote there was a big reward on the men's heads. He would personally see the reward money was paid to Seth's ranch family.

Chapter 45

The rain turned into a steady drizzle. Seth wanted to ride into town and make plans with the traveling preacher to marry him and Sarah. Since his plans had become delayed a few days, he decided to take Sarah with him. She should be in on their plans to marry, but he didn't want to drag her out in the chilly rain. She asked to take Penny with them.

Slipping out of his muddy boots, he stood at the kitchen door. Sarah was slicing ham. She was humming, which reminded him of a hummingbird flitting around the room. Sarah retrieved a tray and another loaf of fresh bread. He loved the way she glided from the stove to the counter without making a sound. "Sarah." Seth eased in his stocking feet toward her. She jumped and whirled.

"Oh my, I didn't hear you come in. Is it still raining?"

"No, it's stopped."

~

"Good, we can be ready to go in a few minutes. I'm making a picnic to take. You and Penny are always hungry." Sarah glanced at Seth and suddenly felt ill at ease.

"What's wrong? You look funny." Sarah frowned at Seth who was staring at her.

He grinned. "You don't want to know what I was thinking."

"Are we still going to town today?"

"Yes, if you still want to go. There's a gentle breeze blowing. It looks to be a nice day after all."

Sarah inched toward Seth. "Yes, I want to go. I'm ready to get married the sooner the better. Can't we do it today? We don't need everyone with us."

"I'm afraid your mama might skin me alive if we marry without her and Stella."

"No, they won't. Remember, I left home to marry George without them. I love you and I don't want to wait." She wrapped her arms around his neck.

"Stop and look at me." Seth removed her arms from around his neck and held them down beside her slim body. "As much as I want to take you right this minute to my bedroom and make mad, passionate love to you, I cannot and will not marry you without our family present. Your mama and Stella, Snake, Coyote, Martha Ann and Mick are like family, and they are as excited about us getting married as we are. We can't disappoint them."

Sarah hung her head and then glanced up at him. "Let's ask the preacher if he will marry us here in the parlor. We can have a nice reception supper."

"I love the idea of having it here, but are you sure you don't want to get married in the church?"

"We haven't even been inside the church in Casper. I want to go to church when the preacher is in town, but let's get married here in our home."

Seth picked Sarah up in his arms and swung her around, then set her back on her feet. "Get ready and let's go make our wedding plans."

~

Late in the afternoon, Seth stood next to the fireplace with Mick at his side. Stella, Mrs. Sullivan, Martha Ann sat on the kitchen chairs that had been moved into the parlor. Georgia Montgomery, the boardinghouse owner, and Mr. and Mrs. Willard Wallace from the dry good stores were the only outside guests who were invited to the small wedding.

There was no music, but Sarah floated into the parlor like an angel. She wore her long hair braided into a crown with a soft white veil covering her hair and face. A satin white shirtwaist with long sleeves was buttoned down the back with twenty-two small pearl buttons beginning at her neck to her waist. Her royal blue skirt flowed around her white slippers. She looked like a doll in the Sears Roebuck catalog, Penny told her while she was dressing.

Stella made Penny a long pink dress with tiny lace on the collar and on the edge of her short sleeves. Like a little princess, she floated in front of Sarah to the fireplace and stood between Seth's legs. She placed her arm around one of his legs and placed two fingers in her mouth.

Martha Ann motioned for the child to come to her, but Penny hid her face. Seth shrugged and took Sarah's hand. Stella took three steps, grabbed Penny and placed her on her lap, whispering something in her ear.

The old preacher stood before the family and friends and announced, "With two hearts in accord, I would like to ask each of them a few questions from the Good Book." He opened his Bible. "Do you, Seth Jenkins, take this woman to be your lawfully wedded wife, to have and to hold, from this day forward, for better or for worse, for richer, or for poorer, in sickness and in health, until death do you part?" Before Seth could answer, he said, "Will you love and cherish her and always be faithful to her?"

"I will." Seth winked at her.

"Do you, Sarah Sullivan, take this man to be your lawfully wedded husband, to have and to hold—"

Her grip tightened on Seth's hand. Tears clouded her eyes, but she blinked them back while she repeated her marriage vows. "I will." Sarah replied.

Seth took Sarah's hand and slipped the wedding band on her finger. "With this ring I thee wed."

"Oh, Seth, I forgot about a ring for you. I'll get one later," she whispered as he kissed her on the neck.

The preacher made the sign of the cross and declared, "I now pronounce you man and wife. You may kiss your bride."

"Don't fret, love. We are married, and that is all I care about." He kissed Sarah and everyone clapped.

The ladies wiped their eyes and Penny said loud enough for everyone to hear. "Can I have cake now?" Everyone laughed.

After the wedding supper was served, Seth and Sarah tried to find private moments to steal a kiss, but there seemed to be someone in every space. It was around six in the evening before everyone took their leave. The men changed their clothes and hurried out to finish the evening chores. Mick and Martha Ann left after Stella fixed them pieces of wedding cake to take home. As

Mr. and Mrs. Wallace were leaving, they thanked Sarah and Seth for including them as guests.

Chapter 46

Sarah went into their bedroom first. She needed help getting undressed but didn't want to ask Stella or Mama. She wanted them to go to bed and go to sleep. This was the first privacy she and Seth had since the wedding.

~

Seth tapped on the door and entered. His lovely bride was standing uncertainly near a small table that he used to place some of his personal items.

Before he could move closer, she held her hand out to stop him from coming closer to her. "Seth, I have something I have to say. I have no idea what is going to take place between us. Oh, I know a little, of course, but I don't want to disappoint you."

As fast as he could, he pulled her in his arms. "Oh baby, please don't be afraid, especially of me. I'll never hurt you." He could lose himself in the pools of her eyes. "Sweetheart, I'm not good with pretty words. I only want to say that I love you so much it scares me to death."

She ran her fingers into his hair, then pulled his face down to hers. "I've never heard prettier words." She brushed her hand over his smooth cheek. "I don't think I will ever tire of looking at your handsome face. You nearly scared me to death the first time I saw you with that bushy beard."

"Are you ready to go to bed?" He looked around, not knowing what ladies did.

"I'm going to need some help with my buttons on the back of

my blouse . . . if you don't mind?"

~

Sarah quickly removed the pins from the long braid that she wore twisted on top of her head. She shook the long strands and peeked out from her hair at her sweet husband, then grabbed her hairbrush and held it in her hand.

~

Seth laughed as his lovely bride turned her back to him. Sweat broke out on his forehead and it wasn't even hot in the room. Sarah lifted her long hair and pulled it all to one side, giving him a view of the buttons.

He looked down her back at the row of tiny objects. He took a button between his big fingers and fumbled with it. This was his honeymoon night and he was trying not to appear nervous, but his fingers were shaking. He stooped down to get a better view of the little loops and fumbled again. How can anyone sew these tiny things? he thought. He fumbled and blinked at the shiny, slippery buttons. The more he tried to get the blasted buttons loose, the more nervous he became. His tongue felt thick and too big for his mouth. How he wanted to make this a special night for both of them, but it wasn't starting off good.

Sarah giggled.

"You think this is funny? My fingers are too big to handle the buttons and loops." Frustrated, he said, "You'll just have to sleep in your top."

Before he knew it, Sarah popped the top three buttons, tearing the top near her neck and pulled the soft white blouse over her head. She grinned at him and posted her hands on her hips.

"Oh man, you're gonna be in trouble with the person who worked on that." Seth grinned and eyed the silky white blouse lying on the floor. Then he looked at his new bride standing before him in her white slip and corset.

~

Sarah laughed out loud this time. "Oh, darling, you're too funny. Come here."

He lowered his face and she nibbled on his lips. He nuzzled his face between her breasts.

Sarah never felt so happy and peaceful in her life. She slipped her arm around his shoulders and smoothed his hair back. Looking deep into his eyes, she spoke softly. "You know, sometimes out of a disaster comes something wonderful. You found me and saved me and loved me." She sighed and laid her head on his chest. "I love you, Seth Jenkins."

"And, I you, Sarah Jenkins."

Epilogue

"Papa, Mama," Penny called and jumped up from the grass where she'd been playing with her new puppy, Spot. She'd chosen the one with the conspicuous chocolate spot in his face, which made him look like he'd put his nose in pudding. Penny thought he was the cutest of Buster's new litter. Penny raced into the barn and screamed again for Seth. "Hurry, Papa, there's people out front."

"Good gravy, child, you're going to keep the old hens from laying their eggs with all that carrying on. Calm down and tell me what's wrong?"

"Nothing's wrong, but there's a wagon filled with Indians. Come quick," she said, latching on to his large, calloused hand.

~

"Indians?" Seth pondered and allowed six-year-old Penny to drag him out into the sunshine to see who'd arrived.

Seth stopped so quickly Penny almost stumbled. "I don't believe it. You finally decided to come. Welcome to my ranch, friend. I am surprised to see you so soon, but nothing could please me more. And look at you, Blue Sky. You look wonderful. Sarah is going to be thrilled. Let me help you down." Seth hurried to the front of the wagon to lift Blue Sky down, then called over his shoulder, "Snake."

When he appeared at the door of the barn, Seth waved for him to help Red Feather with the horses and his wagon.

~

"Howdy, Red Feather," said Snake. He remembered him from clearing the mountain when he and Coyote went to see their father.

"Unhitch his animals and take them into the corral. Park this wagon beside the shady part of the barn," Seth said with a pat on his back.

Snake was happy to help Seth. He hadn't seen his boss smile so much since he brought Miss Sarah home.

~

Blue Sky gave Seth the bundle she was holding. "Be careful with her, my friend. She's only a month old."

As Seth took the small bundle, a little tyke peeked from behind Blue Sky and climbed down using the wagon wheel.

"Holy cow! Look at how big that boy has grown. Penny will be so happy to have someone to boss around."

Seth and Blue Sky laughed, then she took her baby from him and headed to the house. "I go see my friend, Sarah, now."

Seth touched his daughter's arm. "Penny, go find your mama and tell her you have a surprise on the porch." Penny stopped to pick up her puppy, then continue into the house.

"How did you find me?" Seth asked Red Feather.

"You make joke, I am sure. Finding the Jenkins Ranch was the easy part. Everyone knows of your large cattle spread. You are famous in these parts."

Seth tossed back his head with a howl of laughter. "You're kidding, I'm sure."

"This is a nice place you have. Are you sure you want this Indian family working for you?"

"Yes, I am sure, and Sarah is going to be so happy. Wait until you see her." He motioned with his hands at his stomach. Red Feather grinned. "You know her mama and Stella live with us, too."

"In-laws, too. How is that working out for you?" Both men laughed.

"Just fine, very good actually. Both ladies are nice and hard workers, too. They will adore your children."

~

Sarah appeared at the door. "Hush, child. Your grandmother is taking a nap."

"There's a surprise." Penny pointed at the wagon.

Sarah stepped onto the front porch. "I don't believe it. Blue Sky? Oh, Blue Sky." Tears welled up in Sarah's eyes. She hurried to her dearest friend in all the world. "I've prayed that I would get to see you again."

Sarah hugged her tight until Blue Sky pulled back. "You wake baby."

Sarah peered at the beautiful baby girl. "Oh, Blue Sky. Our children will grow up together."

"Did Seth not tell you we were coming? We are going to live here and work for you."

"No, he didn't say a word. He probably didn't want me looking for you every day." She smiled. "I'm so happy you are here. Red Feather can work with Seth, but you will not work. You'll be my friend, and we'll help each other with our babies." Sarah pulled the blanket back and peeked again at the new bundle. "She's beautiful," Sarah said and patted her big belly. "Seth wants a son, but I secretly want a girl child."

"God will decide." Blue Sky called her son over. "Come and meet the woman who brought you into the world."

Sarah playfully slapped her friend on the arm. "You know Seth helped you, while I laid drunk on the floor." She gazed at her husband and shook her head. Now she understood Seth's actions. During the year Seth had hired a few men to work on a cottage in the wooded area.

"Why are you building this nice cottage away from our house?" She'd questioned Seth.

"Well, someone we care about might need a place to live and I want to be able to offer it to them. Who knows, Snake or Coyote might decide to get married."

"That's too funny. Those boys are scared to death of girls."

Seth laughed. "You may be right."

~

At dinner that evening, Seth announced he would take their friends to their new home. Everyone was surprised, but pleased. He also had a letter from his sister-in-law, Mary. She wrote that she was happy. Her son, John, had grown into a happy, healthy boy. The man she married was good to them both, and they had a nice home in the city of Billings. She hoped to send John to Seth's ranch in a couple of summers.

Sarah, Stella and her mama looked pleased with the news of a new home for Blue Sky and of Mary's happy family.

~

Once the men were outside, Red Feather spoke, "Does your woman ever speak about the man she was to marry?"

"No, not to me. We try hard to put that memory from our minds."

"Well, Sarah will not have to ever be afraid of him. Captain Turnberry molested a young Indian girl who lived outside of the fort. Her brother killed him, and sadly now the young brave is on the run from the law."

Seth spoke quietly to Red Feather. "Please don't tell Sarah this bad news. She would worry over the Indian girl and her brother forever. If she ever asks about him, I will tell her. She's happy now and never mentions her near fatal mistake in marrying the man she'd planned to for a couple of years." Seth placed his arm across Red Feather's shoulders, and they walked to the barn to retrieve his covered wagon. "My family is complete now that you are here."

"You and Sarah are happy now. That is good."

"Thankfully, I was able to save her from the pit of hell. I thank God every day for putting me in the right place at the right time. I have been blessed with a wonderful wife, a little girl and this successful ranch. Now, in a few weeks, I will be blessed again with Sarah's love. She is going to give me another part of her soul—a new baby."

The End

<u>Coming this Spring - Untitled</u>

Chapter 1

"Pa! You better not raise your bet using my Betsy or my two prize sows. I raised them from babies and they're the only thing that keeps food on our table," Mary Grace Winters screamed at her foolish, gambling father.

"Oh, Honey, git your sore butt out of this here room before I lock you upstairs. A man's gotta do what he's gotta do when he has a hand as good as mine."

"You gonna up the ante old man or chew with that gal of yours. If you want'a make this pot interesting, why not put your gal up as collateral. I don't need or want a dried-up milk cow." Jake Tyler was the owner of the biggest gold mine near Cripple Creek, Colorado.

"You crazy! I'd never put up my gal, even with this winning hand I'm holding." Moon said, owner of the stage depot and café.

"Pa! What are you doing? I told you that you better not lose my Betsy. If you do, you better not close your eyes because you won't be able to open them in the morning," Mary Grace said as she slammed a platter of hot doughnuts on the pile of money in the center of the table.

"Damn gal, if these doughnuts weren't so good, I'd take you outside and dump you down the well. You're worse than a boil on a man's behind," Jake Tyler shouted as he scooted his chair back from the table.

Mary Grace turned and stormed back to the stove and poured more batter into the pan of hot grease. She'd like to pour the hot grease over that handsome, cocky gold miner's head. She sighed and thought how he has never said anything to her before tonight.

"You know Moon," Jake lowered his voice, "I sure could

use a cook up at my mining camp. How about letting your gal come and cook for my men? She would have her own room and I will pay her a wage each week."

"Are you trying to distract me, sonny boy?" Moon peeked over his hand and glared at his opponent. "What would I do for a cook here? Her good cooking is what brings my customers in this place. I can tell you now it ain't my watered-down liquor or these cards games."

"You can always hire someone to keep coffee on the burner and cook bacon, eggs, and toast for your so called customers. You don't have more than a dozen men who come to eat. I bet you haven't ever paid your girl a dime for all the hard work she does around here."

"Hey, I don't have to pay her. She's got a roof over her head and she gets all the food that she can cook. She don't want for nothing!"

"Are you going to play cards or just keep on jawing about your wager?" Jeffery Sumter looked at Moon. "It's getting late and I'm tired."

"Eat another doughnut," Jake said and continued to stare at Moon.

"I'm out, but I'll take several of these hot treats with me," Jeffrey tossed his cards on the table and stood while stuffing doughnuts in his jacket pockets.

"See you back at the mine, boy." Jake shuffled his five cards in his palms. "What's it going to be old man? Are you raising your bet with your gal as collateral? I'm not accepting that cow."

"Hold on thar a minute. I gotta think. Thar's at least five hundred dollars in that pot." He looked at the money in the center of the table.

"Yep." Jake counted the money in the center of the table and said, "Five hundred, two dollars and 65 cents to be exact."

Moon felt sweat beads on his upper lip. He rubbed his bald head that had gotten him the nickname Moon. He lifted his three aces and two kings. This was the best hand he had all evening. He knew that there was only one ace out, and he was sure no one would be lucky enough to have that one black card.

"Time's up, Moon. Show me your hand or toss them in the pile." Jake smiled at the old man who had been winning all night.

"Lady Luck has been with you tonight and you still have a 50-50 chance of winning."

"My gal is my wager," Moon said as his daughter walked back into the room where the two men were making their final play.

"No Pa! You can't do that. I'm not just a thing you can use as collateral. I will never forgive you for this—win or lose, I will hate you forever." Mary Grace whirled around and ran outside the building.

Moon and Jake didn't look at her or allow her outburst to disturb their final play. Several men had gathered around the table and were interested in this last turn of the cards. A big pot of money and a woman was the most exciting wager most of them has ever witnessed.

"Now or never," mumbled Jake to Moon.

Slowly, Moon showed one card at time. "Three aces," Moon said, with a big smile, "and a pair of Kings." The men mumbled amongst themselves, one patting him on his back.

Just as slow, Jake spread his five cards on the table and said, "A Royal Flush." Jake leaned back in his chair as he watched the blood drain out of Moon's face.

"You cheated, you cheat! You may take all the money, but you'll never take my gal." Moon jumped up from his chair as it slid back and slammed into the wall.

The men all moved away from the table as Jake stood. He leaned over the table as he picked up his winnings and glared into Moon face. With a smile on his face, he said. "I won fair and square and you know it old man. Now, this money is mine and so is your daughter. She will be going with me to my mining camp and be my cook. Nothing more. I will see that she is taken care of and she will be paid for her work."

"She'll never go with you," Moon said as he stood and watched the men file out the door. He wished he had somewhere else to go because his daughter was never going to speak to him again.

"She'll go, but I want you to tell her what my plans are for her. I will be by in the morning to pick her up. I will be driving the supply wagon."

~

217

Early the next morning, Jake walked into the miner's dining hall and found Harry Jamison, an old man with a peg leg sitting on a barrel. He had his wooden leg stretched out in front of his old thin frame while he drank coffee from a tin cup.

"Why aren't you getting breakfast ready?" Jake asked.

"I'm trying hard to stand and hop around, but I'm having a bad day and the sun ain't even come up. Sure glad your hired that youngster, Jimbo, to help me out. He's out in the chicken house gathering eggs."

"Well, I come to tell you that I have hired a young lady to help out with the cooking. I plan to bring her back with me today. I'll let her stay in the bedroom that I built for myself."

"Well boss man, she will be a welcome change around this place. A girl, that's nice. The men will be happy to have someone else's cooking besides mine."

"You might have to help me make her feel at home here. You see, well, her pa put her up as collateral during a card game last night. She may not be too happy to be here, but she will stay even if I have to hogtie her.

"What! You can win a woman in a poker game. Have you gone loco?" Harry couldn't believe what Jake had just told him. He tried to stand but the upper part of his thigh had been rubbed raw. He flopped back on the barrel.

"Don't get your drawers in a wad. I don't want her to be my woman. I want a cook and nothing else." He sat down on a barrel next to the counter where Harry served food. "This young gal has been working for her pa at the café and stage depot. He doesn't pay he,r and she doesn't look like she has anything nice. I'm going to pay her a wage."

"I guess I understand now. But, you better not do anything to her . . . you know what I mean. If you do boss, you'll be standing in front of that old preacher who drops by here once in a while.

"Gosh, old man. I just want her to cook. Just wait until you taste her food. You'll never want her to leave."

~

Jake's first stop in town was at the dry goods store where he dropped off his list of supplies for the mining camp. He drove the flatbed wagon down the street to the café and stage depot. He jumped down and entered the café. It took a minute for his eyes to adjust to the dim light in the room. "Why is it so dark in here, Moon?" Jake asked as he looked around. Over in the corner was a carpet bag and a shotgun laying on the floor. Moon didn't reply to Jake.

"Is your daughter ready to go to my mining camp?" Jake really hoped that the girl would be eager to go with him.

"Afraid not, Jake. I went upstairs this morning and packed her things but she said that she will die before she leaves her room and go anywhere with you."

"Does she understand that I want her to cook for my miners, and nothing else?"

"I explained that to her but she ain't being reasonable. I told you last night that she wouldn't go with you." Moon said, trying to hold back a smirk.

"Which room is hers and what's her name? I don't believe I have ever heard you call her anything but Gal," Jake asked as he placed his foot on the first step of the stairs.

"Mary Grace. She's at the top of the stairs. First door on the right."

Jake walked up the stairs and stopped at the first door. He heard sobbing. He called to Mary Grace, and the crying stopped.

Mary Grace clamped a hand over her mouth and wiped her eyes and runny nose. She whirled around in her plaid shirt that was tucked in the tight denims. She stopped crying and tried to control her heavy breathing. She turned a thoughtful look at the front window. She knew that she couldn't escape the room with him standing in the doorway.

"Miss Mary Grace?" Jake spoke gentle. "Your pa has given you permission to work for me at my mining camp. I need you to help me out by cooking for my men. I am going to pay you a wage, just like I do my men. What do you say?"

Mary Grace opened the door and said very politely, "No thank you." She slammed the door in his face.

Jake turned a disgruntled look and began pounding his fist on her door. "Mary Grace, open this door and let's talk about the wager your pa lost to me last night."

The door flew open and Mary Grace stood with her palms

on her hips. "You go and talk to Pa about the wager. I had no part in it and I wouldn't cross the street with you. Now, leave before I make you sorry that you came up here." The door slammed in his face again and he heard something being pushed up against it on the other side.

Not to be outdone by a young whippersnapper of a gal, Jake took his pocketknife and began removing the screws that held the door on its frame. Once the door was completely removed, Jake stepped around the dresser that she had pushed up against the door. He saw the lovely gal standing across the room glaring at him in disbelief. Jake placed his hands on his hips, took two steps toward Mary Grace and gave her an arrogant smile.

Before he could say anything to her, he felt something hard as a brick hit him directly between the eyes. The room went dark and his head spun. He felt himself sliding downward and he tried to steady himself by reaching for the girl. He saw the walls closing in on him and he lost all consciousness.

Mary Grace eased over to the mine owner. She took her big toe and pushed on his shoulder. He didn't move, but she could tell that he was breathing. He wasn't dead but he would sleep for a while. She would have time to leave on the next stagecoach. She stole enough money from her Pa's secret box to travel to her Aunt Louise's small farm in Wildwoods, Colorado. Her pa's sister had begged her to come now that she wasn't in good health. Mary Grace never wanted to be a nurse, but she wasn't ever going to be a kept woman.

As she walked down the stairs into the café where her pa was making coffee, he looked behind her. "Where's your new boss man?"

"I told him that I refused to work for him so he left. Didn't he tell you what I said?" She asks her pa so innocently.

Mary Grace picked up her carpet bag and shotgun and walked to the back of the café. She looked over her shoulder to make sure her pa wasn't watching her. She hurried out into the alleyway and ran to the stagecoach that would be leaving soon.

A note to my wonderful supportive readers.

It is exciting to know that I began writing in the fall of 2012 and I have
completed my 10th book. This is a milestone for me and I am so excited.
I could not or would not have continued to write if it had not been for all
of your encouragement, love and support. All of your sweet words and
expressions of love for my characters and stories have fed my soul.

I am not a New York Best Seller (Yet) but when you tell me how much   enjoyment you get from reading my stories, I feel like one. I want to express my gratitude to all of you for your continuous support by purchasing   my books. Someone said to me, "Surely, Linda, if they didn't like your   books they wouldn't keep reading them." In my heart I feel that is a true
statement.

Thanks you from the bottom of my heart for being one of my faithful readers.

Social Media Contacts

Amazon Author Page

https;//www.amazon.com/author/lindasealyknowles
Email address:
Lindajk@cox.net
Goodread.com/
Instagram
Facebook
Facebook Blog
https://writerlindasealyknowles.com
Newsletter
Lasso the Heart

Other Books by Linda Sealy Knowles

The Maxwell Saga

Journey to Heaven Knows Where	Book 1
Hannah's Way	Book 2
The Secret	Book 3
Bud's Journey Home	Book 4
Always Jess	Book 5
Abby's New Life	
Joy's Cowboy	
Kathleen of Sweetwater, Texas	
Sunflower Brides	

The Importance of Reviews

Reviews are the foundation of a good book. Please share your experience of meeting my beloved characters with others by placing a short review on Amazon or

Facebook. Readers like to know that it's worth their time to read my book. Your opinion is the *voice* of my writing—good or bad. I appreciate your help with this. Just one line is enough. "Something like: Great story. I enjoyed this book, etc. You don't have to write a book. You can just read mine.

Linda Sealy Knowles is an historical-romance-western writer that brings her love stories and characters to life. She gives God the glory for her talent that has given her much joy and happiness. Since 2012, she has written ten novels. Linda is from Satsuma, Alabama but resides in Niceville, Florida, near her daughter, Kelli, and son, Pete, II. She has three lovely teenage granddaughters.

Made in the USA
Lexington, KY
04 November 2019